LITTLE DYSTOPIAS

a collection

Kyle Aisteach

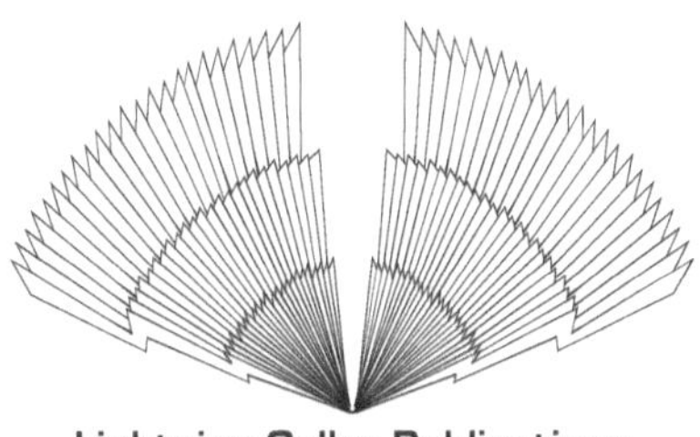

Lightning Cellar Publications

Little Dystopias by Kyle Aisteach

This is a work of fiction. All characters, names, places, and events are the product of the author's imagination or are used fictitiously. Any similarities to actual people, places, or incidents is purely coincidental.

ISBN: 978-1-943305-01-8

Library of Congress Control Number: 2015938855

Published by Lightning Cellar Publications
P.O Box 4204
Fresno, CA 93744

First Edition, October 2015

20150921

For Chris.

ACKNOWLEDGMENTS

I think this is the hardest part of this book to write, because so many people helped in so many ways that it's impossible to list them all. As a collection of shorter works, there are many and varied hands that have touched different parts of the book. So, first and foremost, I need to acknowledge the original editors many of these stories: Wilson da Silva, Damien Broderick, Michael Wills, Christine Clukey, Bruce Bethke, Andrea Jakeman, Daniel Friend, Lynnae Jackson, Rachel Ontiveros, Nyssa Silvester, Savannah Woods, Jordan Ellinger, and Richard Salter.

Feedback on individual stories came from two primary sources: my critique group, Fresno Scifi & Fantasy Writers (FSFW) and the MFA program at Fresno State. FSFW members are too many and too fluid to list, but I need to particularly acknowledge the founder of the group, who first encouraged me to join, Christopher Wood, and to two members in particular whose specific help made individual stories work, Amanda Hsiao and Rob Lopez (both also fine writers whose short stories I think you would enjoy). My cohort in the MFA program also deserves a special shout-out, if only because they put up with me trying to sneak science fiction and fantasy into a literary program for two years: Brandon Baker, Jordy Dakin, Kristen Norton, and Jessica Santillan, as well as the cohorts immediately before and after me (who only put up with me for one year): Matthew Fullerton, Mary Locke, Suren Organessian, Aaron Budiman, Teresa Chacon, Angela Corbett, Loretta Kennedy, Kourtnie McKenzie, Pat Miller, Kamilah Okafor, Owen Torres, and Monique Quintana. The faculty of the MFA program also, obviously, were a huge influence: Steven Church, Corrinne Clegg Hales, John Hales, Tim Skeen, and especially the fiction faculty, Alex Espinoza and Randa Jarrar. Fresno State's creative writing program is inextricably intertwined with the rest of the English department, so I need to collectively acknowledge all the faculty there, and especially two who graciously agreed to serve on my thesis committee despite the fact that they did not get paid for it, and from whom I also learned a great deal: Lisa Weston and Howard V. Hendrix. I also need to thank my vast array of friends who periodically jump in to answer specific questions or to read a random draft to make sure I'm getting my facts right. Stories in this collection specifically benefitted from input from Lee Bennett, Robert Hurt, Ann Leckie, Erin Ryan, and Emily Siskin.

This particular book went through many iterations over quite a stretch of time, and so I need to thank my "first" readers (many of whom won't recognize the final version): Eain Bankins, Deb Danner, Joy Frye, Erin Gordon, Missy Guice, Amanda Hsiao, Carol Keller, HelenJane McKee, Helen Nauert, Chad Neptune, Lisa Peters, Drew Schatt, Jeremy Seip, Rebecca Strong, and Liz Burke Turi.

For invaluable professional advice, I need to thank everyone who participates on the SFWA discussion boards and all the members of Codex Writers' Group.

And, finally, I need to acknowledge you, the reader, without whom this whole endeavor would truly not be possible.

Table of Contents

That One

I'm crap at titles.

The first short story I sold I had titled "Rennie." That's not a good title. It tells you nothing about the story. It doesn't have any "have to read" aura about it. It's a jumble of six letters. That's me. Crap at titles.

Ironically, my first publication was a title. Just a title.

I was fourteen.

There used to be this chain of bookstores called Waldenbooks. Their business model was to invade small storefronts in popular shopping malls and stock lots and lots of books that would appeal to the typical mall rat. They were an early experimenter in customer loyalty cards, and they had a "club" for all the different genres. It was free to join, and each one came with a newsletter that you could pick up by just stopping by the store. The science fiction club's newsletter was called *Xignals*. And one day they announced they were having a "Sure-Fire Title Contest" — looking for great titles for unwritten works, titles like *Conan the Librarian*!

Well, my best friend Laurie Anne and I decided to team up and come up with some sure-fire titles to see if we could win this contest. My personal favorite was *I, Rowboat*, but I had to admit that it was pretty obvious and therefore it was possible someone else would come up with it, too. Of the list we worked up, I thought we had the best shot with our "Incarnations of Mortality" series: *On a Pale Whore, Bearing Our Ass, With a Tangled Brain, Welding a Red Ford*, and *Beating a Mean Brother*. Yes, those were sure to take the top prize and get published in a free newsletter that Waldenbooks gave out to customers of all ages!

There was one title we had brainstormed that neither of us liked. It was terrible. It had no chance of winning. We agreed to cut it. But since I was the one with a typewriter, it fell to me to type up our list and send it in. As I was transcribing my handwritten scrawls, I decided there was no harm in including the lousy title anyway. I mean, it wasn't like it was bad enough to hurt our chances with all of our *good* entries.

Well, when the new *Xignals* came out, I stopped by Waldenbooks and picked it up. Sure enough, they had published the winners.

And, there among them, in glorious print for all Otherworlds Club members to read was our lousy title, the one we both agreed to cut.

Car Wreck: The Next Degeneration.

Laurie Anne and I spent several hours on the phone that evening trying to figure out how we won with a crap title like that.

I'm still baffled.

Yep. Crap at titles.

Fast-forward some 24 years to 2010. Laurie Anne had passed away from some bizarre illness I don't think I could pronounce if you paid me. I had given up a great career in Los Angeles to follow my husband to Fresno. And, frankly, I didn't know what I wanted to do with my life. I'd been a writer off and on my entire adult life — the purely functional kind of writer who does educational screenplays and web content for clueless university departments — and I really missed science fiction. So I cleaned up a half dozen stories I'd been working on — stories with promising titles like "Rennie" and "Viraquae" — and got them, as we say, "into circulation."

Now, I have to digress here for a moment to explain that my husband doesn't much care for science fiction. Well, he's a big *Doctor Who* fan, but that's not really science fiction, he assures me. And he sometimes writes steampunk, but that's not really science fiction, either. And lately he's been getting involved with *Wizard of Oz* fandom, but... well, you get the idea. But he felt guilty about uprooting me and moving me to a city where all the job skills I'd developed over three or four careers were completely useless, so he was very tolerant of my newest obsession. He commiserated with me over every rejection letter. And there were a lot of them. Until one morning in April when *Cosmos* sent me an e-mail.

By this point, I was so used to rejection that when I saw the subject line and who it was from, my brain immediately started trying to figure out who I should send the story to next. When I read the e-mail, it made no sense to me. I read it again. Still baffled. On the third read I finally figured out what Damien Broderick was saying — that they were *buying* "Rennie."

But they wanted to change the title.

Well, I switched instantly to "bouncing of the walls" mode. They could call the story whatever they hell they wanted. I knew I was crap at titles. None of that mattered. *I had sold a story!*

I grabbed my phone and called my husband. As soon as he answered, I screamed, "*Cosmos* just accepted my story!"

"Who?"

My husband doesn't follow science fiction, remember. Apparently he also doesn't follow popular science magazines.

"*Cosmos!*"

"What's that?"

O.K. I should have realized that *Cosmos* isn't a big name in the U.S. They don't really have much circulation here. We writers know who they are. But they're an important market, nonetheless.

"*Cosmos!*" I said. "Australian magazine! Bigger circulation than *Asimov's.*"

"Oh, that's great!" my loving husband sang. "Which story?"

"'Rennie.'"

"Really?" His voice turned incredulous. "Someone bought *that one?*"

Yeah.

"That one."

And that's how my career as a short storyist launched. Talk about bringing someone back down to Earth.

Now, I can't be mad at my husband. Not every story is everyone's cup of tea. And I must admit that I have a love-hate relationship with "that one" myself. Half the time I re-read it and I can't believe I wrote something so good. The rest of the time I re-read it and think I really should change my name before anyone associates it with me.

Even as I write this I don't know if I like it or not. But lots of people do.

Officially, the story is now called "Too Close for Comfort." I'm not sure who on the *Cosmos* staff came up with it. It works for the story. I like it. I can call my story that without having to apologize.

But around my house, we still call it "That One." Somehow, to me, that feels like the right title.

But I'm crap at titles.

Too Close for Comfort

It started with the deposition. It started normally. "State your name and occupation for the record." I glanced at the computer to make sure it was recording.

"Sara Wiedergeburt." She spelled it without me asking.

Dr. Wiedergeburt carried herself with class. She sat erect in the oversized leather chair, wrinkled hands folded on the oak table in front of her, silver-grey hair folded back in a style that should have looked 30 years out of date, but somehow just seemed right on her. "Ph.D. Retired."

"You understand," I said, reading off the notes, "this deposition is in connection with the disposal of the results of experiments in which you participated?" I looked for a non-verbal reaction. "That would be prior to your 'retirement.'"

She inhaled deeply before answering. "If by 'results of experiments,' you mean my daughter," she said, "then yes, I'm aware they want to kill her."

The district attorney had warned us that the participants referred to the Neanderthals as their children. Probably Dr. Wiedergeburt's idea — her field was cognitive psychology. "According to the notes I've got from the depositions of the other participants, they say the experiments were your idea."

"That's correct."

"Can you tell us how they came about?"

She nodded slightly to one side, a very distinctive gesture. "I had a friend in Connecticut at the time who was working on sequencing the Neanderthal genome."

"That would be Dr. David Latham, is that right?"

"Yes." She seemed to relax, crossing her legs and placing her hands on her lap. "You may recall that in the late 1990s, President Clinton ordered a federal funding ban on human cloning."

I just smiled politely. I wasn't born until the following decade, but I've always looked older than I am. Most people don't realize that the lawyers who get stuck taking depositions are the ones with the least seniority, and I considered myself lucky to even have a job, given the economy.

"I was having lunch in the cafeteria with a geneticist colleague of mine, Dr. Babar Kurup," she continued. "He passed away in 2020. He had worked out a reliable way to clone apes. He commented that the process was theoretically ready for human trials. But since the university, like most schools, received federal funding, human cloning was absolutely forbidden. I merely noted that a Neanderthal wasn't technically human, and I knew someone who had access to the genetic sequences."

I stared at her, dumbfounded. "You mean to tell me—"

"—That the greatest paleo-anthropological experiment ever conducted was actually just an attempt to circumvent a stupid human-cloning ban," she finished for me. "Yes."

I remember I felt like laughing, but didn't. "And you didn't think it through beyond that."

She shrugged. "In that moment, no, it was an offhand remark. But Babar, David, and I gave it a lot of thought before we actually proceeded."

"What did you think you were going to do with a Neanderthal child?"

"Exactly what I did." Her tone turned suddenly clipped. "I planned to raise it as my own child. A Neanderthal child. Raised in a human household with a human parent. Brought up in our culture. An experiment that would demonstrate what sort of cognitive and physiological differences there were between *Homo sapiens* and *Homo neanderthalensis* — to let us see what was cultural and what were, in fact, species-specific differences."

"And you thought this would work."

"Yes. My niece is autistic. I saw no reason to predict, even based on low-end estimates of Neanderthal mental abilities, that it would be any harder."

"And, what, you planned to send her to school like all the other kids?"

She smiled through tight lips. "At the time, we did not know that Neanderthals were orange."

I remember just staring. Of course, it would have only been after the cloning that we actually knew what a Neanderthal looked like. Pictures in old textbooks always showed Neanderthals appearing to look like modern humans, but with shallow foreheads. "You planned to pass her off as human."

She closed her eyes and sighed slightly. "Honestly, at the time, I thought she would be human. There were two schools of thought then. One said that Neanderthals were a different species, a genetic dead-end, and that *Homo sapiens* had emerged independently from *Homo erectus*. The other school of thought said that Neanderthals were modern humans, but basically a different ethnic stock, one not found in modern populations. The genetics favored the former theory, but, as you know, I'm not a geneticist."

"And what were you going to do with her when your experiment was done?"

"Again," she remained cool this time, "exactly what I did. Raise her as my child, let her become what she wanted to become, and then do what all parents do."

"And you never thought about the consequences."

"No," she said. "And I still don't. Rennie has done nothing wrong."

"Dr. Wiedergeburt," I said, "a man died."

"Rennie didn't do it."

I looked at the notes. They only said that a clan of Neanderthals deliberately stalked and killed a man. Nothing indicated which of the animals had been involved. "Do you have some evidence of that?"

"She was at home with me when it happened." She stared at the table. "But, I'm her mother. Of course I'd say that."

"You're aware of the laws that prohibit keeping and raising dangerous animals, right?"

"She's not an animal. Mr. Jackson, I need you to understand that. I accept now that she's a different species, but… she thinks. She has hopes. She has dreams. The differences between our species — they're so minor. If it weren't for the skin color and the body hair, you'd never doubt she was human."

I let myself go down the tangent. "What are the differences?"

She seemed to consider for a long time before answering. "For one thing, she only gestated seven months. When I had the embryo implanted, we just assumed I'd carry her to a normal human term. But she came out two months early, and appeared to be fully developed. Orange and covered with body hair, but fully developed. After that, we warned the obstetricians first."

That was quite an image. But either she hadn't been joking or her timing was acute enough to know when to press on, because she continued immediately. "I named her Rennie. It's short for Renaissance. Sort of a bad joke, actually."

My mother's name was Renée, a more common take on the same theme.

"She grew quickly. Very strong. Linebacker build, and we had cloned one of the smaller female samples. Amazing sense of smell. She can track me like a bloodhound. But she's red-green color-blind. Another contribution to our gene pool from the genetic 'dead-end.' We found, observing her, that she's much more literal than the average human. Genuinely atheistic. She and the later Neanderthal children all sincerely don't understand how we can imagine a God that can't be seen or touched. And really, that's it. Skin color, body hair, sense of smell, color blindness, different sense of symbolic representation. That's all the differences there are. Somehow that was enough to let our species out-compete their species 25,000 years ago. And really, except for the skin color, I could name *Homo sapiens* who exhibit every trait we've observed in a Neanderthal, behaviorally or physiologically. Even the body hair."

"How many clones did you end up making?"

"Twelve." There were fifteen being held, which meant three were subsequently bred. "When Rennie was two and the brouhaha had died down, we decided it was worthwhile to try again, to ensure that we had a broader sample base. So we didn't conclude, for example, that all Neanderthals were good at math because Rennie was. She was counting at eighteen months and adding at two. And it's a good thing we did, because Rennie was unique in that. The second one, Joseph — that was Maria Rodriguez's son — can barely add to this day. But, oh, what a talker he is."

"Was he one of the ones who killed Dr. Wanaker?"

She exhaled deeply and studied the bamboo floor. "I believe so, yes. He was always very protective of Rennie."

The notes didn't give me any hint of what she might mean. "I'm sorry?"

She looked directly into my eyes. She had piercing gray eyes, the kind that seem as though they can pull thought and emotion directly from the minds of others. "Didn't they tell you the circumstances, Mr. Jackson?"

"I have here that a group of five male and two female Neanderthals stalked and later killed Dr. Wanaker at his home. Dozens of witnesses saw them drive him off the roof and then jump and cheer as he convulsed on the sidewalk. They made no effort to summon help, and showed no remorse."

"They also didn't resist when the police placed them into custody." She folded her arms. "Nor did the others, when officials came around to take them, too. And if there hadn't been so much debate about how to kill them, they would have all been executed without due process before we got the injunction."

It's always a little annoying when laypeople spit out a vague legal principle out of context, but I pressed on. "Dr. Wiedergeburt, the Neanderthals, by your own admission, are not human. Therefore they are animals. That means they're dealt with according to the laws regulating any other animal. And an animal that attacks a human is, by law, properly put down."

"Dr. Wanaker raped Rennie."

That stopped me cold. But, of course, manipulating emotions was her expertise. "That's a rather sensationalistic accusation."

"He submitted a paper about it!" She nearly spat, the biggest crack I'd seen in her demeanor. "Rennie has always been very passive. Especially around men. I'm not sure why. She certainly didn't get it from me."

That I could see. "Is this paper available anywhere?"

She directed me to a preprint online. I scanned it quickly, but it was written in technical jargon. "In a nutshell," she explained, "it tells how he informed — not asked — Rennie that he was going to see if modern humans and Neanderthals could interbreed by impregnating her, and proceeded to try. On four separate occasions. She didn't tell me, of course, until afterward, when I asked her at the zoo what Joseph and the others had been thinking."

I scanned through some more. It did seem to corroborate what she was saying, but none of that would change the law. "I don't think that's going to affect the case."

She stood up and walked over to the window, looking out across the rooftops below. Our office had one of the best views in the city, if you were lucky enough to be near a window. "Our lawyers agree," she said. "The first step is to get them declared legal persons. Then, well, if we can get a fair trial we might use that as a mitigating factor." She turned back to me, her arms folded authoritatively. "I'm not asking you to condone what they did. None of us do. Rennie doesn't. I'm just asking you to accept that they're not animals. They protected one of their own."

"Dr. Wiedergeburt, I'm afraid I'm only here to take your deposition."

She smiled. Genuinely, as best I could tell. "Of course." She sat back down.

"Where did the Neanderthals learn to kill?"

I remember the cold look that came across her face to this day. It literally sent a chill down my spine. You can almost hear the expression on the recording. "That would be Dr. Llorneil's contribution." Again, she spelled it. "He was interested in studying Neanderthal acquisition of life skills. So he set out teaching them best-guess reconstructions of Neanderthal technology. Stoneworking. Leather crafts. Pitch-glue making — they never did figure that one out, Lord knows how the prehistoric Neanderthals did it. And, yes, hunting. I have no idea what he got out of it, but the children seemed to enjoy it."

"He thought these skills were innate or something?"

"Something like that." She paused as if trying to recall something. "*Homo habilis* made stone tools, but showed no evidence of evolution in toolmaking. So it's thought that they made tools the way birds make nests, on instinct, not intellect."

"And he taught them to chase prey with fire and sticks?" I asked.

"It's thought that they hunted larger prey by chasing it off cliffs, yes." Her voice had gone flat, resigned. "The murder of Dr. Wanaker is exactly what Dr. Llorneil taught them to do... only with human prey and a city environment."

"And no one thought that what they were being taught might be dangerous?"

She exhaled strenuously. "You don't expect your children to grow up to be murderers, Mr. Jackson. No parent does. In hindsight, I think we were grateful for the break. We had to teach them ourselves. We couldn't send them to school, you know. No, ten families, twelve children, and one really raucous home school. And now three of them have children of their own..." She just shook her head as she trailed off into silence.

I waited a moment before pressing on. "Do you feel you could have done something differently to prevent what happened to Dr. Wanaker?"

She pierced me with those eyes again. "You mean would I advise another mother raising a Neanderthal child to do things differently, or was there something I should have known at the time?"

"Either."

"I did the best I could. We all did. We did nothing that any ten other families wouldn't have done. But obviously, we learned a lot in the process. Just as any grandmother has more experience than any new mother, yes, I could think of things I'd do differently. I still regret losing my temper when she chewed up my African woodcarving."

I let a laugh escape. "That wasn't on your list of differences in the species."

"That's because my brother also teethed on anything and everything," she said.

"Did you have any other children?" I realized only after the words came out how I had phrased the question.

"No," she said. "I never married. I was 37 when Rennie was born. I think that was part of the reason I was so ready to volunteer."

"Just one more question, Dr. Wiedergeburt. Were there any warning signs of violent tendencies among the Neanderthals?"

She stood up and walked to the window again, hesitating a long time before answering. "No more so than with any other child."

"But you had no children."

"I've studied child development extensively," she said quietly, not turning around, "and written two books on the subject."

"Very good," I said, bringing the recorder back to the foreground. "Do you have anything to add?"

"Just that they're people," she said, still not turning around.

"Thank you," I said, pressing *stop* on the recorder.

"Is the recorder off?"

"Yes."

She finally turned back around. Her whole demeanor had changed. Suddenly she looked frail, vulnerable. "Mr. Jackson, there are fifteen scared people being held in a zoo. A zoo, Mr. Jackson."

"Dr. Wiedergeburt —"

"I know," she said, holding her hands up placatingly. "I know that officially you're powerless to do anything. But I'm not asking officially. I'm appealing to your humanity. They're trying to kill my daughter."

"There's really nothing I can do," I said, quite sincerely.

"Yes," her voice dropped a register as she sat back down across from me, reaching out to rest her hand on mine. Her skin felt leathery, but her touch was gentle. "Actually, there is."

"I'm just —"

"A junior lawyer at a law firm hired to take depositions for the government, yes," she said. "But tell me, when was the last time you saw a dangerous animal case where the animals in question spoke English and could speak for themselves?"

She was, of course, correct. The Neanderthals weren't human, but they weren't ordinary animals either.

She apparently took her cue from my reaction, because she continued, more earnestly. "Would it be unheard of for your firm to depose everyone involved in the case?"

The prosecutors really didn't seem to have given any thought to interviewing the Neanderthals. It would be unprecedented. "You think it will help your case." Of course, under discovery rules, the district attorney would need to turn over any and all depositions to her lawyer.

"Having all sides out certainly wouldn't hurt anyone's case, unless the case is based on fallacy."

I understood. "If I can get access."

She grinned wickedly. "The zoo staff is pretty accommodating. Especially if they think your presence might help calm their wards."

"I assume they're not happy about keeping them?"

"No," she said. "Even the ones who don't think the Neanderthals are human agree that they're human enough..." She looked down at our hands.

"Then, what, jail?" I asked. "Put them in with human inmates? Isn't that asking for more trouble?"

She looked directly into my eyes again. "And that, Mr. Jackson, is the part of the equation that we didn't really consider. All of us involved in the experiment, we believed, we knew, that Neanderthals were human — or close enough that we could raise them as human."

"But they're not."

"No," she admitted. "Off the record. Or even on it, they're not.

They're Neanderthals. Very, oh, so very nearly human, but not human."

"But not animals," I said.

"No more so than you or me," she said. "People. Different. The same. People."

"So what do you want me to do?" I asked.

She inhaled deeply, letting go of my hand. "I'm a mother, Mr. Jackson. And my daughter is all grown up. It's time for her to be on her own."

Again, I had no idea what she was getting at.

"Mr. Jackson," she said, voice dropping to a near whisper. "They're perfectly capable of surviving in the wild."

Neanderthals. In the "wild." It seemed an even bigger recipe for disaster, and certainly not legal. "We're talking about a potentially dangerous species," I said.

"One that, if we believe the paleontologists, we competed with for tens of thousands of years," she said. "That's the part of the experiment that went wrong, you see. Two species with identical needs cannot exist in the same biome. Now that they're established, they must compete with us. And we must compete with them."

"Now it sounds like you're arguing for putting them down," I said.

"No," she said deliberately. "The part you're missing is 'in the same biome.' If they were located elsewhere—"

"Our species wouldn't come into contact," I finished for her. "At least not for now."

She nodded. "Believe me, I'd rather have Rennie just come home. But we're past that point now. But, they're well-suited to living in cold climates, where we don't do as well. The Yukon, maybe."

I had to admit, it was a more pleasant alternative to consider than simply killing them all. "What can I do? Legally, I mean."

"For starters," she said, "get depositions from them all. And then, well, you know what to do from there."

And I did. "You realize you're just delaying the inevitable."

She nodded. "I can hope that as a species, we've learned better."

"You can hope." I stood up, making myself as professional sounding as I could. "Dr. Wiedergeburt, I'm afraid that I'm in no official capacity to help you."

She laughed, rising, and held out her hand to shake mine. "Then I shall leave you to your unofficial capacity."

I shook her hand. She was a smart lady. "You have a good day, Dr. Wiedergeburt," I said, and slipped my computer into my hip pocket.

I walked her to the elevator, which she entered silently. As I headed back to my cubicle, I pulled out the computer again and scanned through my schedule. I had time after lunch to run down to the zoo and take a few depositions — twelve, perhaps. Plus a few zookeepers.

And that's how, in my first year as a lawyer, I began my criminal career.

Research Fail

When people try to classify me as a writer, I'm usually either lumped in with the gay and lesbian genre (despite the fact that I've never actually sold a QUILTBAG story) or I'm considered a "hard science fiction" writer, a writer of stories that puts the emphasis on getting the science right. I don't really mind either label, but I also feel guilty taking on the hard-SF label when I often write stories where the technology is something I know is impossible and where I have to do a lot of hand-waving to convince the reader to accept it. Time travel is the classic example. I know the physics. I get the physics. We're never going to invent a machine that lets us physically pop back in time to a point before the machine was invented – at least, not based on any version of physics as we now understand it.

What I am, however, is a research-oriented writer. Even when I've decided to go ahead and let the science be wrong in order to play with a popular science fiction trope, I do strive to get my facts right.

"The Survivors' Menagerie" started out as an idea I had while nursing one of my pastimes: I'm a *Titanic* geek. One of my sources mentioned that a group of passengers was escorted from the boat deck back down into the bowels of the ship with the intention that they could board the lifeboats that had already been lowered through the passenger loading doors much closer to the waterline. This group went below decks and was never heard from again. I checked several sources, and all the witnesses simply called it "a group." No mention of what size group it was. No mention of who was or was not in it.

Now, one thing you have to remember about *Titanic* is that, contrary to the myth, very few women and children died. Many of the ones that did are known to have refused spots in lifeboats. Third-class women and children were not locked away from the boat deck, and, in fact, were actively being sought out and escorted to the boats. So if we assume that "a group" is, say, 80 or 90 women and children, this lost expedition to the passenger loading doors could account for most if not all of the women and children who wanted to evacuate but didn't.

Well, my writer brain, of course, started thinking. What did happen to them? Obviously they got trapped in the hull of the ship somehow. There's no evidence of the passenger loading doors having been opened, and recent explorations indicate that the scissor gates inside them were still closed and locked when the ship sank. So what if, *Millennium*-style, time travelers from the future snatched them away?

I want to emphasize to all you writers out there that you should never, ever start writing based on an initial idea like this. That would have been a terrible story. John Varley did a great job with this premise in the early 80s, but nowadays it's done to death. However, it did get me wondering why someone might want to steal a bunch of *Titanic* victims away like that. And my brain slowly built the historical research institute. There's nothing like a primary source for studying history. And what better primary source than an actual, living person, right? Grab a group of people who you know died but whose bodies were never found or won't be missed, resettle them in the present day, and you've got a living laboratory.

Of course, it would be silly to limit yourself to just *Titanic*. You could actually go all John Varley with the 9/11 airplanes, or go back to a time when bodies were dumped before they were really dead. You can steal people from most any major historical event. It's an ethical quagmire, but a historian's paradise. And the ethics of it fascinated me. So I started mapping out a story, which means I started doing research.

I grabbed my deck plans of *Titanic* to see where it would be plausible that this group of victims got isolated and trapped.

And what I found was that my scenario didn't make any sense. At every point along the way, this group was in wide-open, public spaces, in full view of other passengers. Since survivors were at most every point in the ship at various points during the sinking, there was no way for this group of victims to be removed without witnesses – witnesses who lived to tell the story. The real-life mystery of what happened to this group of women and children deepened.

I did, of course, have the option of ignoring the facts and writing my story anyway. I mean, I was asking the reader to accept *time travel*, for crying out loud, who's going to notice a little detail like the fact that there was no way to *actually* get your hands on the human research subjects?

But that's not the type of writer I am.

I abandoned the concept.

But then, ultimately, I started to wonder what would happen if the scientists who built this research center made the exact same mistake I had made. What if they, too, had just assumed it would be straightforward to rescue substantial groups of people, and instead found that real life is messy, and real disasters are disordered and chaotic?

The story that resulted is radically different from the one I set out to write, but I think it's stronger for the research fail. It focuses much more tightly on individuals and their problems and less on the more abstract issues.

And it lets me counter anyone who accuses me of writing hard science fiction by pointing out that I wrote and published a cliché time-travel story.

Ignore the fact that it's still overly researched.

The Survivors' Menagerie

The waves crashed against the rocks as a grey sky pressed down on the choppy, silver water. Hannah's skirts clung to her ankles as the wind seemed to push her back from the water's edge, pressing its cold, salty fingers into her eyes and nose. Somewhere, somewhere across this vast ocean lay Donoughmore. What did it look like now?

"Hannah?"

Hannah didn't need to turn. She knew the voice. That excited American accent.

"If ye want me to stay inside, ye might consider locking the doors, so ye know," Hannah said.

"You're not a prisoner, Hannah." Chloe stepped up beside her. As usual, she wore an outfit comprised entirely of undergarments. All women dressed that way now, Hannah had been assured. And if the women Hannah had met over the past few months were any indication, it was true. "We just worry about you."

Hannah looked back out over the Atlantic. The late-morning sun glinted briefly off a dolphin breaching the surface. Hannah wondered if she could ride it home. "Ye ought to've left me on that ship, ye know."

They'd shown her pictures of that ship — a rusted, crushed hulk disintegrating into the sand, her fellow passengers' personal affects still strewn across the sea floor, occasionally a pair of leather shoes where a body no longer lay. Her own shoes should have been down there with them.

The wind freed a lock of Hannah's hair from the hairpin they'd made for her. Chloe had suggested several times that Hannah adopt the new custom of short hair, but somehow that just seemed obscene.

Gradually, Hannah realized that Chloe had remained uncharacteristically silent. Hannah turned and studied the older woman — the older woman who was actually 118 years her junior. A bit of the sea's salty spray clung to the crow's feet around Chloe's eyes. When she finally spoke, she spoke quietly, the sound almost completely absorbed by the wind. "You were our first, you know."

"I was." Hannah sat down on a lichen-covered rock. "Ye asked me if I wanted to live, so ye did. But the devil if I'm going to live in a menagerie."

"It's not a menagerie, Hannah!"

"So ye say, but what would ye call it, then? People come through to gawk at me, so they do. They say 'research,' but really they're thinking, 'Look at the odd little woman from 1912.' I'm a specimen, that's what I am."

Chloe grimaced down at another rock before dusting it off with her fingertips and sitting down on it gingerly, as if afraid of soiling the bloomers she paraded around in. "O.K." Chloe turned back to the ocean briefly before continuing. "O.K., fair enough. You're a scientific curiosity. But you're alive."

"Sure I'm alive." Hannah kicked at the surf-rounded pebbles under her feet. "Family dead. Friends dead. Just ye imagine, Miss Chloe, just ye imagine for maybe five minutes, if ye will, that I grabbed yer hand and said, 'Come with me, and by the way, everyone and everything ye know in the whole of God's green Earth is dead and gone a century and a half now.' Can ye imagine that, Miss Chloe?"

"I can only imagine that," Chloe said.

"I want to go home," Hannah said to the sea. "I want to see where me father's buried. I want to know what became of me brothers and of me sisters. I want to see me church. Have they torn down me church, now?"

"No. No, it's still there. But I don't think you'd recognize it. It was heavily modified during the Catholic Reconstruction."

"There's not even a God any more, is there, now?" Hannah felt the sting of her own tears. "The Church changed who God is while I was gone, so they did."

Chloe held out her hand. "Come back to the facility, Hannah."

A gull clucked. The waves crashed. And Hannah wondered if she could swim all the way to the bottom where that great liner slept.

• • •

Burning pain in his chest snapped Iamus awake. It was day. No. It was night. The strange, fireless light had fooled him again. It was night outside the unbreakable window. But the room was bright as day. Brighter.

Iamus pressed his hand to his chest and could feel the strange bumps where they had somehow closed his wounds. But the wounds still seared.

He dragged himself out of the bunk — the bunk that was simultaneously too hard and too soft, made of a metal that weighed far too little — and turned to the mirror that filled the wall. They always came when he addressed the mirror. "What have you done to me? I'm dying!"

The click. Iamus hadn't worked out how the lock worked, exactly, but it clicked just like any other lock. The door opened and the tall man who thought he spoke Latin stood there. "Be calm, and have peace," the tall man said, ridiculously formally. Iamus only understood the accent because when he had first been brought here he had insisted that his captors write down what they were trying to say. Of course, they had not known how to write their letters properly.

"I'm burning inside!" Iamus said.

The tall man entered and approached slowly, the door clicking again as it closed, the hinges eerily silent. Iamus hadn't been able to damage the door or the hinges, though they didn't feel like iron.

Iamus lunged. The tall man recoiled. Iamus caught the man's neck easily and slammed his body against the mirror. It rang like a drum. "What are you doing to me?" Iamus insisted.

The tall man gasped, his face reddening. Iamus' training had kicked in instinctively; he wasn't strangling the man, just making him uncomfortable. Making an opponent uncomfortable makes for a more satisfying show than killing him. Iamus pressed his body firmly against the tall man to keep him from squirming away. "You can talk," Iamus said. "Tell me where I am!"

Something hard, concealed in the man's garments, poked against Iamus' hip. He reached down with his left hand and pulled at it. A small, rectangular object slid out of the fold. Iamus slipped it under his own belt.

The door clicked again. Iamus didn't need to look. The large men who didn't speak any Latin would be there.

Iamus threw the tall man toward the door. He bounced once and slid along the smooth, oily surface toward the two large men. They grabbed him and pulled back out of the room. The door clicked shut behind them.

The pain had subsided a bit. Iamus turned his back to the mirror. He didn't know how they could see through the mirror, but that was clearly how they watched him. He stalked into the small room in the back, the one with the water-filled toilet, the washbasin with running water, and the larger basin that seemed to be intended as a tiny bath. They didn't seem to watch him in that room.

The object Iamus had taken from the tall man had an engraving of the man's bust on it, colored so naturally that almost looked like a miniature version of the man stared out at him, not like any painting. It was completely smooth to the touch, and had writing on it. Some of the letters were proper engraved Latin letters and some of them seemed like they could be variations of Latin letters.

Iamus wondered what sort of barbarians these people were.

. . .

Noah selected an English muffin to go with his eggs and Canadian bacon, and moved away from the food trough. Over on the far end of the common room, Chloe huddled with her research assistant, Thom, discussing something furtively near the door to the "staff only" section of the facility. Occasionally one of them would glance at the door to the room of the gladiator, Iamus, so it was reasonable to assume that it had to do with the ruckus he had kicked up again last night.

The facility had been built to accommodate a couple hundred, but thus far it only had a tiny fraction of that. There were twenty or so researchers, and, including the gladiator who still wasn't allowed out of his room, a half dozen research subjects. The woman in the uniform Noah didn't recognize stood by the bay windows, nursing a cup of coffee. Noah hadn't learned her name yet. She still seemed shell-shocked, never speaking. Noah preferred to let the staff deal with her. François, the French soldier, didn't seem to be up yet. The hippie, Bobby, sat at a table with three of the research team. Hannah, the girl from *Titanic*, sat alone at one of the tables with her book of crossword puzzles. Noah moved over to her.

"Mind if I join you, Hannah?"

"Please, Mr. Noah," she responded, motioning him to the chair opposite her. "'Tis actually quite impossible to do a crossword when ye don't know three-quarters of the references, so it is."

Noah sat down, and tried the eggs. Powdery, as usual. "I understand you escaped again yesterday."

"Escaped? I'm told that I just went for a walk."

"Is that what they said?" Noah asked. The Varidura™ floor shifted to a warmer amber tone to compensate as the sunlight broke through the clouds and streamed through the window onto the silent woman. Noah wasn't sure if whoever was funding the research had bought into the hype about Varidura™ being the only floor for high-traffic areas, or if they just thought it was actually beneficial to continually remind people from different eras that they weren't in Kansas anymore. He would have preferred a simple, timeless terrazzo. One that didn't change color. "I'm curious how you got out."

"I walked over and opened the door, so I did."

The only door to the outside in this part of the facility was the emergency exit, behind the security desk, on the far side of the common room. "It's alarmed, isn't it?"

"Well, so it is." Hannah leaned forward and smirked. "But, see, it has this clever little switch on it labeled 'off' which ye can flip if ye're smart."

Noah stared at the door. "And you just walked out?"

"I'm Irish, so I am. We're invisible."

"Not so much any more," Noah said absently. "At least, not where I come from."

"If ye say so." Hannah sat back in her chair. "So what year did they snatch ye out of, Mr. Noah?"

"2042."

"Ah, a baby by comparison, so you are. And so what great disaster where ye supposed to be a part of, then?"

"None as far as I know. I went out for a hike, and Chloe appeared and told me I had disappeared and my body was never found. I was her thesis advisor."

"And let me guess, now," Hannah's voice dropped half an octave, "she ne'er realized ye loved another."

Noah had been married at the time. "And they say Edwardian ladies were sheltered."

Hannah scoffed slightly. "So ye know, ladies belong to another class and George was king, if ye must know. And, so ye know, by taking ye, she guaranteed yer body would ne'er be found, so she did."

"The thought had occurred to me." Noah finished his eggs and decided against taking his tray back to the service conveyor.

"So does that mean she was working on her time machine then?"

"Actually, temporal physics was my field," Noah said, suddenly feeling his "professor" instinct taking over. "We were working on sending subatomic particles as part of a communications and computing system. The idea of using it for transportation was… well, they'd've thought we'd gone walkabout. The advances Chloe made are… something."

Hannah nodded blankly. "So I suppose ye find it harder than H.G. Wells made it sound, now?"

"Much," Noah said with a chuckle.

"So why aren't ye in there, working with them?"

Noah felt the anger rise up through his neck. "I have a daughter, you know. She'd be 36 now. And here I am, alive, and I can't even tell her what happened." Hannah's gaze had shifted to the large picture windows across the room, a wistful look in her eye. "Oh, I'm sorry," Noah said. "You're family's completely gone, aren't they?"

"To be honest to God, me family and me, we had differences," Hannah said. "Bought the ticket and left without saying goodbye, so I did. £17. Too late now."

"You had a future. You had a life."

"Which would have ended that night, so I'm told. Lost at sea, so I was, body ne'er found, or ne'er identified. But I'm an old-fashioned girl, now. I expected heaven. Instead I got a menagerie, so I did."

"Yes," Noah said. "And I wonder why our keepers are locking themselves in here with us."

Noah stood up and marched toward the emergency door.

One of the guards stood up from behind the security desk. "We'd prefer if you didn't use that door, Doctor," the guard said to him.

Noah was quite sure of that. He wondered if he could learn Hannah's trick of turning invisible.

• • •

Iamus pushed the strange lever by the door upwards, and the fireless light brightened again. He pushed it downward and it dimmed. By pushing it all the way to the bottom of the little box built into the wall, he could make the light go out altogether, the only light in the room then coming through the unbreakable window. Iamus had control of the light. And the people who watched through the mirror wouldn't be able to see in the dark.

The lock on the door clicked. He had gotten too close to it with the strange engraved thing under his belt. Iamus stepped away. He didn't want them to realize he had learned how to operate the lock.

Iamus scanned the room. The blanket on the bed was surprisingly sturdy for its weight. It would work like a net. Now, he just needed a weapon.

• • •

The rain left streaks down the glass. Outside, a gull shook its head, futilely refusing to be wet. Behind Hannah, Chloe chattered to some of her staff about which of her family members had fled America, and to where, and which hadn't made it out in time.

Somewhere to the south of them, the Land of Opportunity was no more. At least, if the stories were true.

But somehow, Hannah preferred to believe that it was still 1912. And somewhere in space-time, if her professor had explained it correctly — yes, Hannah decided, Mr. Noah was still a professor even if he was out of his own time as well — somewhere in space-time, it still was.

• • •

The sun had set, its long shadows finally blending into the darkness. The window in his cell faced north as much as west, but Iamus had been able to watch Apollo's chariot disappear behind the craggy rocks over the next hill. Even at midday the shadows were longer than they were in Rome, so Iamus knew he was in the north, somewhere. Farther north than he'd ever been, though. He was born in Rome, and had only traveled for the games. But if he could find a road and head south, eventually he should be able to make his way back to civilization.

Iamus turned. Darkness had spread through the room, a faint hint of twilight coming through the window. In the mirror, six tiny green lights shone as if coming from behind it. On the lever that controlled the light in the ceiling, a red light shone. Iamus reached back and pulled the window blind down to prevent whoever was watching from figuring out what he was doing in the backlight.

The table wasn't hard to find in the dark. Iamus felt his hand along it until he located the leg. Placing one foot on the table, he yanked the table leg sharply. It snapped satisfyingly, the table sliding away from his foot as he came up with the sharpened shard of the leg. With his left hand, Iamus pulled the blanket off the bed, and swung it a few times until he found a balance point. Thrusting spear and net weren't his specialty — and Iamus had never seen someone fight with that particular combination — but it would have to do. It wouldn't be unlike fighting as the fisherman, with trident and net, and little armor. Iamus wished he had armor.

Iamus focused like he would before the games, and moved toward the red light.

He found the door handle. The door unlocked exactly as before. Slipping the strange key back into his tunic, Iamus readied his weapons again and pulled the door open.

Bright light streamed into the room from the outer basilica. It was huge — three stories tall, with balconied walks on all sides leading to more doors like his. Iamus seemed to be on the ground floor. Two dozen tables stood at the center of the room, and on one wall an enormous window looked out into the darkness, several misshapen couches gathered in front of it. About a dozen people populated the space, all dressed in strange, barbarian attire. Thus far they hadn't noticed him. A door stood by the enormous window, and between it and him stood a dais, with a desk on it that two men in identical clothing sat behind. Identical clothing meant uniform, which meant the two men were either priests or soldiers. The first rule of the games with an unknown objective is that defenders place themselves between you and your objective. That door was his objective.

Somebody shouted as Iamus began to move across the open room. People began to scatter, but the two soldiers stood and flanked their desk to set up a line in front of him. They pulled black, chevron-shaped objects from their belts and pointed them at Iamus, as if to ward him back.

The old woman with the Greek name, Chloe, ran past Iamus and stood in front of him, holding her hand out. "Iamus, stop, I pray you," she said. Her Latin was better than the rest, mostly because she had taken the time to try to learn how to pronounce it correctly.

"Stand aside, barbarian," Iamus said, pointing the improvised spear and starting the blanket spinning.

"Iamus, put down the… arbor," the old woman said.

Iamus swung the blanket, catching her hand with it. He yanked it aside and she fell with a yelp. He continued toward the door.

The two soldiers shouted in a language Iamus didn't know.

"Stop!" the old woman screamed from behind him.

One of the soldiers pressed his shoulder closer to the other soldier. "Stop," he ordered hesitantly, his accent almost incomprehensible.

Iamus charged.

Four sounds like thunder echoed through the enormous room. Someone screamed. Iamus' legs stopped moving. As the pain registered, Iamus realized he was screaming.

Blood streamed out of his chest and stomach. "Glory to the Emperor," he forced himself to say, "…who am about to die… you…"

Iamus' legs gave out from under him.

• • •

Several people cried. The five remaining research subjects and the entire staff of the research facility had gathered in the common room. Most of the blood had been mopped up, but several splatters still clung to the railing above Noah's head.

Chloe, blanched and still trembling, stood by the door to the staff-only wing. "Obviously," she was saying, "what happened here tonight was a terrible tragedy, and the last thing any of us wanted. I've asked the university to send up one of our crisis counselors. She should be here in the morning, for anyone who wants to talk."

One of the staff members translated for François. There were a few additional murmurs, and a general sense of unease.

A loud, strong voice cut through the room. "Is that what you have in store for the rest of us?" It had come from the silent woman in the uniform Noah had never identified.

"No, no, of course not," Chloe said, her voice cracking. "Iamus was a… difficult situation. He wasn't a planned take. We were investigating the Flavian Amphitheatre, and he was brought into the *spoliarium* — that's where the bodies of the dead gladiators were processed. Dr. Mancini and I realized he wasn't actually dead, and that his injuries might be survivable with modern medicine. Nobody was paying attention, and we didn't really think much beyond that."

Noah thought that Chloe was again not thinking through her actions. He wasn't sure what he would have done if a Roman gladiator had been killed by security guards in a facility where he was doing unauthorized time-travel research, but he was pretty sure that hiding the body in the walk-in freezer without reporting anything would not be the best choice.

"With the rest of you," Chloe was still saying, "you were pulled out before… The plan all along was that if anyone truly couldn't adjust and would rather go back and face your demise in your own time, we could simply put you back. Of course, we had also thought we'd be able to pull out more people from each of your times, but it proved surprisingly difficult to isolate subjects. Late enough in the series of events that you wouldn't be missed, that is. But since we had done emergency surgery and fixed Iamus' wounds, if we put him back he would have sprung up from his stretcher miraculously healed. But he obviously wasn't adjusting well. It was a terrible situation and I take full responsibility."

A truly responsible person would have called the Royal Canadian Mounted Police and explained the whole situation. Noah stood up and wandered over to the window. It appeared to be raining again. Periodically a drop caught the light coming from the inside and flashed silver as it passed the window.

"Miss Chloe," the girl from *Titanic* said, "it seems to me that you might've overlooked some of the ethics before ye started yer research, now."

"In retrospect, I concur with that, Hannah," Chloe said, her voice surprisingly strong. "From our point of view, you were all dead when we started. Even in our field, it's hard to think of a dead person as a living, breathing individual."

"So what do we do?" one staff member asked. "I'm not keeping a body in my freezer. Not if you expect me to keep food there."

There was a long pause as the principal investigators of the various science teams looked at each other. "We haven't decided yet," Dr. Mancini said.

Another staff member stood up angrily. "Look! I don't know about the rest of you, but I just barely made it out of the States alive," he barked. "My family didn't. I don't want to risk the Canadians deciding to send us back."

"That's one of the issues we're considering," Chloe said.

Thom sprang from his seat and shouted across the crowd, "And how the hell did you not notice that he had your key card?"

"I had to be carried back to my room!" one of the grad students shouted back.

The argument held everyone's attention pretty thoroughly. Noah moved over to the emergency door. As Hannah had promised, the door alarm had an inconspicuous on-off switch on the bottom.

"Obviously, if there's nothing to alert the Canadian government, there's no immediate risk," Dr. Mancini said. It struck Noah as an attempt to stop the accusations from flying.

"You're not keeping a dead body in my freezer!"

"That's a temporary solution."

"We should've called the R.C.M.P. right away!"

"There are too many of us here who can't take the risk."

"Unless ye're planning to take a bullet-riddled body and drop it back in the Colosseum, it seems like that would just be a matter of time, so it would."

Noah clicked the alarm off, and quietly slipped out through the door. The cold hit him like a blast. He hadn't been cold in several weeks. He could hear the ocean, which meant he knew which way the city was. He had visited here before, back when the land contained only a small wildlife research station.

Noah took off running into the rainy night.

. . .

Drawn, ashen faces. Tightened lips. Thin, forced smiles. Hannah had seen the expressions before, countless times. They were the expressions that parents, police officers, and government officials had when they were frightfully worried, but trying not to worry anyone else. And the staff still had them that morning.

The sun had come out again, rising over the Atlantic and streaming in through the main windows. Chloe sat on one of the sofas, her feet up on the cushion in front of her, her chin on her knees, staring out at the sea. She wore one of those expressions. Hannah sat down beside her.

"I need to go back, now, Miss Chloe."

Chloe turned to her and smiled slightly. "I know," she said. "Just let me know when you're ready."

. . .

The hard part had been finding someplace to cross the river. For some reason, the one bridge that had been there forty years ago now lay twisted and broken in the waves, rusted and overgrown. But by following the river upstream back to what had once been a vacation community, he found another bridge, and had reached the outskirts of the city right around dawn.

The city hadn't changed much. The hairstyles on the billboards were different, as were the names of the products being advertised, but on the whole it was the same little town he had known so many years ago.

Police stations aren't the easiest things to find, and the city had a distinct paucity of pedestrians to ask so early in the morning. But by following the transit lines, he finally came across one.

The desk officer looked up as Noah entered. "Can I help you, sir?"

"Yes," Noah said, and then suddenly didn't know where to begin. "I'm sorry, could you start by telling me today's date."

"Fifth of September," the desk officer said.

"What year?"

"Are you feeling disoriented, sir?"

"Um, perhaps," Noah said. "What year is it?"

"'62."

"In that case I'm not feeling disoriented," Noah said, though he was sure he must've looked quite a fright, having spent the night running through a rainstorm and then drip-drying on the walk into town. "My name is Noah Broadbent. I'm a research physicist from Sioux City, Iowa. I believe I should've been reported missing about 20 years ago."

The desk officer raised an eyebrow. "20 years?"

I'm happy to provide you a biometric sample to prove my identity," Noah said.

"Now I want you to think very carefully about that," the desk officer said. "If the American government is looking for you and I query their database with your biometrics, they're going to march right up here and take you back."

"But we're in Canada, aren't we?"

"That's not going to stop anyone."

"Well, look, I'm not wanted, I'm just missing."

"That's much the same thing, as far as the Americans are concerned."

Noah stared at the man. He seemed to be in earnest. And yet what he was saying made no sense. "Why is everyone so afraid of the American government all of a sudden?"

The desk officer grimaced and bit down on the catch end of his writing stylus. "Look, I'm going to do you a favor," he said. "Now, I'll admit this is partly because I'm not in a hurry to mix up with the Americans, but it's for your own good, too. I'm not going to look you up in the American identity databases until you've been checked out by Mental Health Services. If you're sane, you've got nothing to worry about. If you're confused, then they'll be able to help. Does that sound acceptable to you?"

Noah wasn't sure he was ever sane. But if there was, in fact, some reason to fear the American government, it did seem prudent to get the facts from someone who didn't have a vested interest in keeping him in the dark. "Sure," Noah said.

The double-locked doors buzzed. "Just step right through that door, and someone will take you down to the holding area."

. . .

The whole room whined like the wind pushing through the cracks in a stone wall. That sound had given rise to the legends of the banshees, so it was told. And now it seemed as if a banshee wailed for Hannah. The sound actually came from the fans in the machinery, Hannah knew, but still, it seemed poetically appropriate.

The time machine looked much like it had when Hannah had first arrived, but clutter had overtaken the room around it. Hannah had put back on the dressing gown and shoes she had been wearing that night, and now she stood beside the octagonal platform ready to step back… well… right where she had left off.

Most of the research team either stood around the machinery on the periphery of the room or stood behind the glass wall in the observation chamber.

Chloe walked into the room, hugging Hannah's life vest to her chest. She sighed a bit as she handed it over. "We had to stitch it back up again. Some of the team had taken some of the seams out to try to identify where the cork inside was grown, and another one wanted to do some drop-tests on a good copy of it. No one should notice."

Hannah put the life vest back on, trying to remember how it was supposed to fit. Chloe helped her with it, choking back a sob.

"Ne'er be sad, now, Miss Chloe. For I was dead for a century and half before ye met me."

"I know," Chloe said, adjusting the life vest and stepping back to inspect her handiwork. "But I've grown quite fond of you, and I'm never going to see you again."

"I would say I'll miss ye, too, Miss Chloe, but I suspect me future is a bit short to spend too much time missing people, so it is."

Chloe laughed through a sob.

"Chloe," came a tinny voice over a speaker from the observation room. "Noah didn't come to breakfast. We just checked his room. We can't find him anywhere and the exit alarm has been disabled again."

"Goddamn Canadian fire code!" Chloe exclaimed. "He'll be on foot, but he knows the area, so he's probably headed into town. I don't want to keep Hannah waiting."

Several people in the observation room slipped out. Hannah pointed to the octagon, where she had been standing when this room first appeared around her. "I stand here, do I now?"

"Yes," Chloe said. "Would you like me to come with you?"

"If ye're putting me back right where ye found me, I suspect I can find me own way out of the ladies' lav," Hannah said, climbing onto the octagon.

Chloe laughed again, sniffling as she did, tears running down both cheeks. "Counting down in three- two- one-"

"Bye now," Hannah said.

She felt suddenly off-balance, as if the floor dropped out from under her momentarily. When she caught her footing, the floor was tilted. The linoleum tile floor. In the ladies' lavatory with the grand oak paneling. Hannah swung the door open and walked up the short hallway to where the group was assembled. The crewmember who had led them below decks still argued with the porter.

"My orders were to bring these ladies below and load them into the boats through the passenger loading doors at the waterline."

"I'm quite sure this isn't where he meant. This is the first class reception area. And besides, we're nowhere near the waterline, nor are we likely to be. He probably meant the third-class entrance on E deck."

"How do we get there?"

"Take this staircase down and follow the starboard passage forward. Once you go through into the third-class section, the doors are right there, port and starboard."

"Very well." The crewmember turned to the mass of about 80 women. Hannah slipped back into the group through the arched opening. "Ladies," he announced, "we're going to go down one more deck. Everyone follow me, please."

The great iron ship moaned, as if warning them that going deeper into her bowels was suicide. The group shuffled back toward the grand, wooden staircase, ignoring the omens.

• • •

The Mounties flanked Noah as they walked up to the front door of the university research facility. The one on the right pressed the buzzer. "Yes?" came a voice over the speaker.

"Royal Canadian Mounted Police."

There was an ominous pause. "I'll be right down."

The other Mountie turned to Noah. "What sort of research did you say they're doing here?"

"Temporal physics," Noah said. "Mapping, characterizing, and manipulating the fourth dimension of space-time."

The door opened, and one of the grad students stood there. Noah had never managed to learn his name. There were too many staff and Noah had found the whole experience too overwhelming to grill people repeatedly on who they were. "Noah! We've been looking everywhere for you!"

The Mountie on Noah's right produced a warrant. "I'm afraid we're going to have to take a look around."

The grad student scanned the warrant. "Of course. Come on in. Do you mind if I make a copy of this?"

"We'll provide a copy along with a seizure report if we have to take anything when we leave," the Mountie said, stepping into the lobby. Noah had never been in this room before. It was tastefully decorated with old-fashioned leather furniture and pictures of the university from its early days in the 20th century.

The grad student shot Noah a pleading glance. "What can I show you first?"

"The research lab, if you don't mind," the other Mountie responded. "And then we'll need to check out your power generators."

Chloe emerged from one of the side offices, hovering under a potted tree.

"Of course," the grad student said, leading them away from Noah. "The research equipment is all down at the end of the hall here."

Chloe swooped in as soon as they were out of earshot. "Are you insane?" she whispered through clenched teeth. "They're going to ship us all back to America!" She motioned furiously for some of the other staff to come over to her.

"What is going on in America?" Noah insisted. The mental health service worker who had interviewed him had just smiled pityingly when he asked her to catch him up.

"The Constitution can be suspended in an emergency, and right now, disagreeing with the government constitutes an emergency." She grabbed two of the staffers. "Get Iamus' body out of the freezer, and get it up here without the Mounties seeing it. Get his clothes and equipment, get the body dressed, and be ready to get it into the lab the instant they're done poking around in it."

"What are you going to do?" Noah asked.

Chloe turned to him, fury flashing in her eyes. "I'm going to dump his bullet-riddled body back in the *spoliarium* and pray to God the archaeologists never find him."

. . .

An electric light in a cage cast beams out through the smoke from countless cigarettes, dim compared to the lights they used in the facility. The scent of the thousand men who had been calling the ship home since Queenstown mixed with the smell of tobacco and the remnants of their last meal.

And now, they waited.

The crewmember had vanished to look for someone with the keys to the Bostwick Gates that sealed the passenger loading doors, and probably to get reinforcements as well. Over a hundred men, upon learning that the women would be loaded into boats out of these doors, had assembled here. Not all of them appeared ready to stand aside.

Hannah heard a brief phrase in an odd tongue, and she looked and noticed a dark-skinned woman, probably an Arab, talking to a young boy and a young girl. Hannah looked more closely at the rest of the group. A few of the ladies had children, mostly babies.

When Chloe had taken her, she had mentioned that they had

wanted to rescue this entire group, but they were surprised that some of the people in the group had survived, or that their bodies had been found and identified later. They had apparently thought it was a group of only 20 or so who had been led below decks to load into boats at the waterline and subsequently vanished. Hannah had been the only one they had been able to isolate, when she wandered off to use the lavatory.

Not all these people were going to die here, below decks.

About twenty feet forward, water had started to come up through a stairwell, also seeping up between the floorboards. A strange, greenish glow lit up the water.

This ship had electric lights.

"Electricity and water," Hannah said aloud.

"What?" the Arab woman said. Her son — he looked to be about seven — buried his face in her skirts sleepily as her daughter, probably about ten, swayed in her spot.

"We had best start moving out of here, now," Hannah said strongly. "This ship has electric lights, and if we're here when the water gets here, we'll all be electrocuted, so we will."

"The crewman said to wait here, so he did," one woman called back from the far side of the group.

"And where is he, now?" Hannah responded. "Let's go, now. Everybody up the stairs." The staircases nearest them didn't have water coming up them yet. Hannah was still a bit nervous that their steel frames might already be electrified, but it was certainly better than staying put. The wood treads and handrail were probably safe enough.

One of the men, seated on the staircase on the far side of the ship yelled back in a Cockney accent, "They're not letting 3rd class up on the boat deck yet, anyway."

"We were all on the boat deck, so we were," Hannah barked back. "They're letting the women and children through, now. Everyone up!"

"Yer wasting yer breath," another man, on the nearer staircase, said. "The decks are clogged, so they are. You'll ne'er get through."

"Then we go this way," Hannah said, and marched toward the back of the ship, into the mouth of a long corridor, which now sloped uphill at an uncomfortable angle. "Who's with me, now?"

The Arab lady grabbed her children by the hands and marched

after Hannah. Everyone else just stared at her as she walked past.

Hannah paused in the arch of the corridor and looked back. "I'm just telling ye," Hannah said. "Go yer way or mine, but if ye stay here, ye'll die. I know that, so I do. I know that."

Hannah climbed up the corridor. The Arab lady trotted behind her. "Do you know where you're going?" Her English was actually pretty good, despite the accent.

"The stewards have their quarters down here, so they do," Hannah said. "So there must be doors back into the 1st and 2nd class areas."

After a moment Hannah found what she needed. An emergency hatch that swung inward, and if her estimates were right it was about as far up the corridor as they had walked down from the grand staircase.

She studied the latch. "Do ye have something we might be able to stick in here?" she asked.

"Your hairpin," the Arab woman said.

Hannah's hand instinctively went to her hair. It was up. She had left her hairpin in her cabin when the steward had woken her up. Her hair had been down when Chloe pulled her off the ship. She took out the iridescent plastic hairpin the staff at the facility had made for her, letting her hair again fall down around her life vest.

The hairpin was exactly the right size to fit into the latch on the emergency door. Down the corridor, Hannah heard the hiss of water and the shrieks of women as it reached them. Inserting the pin, she yanked hard on the hatch, and it swung open with a clang. Sure enough, the base of the grand staircase lay right in front of them.

Hannah grabbed the Arab woman's son and lifted him through the hatch, noting that he was a bit heavy to carry much farther than that. The little girl stepped through next, followed by Hannah and the Arab. Hannah leaned back through the hatch. "I've got a hatch open here, now!" she yelled as loud as she could.

Hissing and shrieking were her only answers.

"All right, now," Hannah said. "Up the stairs, all the way to the top!"

The 1st class reception room above them still had gentlemen seated in it, enjoying drinks as the ship sank beneath them. "There's water on the deck below you, now," Hannah called out as they rounded the landing to the next flight. The gentlemen didn't move. Irish women are invisible, after all, and rarely know what they're talking about.

The next deck was mostly cabins, just a few couches lining the wall as they rounded the landing. On their way up the next flight, the little boy stopped and said something to his mother. She responded, and he sank down onto a step. "He's tired," the Arab woman said. "He needs to rest."

"We have to keep moving, so we do," Hannah said. "These stairs, they're made of wood, now, and wood floats. So when the water gets to the bottom of these stairs, then pop, pop, pop, they'll float up and these stairs here will come crashing down, so they will." That was how they had explained the damage to her when they showed her the pictures of the wreck. "We've got to get all the way to the top just as fast as we can."

The Arab woman nodded, and pulled her son to his feet. He whined, but she barked at him sternly, and they were moving again.

Hannah coaxed the children up two more flights to the promenade deck. A quick glance confirmed that there were no boats loading at this level, so she waved the Arab to keep going up to the top.

They emerged on the boat deck and Hannah charged out the doors into the freezing air. The band still played a ragtime tune, out of tune with the cold. The lifeboat davits hung out over the rail, empty.

"Are there any other women and children?" a voice called from her left side.

"Here!" Hannah yelled. The Arab woman had just arrived behind her with the children. Hannah grabbed her and steered her toward the increasingly low-in-the-water bow, nearly blind in the dim deck light. "Women and children here, now!"

Up ahead, Hannah could just make out one last lifeboat, all the way forward, looking almost completely full as it hung by the rail.

The Arab woman seemed to realize the urgency. She grabbed her children and began to run, weaving through the crowd of gentlemen on the deck.

"Women and children, coming through, now," Hannah barked as she weaved through the crowd, keeping an eye on the children in front of her.

When they arrived at the boat, an officer turned to her. She didn't let him speak. "Get the children in the boat, now."

The officer lifted the little girl in, and a gentleman with a moustache lifted the boy in, and then helped the Arab woman in after him.

"Now you, miss," the officer said to Hannah.

Hannah looked over the rail. She couldn't see the water in the blackness, though she knew it was probably only ten feet below now.

"Now I know it's a frightful sight," the gentleman said, "but if you don't look down, you can step right in quite safely."

Hannah knew she hadn't gotten into the lifeboat. If she had, Chloe would never have taken her.

And yet, she knew this ship would sink. And she knew the water was cold as ice.

"The devil with dying," Hannah said. She sat on the rail and spun her legs around into the lifeboat.

"Any other women and children?" the officer hollered. He waited a moment, to no response. "Right, then, lower away!"

The pulleys creaked and the boat began to rock. The gentleman with the moustache stepped into the lifeboat just as it began to move, taking the seat on the edge of the boat beside Hannah.

As the boat passed the promenade deck, the faces of gentlemen being left behind to die peered out the glass at them curiously.

"By Jove, what have I done?" the gentleman with the moustache said quietly.

And Hannah wondered the exact same thing.

• • •

Iamus' body was stiff and cold as it lay on the floor. The old woman with the Greek name, Chloe, barked orders in her barbarian language to two younger men. They seemed flustered. The old woman stood on an octagonal platform and motioned with both hands towards Iamus.

One of the young men pointed at the old woman, yammering in their odd language. She looked down at her barbarian clothes, and then quickly ducked out of the room. She returned a moment later with a long, black cloak. She slipped the cloak on and put the hood up as she stepped back onto the octagon.

The two younger men then picked Iamus up and leaned him against her shoulder. She was taller than Iamus, but not as strong as a tall woman ought to be. She had to struggle, holding onto his breastplate, to keep him from slumping off the octagon.

And then, all at once, they were back in the spoliarium. Torchlight flickered on the rough-hewn walls, and the stench of blood, sweat, and decay filled the air. The stretcher Iamus had been carried out of the arena on lay vacant on the floor. The old woman gave him a push, and he collapsed back onto it. She bent down and tried to position his body back on the stretcher properly.

The two men who were stripping the armor off the bodies looked up just then. "Who are you?" the older one barked.

The cloaked old woman looked up, and backed into the corner.

The two men darted across the room, leaping Iamus' body, but the old woman had vanished before they got there.

"Look at this," the younger man said. "He's cold, and the blood on his armor is dried up, like he was killed a month ago."

The older man pulled off Iamus' breastplate. "And these aren't sword wounds."

"I don't understand," the younger man said.

And thus, for three centuries the story was told that Libitina, goddess of death, herself walked in the spoliarium, healing anyone brought there prematurely, but coldly re-dispatching them if no one noticed soon enough.

. . .

Noah sat cross-legged on the leather couch as Chloe emerged from the time-travel lab, a black coat draped over her arm. She marched purposefully over to Dr. Mancini. "Where are the Mounties?"

"They're in the common room, interviewing Bobby and François."

"Have they been down to the power station yet?"

"Yes. The permits are posted. It's fine."

"No," Chloe said, then she turned to Noah. "You were right, Noah."

Noah stood up. "About what?"

Chloe handed Dr. Mancini her coat. "Get everyone out of the building."

She walked over to the wall and pulled the fire alarm. The klaxon blared and the emergency lights began strobing the path to the nearest exit. Chloe vanished into the stairwell.

One of the Mounties appeared in the doorway at the far end of the foyer, the one that led to the common room. "What the hell is going on?" he bellowed.

Gradually, it dawned on Noah. "Chloe, no!" he yelled, and dashed for the stairwell.

As the door swung shut behind him, Noah heard Dr. Mancini saying, "Get everyone out of the building. We assemble on the beach and the transit stop."

The stairs went both up and down, but if Chloe was interested in the power station, she would have gone down. Power stations were in basements, normally. Noah pursued.

The basement stretched out under the entire T-shaped structure as one enormous room, the occasional steel column holding up the I-beams that formed the bones of the building. Hydrogen tanks lined the walls. The power station glowed up ahead, under the common room.

A clang echoed through the basement, followed by a hiss. "Chloe!" Noah yelled.

"Noah, get out of here!" Another clang. More hissing.

Noah ran toward the source of the sound, "Chloe, you're going to get yourself killed!" He rounded the corner just as Chloe swung a large wrench, breaking the valve off of a third hydrogen tank.

"That'll save me a trip back to America." She broke open a fourth hydrogen tank. "If you're not going to leave, at least go upstairs and scatter the components of the displacement controls. We don't want anyone reconstituting it after the fire." She broke off another valve and then marched for the far wall. "Displacement control. It's still based on your designs. You should recognize it."

Noah had seen her like this before, but never so intense. It was useless trying to reason with her.

He wondered if he should say goodbye.

"Noah, go!"

Noah turned and ran back to the stairwell, taking the steps two at a time. He burst back out into the lobby to find both Mounties grilling Dr. Mancini. "It's a hydrogen leak," Noah said. "Get everyone out. Don't do anything that might cause a spark. I'm calling the fire department."

Nobody spoke as Noah dashed into the time-travel lab. The door wasn't locked. One of the grad students stood vigil over the apparatus, ignoring the ear-splitting wails of the fire alarm. "Get out of the building," Noah said. "Which one is the displacement control?"

The young woman pointed. Noah nodded and started releasing the magnetic catches on its casing. "If you can pull anything off of it, put it in your pocket, and then get out of here before the whole building goes boom."

The student nodded, shoving an interactive panel into her pocket. She moved for the door slowly at first, and then broke into a run.

As the access panel came off, Noah could see that it truly was based on his designs. Much more powerful, of course, but the same basic premise. The central control unit would be the key to making it work, and without it, the whole machine was just a collection of random electronics.

And Chloe had cleverly designed the system so that the central control unit was a nondescript chip off to the side of the CPU. Noah wrestled it off of its connector plate, and pocketed it.

The octagonal coupling system in the middle of the room would also be informative to anyone who found it. Fortunately, it was highly flammable if the gas tubes inside were breached. Noah pulled up floor plates until he found the feed hose. A quick search of one of the desks turned up a knife, and he cut the line.

Belatedly, he realized he hadn't called the fire department as promised. He walked over to the videocon and pressed the fire symbol. A young man in a dispatch uniform, unchanged since Noah's last visit to Canada, appeared on the screen. "We have your alarm, what's the nature of the emergency?"

"Hydrogen leak," Noah said.

"We're on our way."

Noah cut the connection and headed back out into the lobby. It was now empty of people, and Noah could feel himself growing light-headed. The hydrogen gas was almost certainly rising. He ducked back into the common room, scanning for stragglers, and especially looking for anyone who might have passed out. He then headed across the common room to the emergency door, which stood open.

The other residents and most of the staff had assembled down the hill on the rocky beach. Noah clambered down toward them.

Noah never heard the explosion. The heat seared his back, and he felt as if someone had run into him with a car. The rocks came up on him quickly. He had already bounced once before he realized he had been thrown to the ground. He didn't hear anything as he stood back up, his ribs protesting, and saw the entire research facility engulfed in flames.

One of the Mounties walked up to him, his mouth moving but no sound coming out. Noah didn't need to hear what he was saying to know that he was very, very annoyed.

And thus, it came to pass that Canada never again allowed American research on Canadian soil without a letter of accountability from the government of the United States.

. . .

It was raining in America when the rescue ship arrived, the skies over New York a not-quite-black shade of grey as the city lights bled into the dreary night. Hannah wore a dress that a lady had been kind enough to give her, and she had about $200 the wealthier survivors and passengers from the rescue ship had collected to help out those whom the sinking had left destitute.

Every time the crew of the rescue ship had come around taking names, Hannah had simply slipped away onto another part of the ship. Most of the survivors gave their names eagerly, many times, hoping to get word to loved ones that they were safe, or hoping their husbands had been picked up by another ship. Now that her family was alive again, Hannah really didn't care if they thought she was dead.

But here, in the terminal, there would be one last obstacle to overcome.

The floors of the massive granite and iron terminal building were slick where the rain had been trodden in. There was a separate queue for immigrants. Already over a hundred of her fellow survivors stood in a jagged row, waiting to give their names one more time. Hannah knew enough about America to know that you didn't really need to go through that line if you could avoid it.

Mrs. Astor marched across the terminal toward the street. Hannah dropped in behind and beside her like she was her maid.

Slowly, Mrs. Astor stopped, the echoes of her footsteps dying away belatedly. She turned around and looked right at Hannah. She had been crying. Her eyes were swollen and red, and tear tracks ran across the powder on her youthful cheeks.

Mrs. Astor's gaze shifted to the sign for the immigrants' queue, then back to Hannah. She grinned slightly. Hannah could only shrug.

Mrs. Astor turned around, her hat snapping briskly from the sudden move, and resumed marching toward the exit. Hannah kept pace behind her. They walked right past the immigration line, with no one taking Hannah's name.

And thus, Hannah's body was never found by the recovery vessel that had set sail the day before.

On the street, an enormous crowd had gathered, peering through rain and darkness for the survivors. Reporters shouted questions, as dozens of police officers fought to hold them back.

Once outside, Hannah simply split from Mrs. Astor and let the crowd envelop her. Irish girls were invisible, after all. Her only regret was that she would never get the chance to thank the lady for the service.

Hannah turned around and looked back at the terminal, just like all the other curious onlookers. The iron arch with "Cunard Line" written across it was barely visible in the street light, and the stone facade looked more like a mausoleum than a terminal. Not a single person in the crowd suspected that she was one of the survivors they were so desperate to see, to touch, to interview.

As someone pressed forward for a better view, Hannah would let them pass. And soon, she was at the back of the crowd.

The lights of the skyscrapers flickered against the night sky, a steady drizzle making Hannah damp, but not quite wet.

Hannah crossed the street and walked along what the sign said was W. 13th Street.

She didn't know where she was going, but she had some money, and she had hope.

New York was a very modern city. Hannah had read that most of these skyscrapers were only a few years old, and more were being built all the time.

But Hannah had seen the future, and somehow twinkling lights against a night sky didn't feel breathtaking to her.

She didn't know why she wanted it, but somewhere up in Canada there was a parcel of land on a small island Hannah figured she should buy. It would make a lovely home for wild animals.

And she didn't know if he would listen, but somewhere in America there was almost certainly a physicist who needed an assistant who understood the four-dimensional nature of the universe.

And so, Hannah disappeared into the misty night.

Little Dystopias

A common complaint I hear about contemporary science fiction is that it's bleak and pessimistic. Gone are the days when science fiction was all about how wonderful the future is going to be.

Well, there's a good reason for that. If there isn't something *wrong*, there's no story to be told. Problems make for much more interesting reading than everything being hunky-dory.

Personally, I find the prospect of colonizing Venus quite exciting. The technology to do so doesn't exist yet, but the theoretical foundations are all there. Someday, perhaps not too far in the future, we really could send humans off to live on our sister planet. This is wonderful! This is the future! This isn't a story....

It's my job as a writer to flip that gleeful vision of what can be over and to examine its underside. What's going to go wrong? What is going to be unsavory, or painful, or unacceptable? That's where the tension and the drama lie, and therefore that's where my story is. So it's my job to take these wonderful visions of the future and break them. I take utopian visions and make little dystopias out of them.

So, Venus. Colonization happening – woo hoo! But this is an alien planet. The day is longer than the year. There's no magnetic field, which means there's no protection from the Sun's harmful radiation. The temperature and pressure are really only bearable at high altitude, ironically about the same place where the clouds are made of sulfuric acid. And then there's that soupy, soupy atmosphere. So, Venus. Colonization happening – are you mad?!

That's my job. Those of you who want happy visions of the future, I recommend the various science and technology journals. And even there, you're going to have to pick carefully.

It's my job to do this to my characters, too. When was the last time you heard someone tell a riveting story about the time their day went just fine and nothing bad happened? No, the good stories are the ones that happen when all the chips come down, when something truly terrible is going on and the person has to give all they've got (and then some) just to get through it. So my characters may be well-adjusted, loving, happy people most of the time, but that's not the story I'm going to tell. Again, I'm going to flip them over and see what's wrong with them. And then I'm going to throw a situation at them that pushes those traits to the forefront.

None of this means I don't believe the future can be better, or that I don't think people can do better than we have in the past. And I think that even as I break good people and expose the dark side of ideals, I'm still pointing toward a brighter future. But I think it's your job, as a reader, to look at where my stories are set, what my characters are willing to do, and to extrapolate for yourselves what that means for when things are going well. Is that a future you want to live in? If so, work towards it. If not, work to make the changes today that will steer us in another direction.

After all, the future isn't in my hands. It's in ours.

Pressure and the Argument Tree

It takes about two hours for a person to fall the 55 kilometers through the soupy atmosphere from the dirigible city to the surface of Venus. They're dead long before they hit the ground. They're roasted and charred. And usually — usually — they do, in fact, hit the ground. Every once in a while, however, someone's environment suit has enough air to go neutrally buoyant. And then the body simply stops falling and drifts away.

Keats Lowdenville had just settled into the monotony of the chase when the radio woke up with the voice of his wife, Dorothy. "Thank you so much for leaving without saying anything." Her voice sounded clipped, argumentative.

Keats checked. It was pre-recorded. As usual, instead of starting a conversation, she had spent hours recording an argument tree, anticipating everything he might say in response to her and programming the computer to spit out whatever response was most appropriate.

The Venus Surface Rover had a slower terminal velocity than a human body. It had taken Keats four hours before he touched bottom and could go in search of the latest victim's remains, only to discover that they were no longer there. It had taken another 20 minutes to disconnect the guide line from the two-meter-thick anchor cable, report the drifter, and set the V.S.R.'s insectoid feet to the task of clambering across the basalt plain in the valiant hope that the body was drifting close enough to the ground for his grapple line to catch it.

Dorothy, no doubt, was off at work trying to get the crops to adapt to the high solar-radiation environment, leaving Keats not only chasing a runaway dead body, but also posting arguments back to his not-listening wife. It was a tedious way to fight. "I left 30 minutes before my shift. You were asleep."

"And how am I supposed to keep track of your schedule?" It was no worse a response than he'd have gotten if he'd actually been talking to her.

"It's posted. The same place as yours."

On the surface, the only light was a dim, orange glow filtering down through the clouds. Up in the dirigible city, the sunlight was almost twice as bright as on Earth. Down here, it felt like the murky depths of Hell itself.

Keats felt like someone was shoving his eardrums into his skull. The pressure at the surface was about the equivalent of a dive to 90 meters on Earth. The V.S.R. did nothing to relieve the pressure. Every time Keats came down this low, he had to decompress for at least 12 hours on the way back up.

During the long pause while the argument tree was stumped, he noticed a signal he shouldn't be getting from the dead body.

"Control, this is V.S.R.," Keats reported. "I'm getting vital signs from the victim."

Keats didn't like the length of the silence that followed.

"We're not getting anything up here, but you're a lot closer than we are." Keats recognized the voice as Mildred's, which meant there had been a shift change. A glance at his panel confirmed that he'd been down almost six hours. That upped his decompression time to 18 hours. "It's most likely the heat short-circuiting it. Even if she could handle the pressure, those suits can't protect her from the temperature. Her re-breather should be fully melted by now."

"That's what I thought," Keats said. "Thank you, Control."

Keats pressed on across what should have been a sea floor. The organizers had promised that the terraforming would take 5-10 years. Fifteen years later, they still hadn't gotten any plant life to take hold; the clouds surrounding the dirigible city were still composed of deadly acid, and the surface remained stubbornly unchanged.

The argument tree had apparently either worked out a response or queried Dorothy at work because it started up again: "Have you ever considered what your work schedule does to me? I need a husband, not a roommate."

Dorothy had her own ridiculously long shifts, of course. Everyone on Venus did, but she'd have answers for all the logically related points. "If you need someone to keep you company, why don't you go down and talk to Blythe and Evan Tinswaddie. Their daughter fell this morning. I'm sure they'd appreciate condolences."

Dorothy never bothered to keep track of anyone else's problems, so Keats was sure she couldn't have anticipated that response. She would either have to actually talk to him or spend a significant chunk of additional time programming a new argument branch. Or concede the argument…but that was like asking for snow on Christmas Day on Venus.

Even inside the V.S.R., with the cooling system running at full, Keats sweated profusely.

His ears popped again. A high-pressure system was making the surface worse than usual, and oxygen toxicity was a very real risk. Keats adjusted the oxygen mix — a slow process since the control panels were now scaldingly hot.

The dead body's locator beacon was coming from way too high of an angle.

"Control, this is V.S.R. Could you help me re-triangulate my target, please?"

"Sure thing, V.S.R. Pulling your data now." Letting Control pull the data remotely was always preferable to working the controls himself. After this long on the surface, controls that weren't insulated could literally burn. The V.S.R. had a cooling system, of course, but keeping 500 degrees centigrade at bay was a function of slowing the conduction, not preventing it.

"Huh," the voice of Mildred in Control came over the radio. "I'm guessing you're wondering why it looks like she's six kilometers above you?"

"That would be my question, yes. Never heard of a body going neutrally buoyant that high up before."

"Well, she was installing a new hydrogen tank when she fell. Might still be clipped to her."

"If you agree she's really that high up, then I can't do anything from the surface level. I'm going to abort and come back up. Can you give me a direction to the nearest anchor cable?"

"Sure thing. Give us a minute."

Keats passed the time by flushing the V.S.R.'s body coolant and listening to the breakups in the locator signal on the dead body.

As if emerging from the orange haze in front of him, he heard the pattern.

The locator beacon put out a steady C-sharp. Interruptions in the signal weren't uncommon, especially through this much atmosphere, but the dropouts were coming in a predictable rhythm. Three short clicks, three long clicks, three short clicks, steady locator tone, repeat. Somebody was interrupting the locator beacon to send an old-fashioned S.O.S.

"Mildred, can you hear the locator tone?"

"Sure thing, Keats, why?"

"Do me a favor and listen to the dropouts."

Keats listened too. It was still there. The pattern was definitely still there: S-O-S.

"It's not possible," Mildred's voice came back.

"Give me another explanation, then."

Dorothy's voice interrupted. "O.K., whatever, don't change the subject." Keats wondered momentarily if she had actually recorded the trope as a new response or just manually pointed the argument tree to an unrelated branch, still safely arguing only in her own mind while he tried to figure out how to save a life.

"And do me a favor and block messages from my wife," Keats said.

"Yeah," Mildred's voice said. "It looks like those interruptions are at the source."

"How long ago did she fall?"

"Fourteen hours."

"We have to get to that suit," Keats said.

"I'll check with the organizers and see if we have anything that can operate at that altitude."

"Any chance she's drifting near an anchor cable?"

"Not close enough to be useful. Not for the next several weeks, probably."

"Then get me to the nearest one upwind of her."

"Fifteen degrees, 535 meters. What are you thinking?"

Keats grabbed the controls, his gloves doing little to stop the heat, and steered the V.S.R. at its best speed toward the cable. His battery warning sounded almost immediately. After this long at the surface, he was meant to move slowly and steadily.

"Keats, what are you thinking?" Keats' heat-addled mind heard the voice as Dorothy's at first, but he belatedly realized it was Mildred again.

"I may be able to get close enough to her if I jump."

He heard the sound of Mildred's mic opening, but she didn't say anything.

Keats maneuvered the nose of the V.S.R. up to the cable. Ascending required him to clip in by the V.S.R.'s nose — logical if your goal is to inspect the cable, but putting a two-meter-thick cable right in front of the only viewport seriously inhibited one's ability to see anything else. He'd be blind until he actually released, and he hoped he'd be pointed in the right direction then.

Dorothy's voice interjected. "Don't ignore me, Keats!"

"Dorothy, Venus is in a lower energy orbit than Earth. Going back to Earth uses an order of magnitude more energy. Without surface operations, there's no way to launch a rocket large enough to return a person. We're here, whether we like it or not."

Dorothy's argument tree had apparently anticipated the non sequitur, however, because it responded very quickly. "Why do you assume this is about that?"

"Because it's always about that, Dorothy, so we can either talk about it or not. Either way, I'm done until you're ready to kill the argument tree and actually communicate."

"Oh, real mature, Keats. Real mature. Glad to see you're such a big boy."

"Mildred, please block those messages."

"I'm working on it. She's a damned good programmer."

He didn't blame Dorothy for missing Earth. He missed Earth. He missed parasailing on their honeymoon, the one time they were truly happy. He missed day trips to the beach with her family, who had never warmed up to him. He missed the low-wage job and the tiny apartment they shared with two other professional families. He even missed the technical diving stint — a job he couldn't wait to quit and never would have applied for if he had realized it would get him drafted to be the V.S.R. driver. All those little stresses on Earth were better than life on Hell.

The battery warning indicator grew steadily more insistent as Keats ascended too quickly. When he had reached an altitude of eight kilometers, he could tell the fallen suit was now comfortably below him and not so far afield.

"Control, this is V.S.R. Could you help me triangulate one more time?"

John's voice responded. "Keats, the organizers don't like this plan." John wasn't scheduled to be back until tomorrow, but he had a lot more experience than Mildred. The organizers were clearly taking the situation seriously. "That's the only V.S.R. we've got."

"Just help me get a good vector to that suit."

The vector appeared on the monitor. Yes… Keats estimated he was high enough to parasail over to it. He spread the V.S.R.'s legs to maximize the surface area, and released the ascender clamps.

Keats' stomach lurched up into his lungs momentarily until the legs caught enough atmosphere to slow him down again. The urine catch rattled out of its cubby but mercifully didn't spill.

Then Keats saw it. He shouldn't have been able to see a suit at this distance, several hundred meters off and almost two kilometers below, but he saw it. A moment later he resolved it: a huge tank, its ribs visible, its skin stretched painfully inward by the atmospheric pressure.

Keats threw his body weight forward to tip the V.S.R. in the right direction. The parasail analogy only went so far. No one had ever tried to steer the V.S.R. in free-fall before. Keats went momentarily weightless as the nose tipped too far. He threw himself back to level out again.

"O.K., Control, I can't see. I'm going to need you to tell me when I'm right over her."

"You're probably already close enough to use the grapple," John said.

"I'd rather use the remote manipulator arms if I can."

"O.K. You need to head slightly north," Mildred's voice said.

Keats tipped to his right, again momentarily catching sight of the tank, much closer and still below him.

"Right there," Mildred said. "I don't know your relative altitude."

"Neither do I," Keats replied. "I'm improvising."

"If you can stand the heat," John said, "try venting a little coolant to see if you can set yourself up into a slight spin. That way, you can see her as you pass."

"Good idea, John."

He had to vent more than a little coolant to get the spin going. The urine catch on the floor began to steam, but it worked. Every thirty seconds or so, he saw the tank, closer below him each time.

The controls for the manipulator arms were so hot he felt his skin burning even through the gloves, but he held each firmly.

He reached left with both arms. The tank came into view, right in front of him but just slightly out of reach. He threw his weight forward, falling faster, and reached up with the right manipulator arm. Its fingers found one of the ribs. He released his grip.

The manipulator hand automatically snapped shut, grabbing the tank's rib firmly.

"I've got it!" Keats barked, throwing his weight back again to slow his plunge.

"Great!" John exclaimed. "Now what?"

Keats was still falling. Not as fast, but still falling. And he couldn't see the fallen suit attached to the tank anywhere.

On a hunch, Keats switched over to the close-range suit-to-suit frequency. "Dr. Tinswaddie, can you hear me?"

"Yes," came a weak female voice in response. "Yes, I'm in the tank. Thank God."

"Hang on, I've got the tank." Keats switched back to the control frequency. "She's alive. She sounds weak, but she's alive. Inside the tank."

He realized what she had done. As she had fallen, she had climbed inside the tank and purged the gas out of it, creating a vacuum to protect herself from the worst of the heat. Her rebreather wouldn't keep operating much longer, though, and if they kept descending, the atmospheric pressure would eventually pop the tank.

"Keats," Mildred's voice said, "do you think you can use the grapple on the anchor cable?"

"That's the plan," Keats said.

Another uncomfortable silence.

"Acknowledged," John said.

"Keats," Dorothy's voice interrupted, "this is inexcusable!"

The pressure was pushing on Keats' ears, eyes, and chest again. He had no idea what his altitude was, but his oxygen mix was probably off.

Keats roared as he threw his weight backwards to steer the V.S.R. and the tank towards another anchor cable. Holding the tank had stopped his spin, but now he couldn't see where he was going.

"Now!" John's voice said. "Keats, now!"

Keats fired the grapple. The spool on the top of the V.S.R. buzzed as the cable spun out behind the rocket-powered claw.

And then the spool stopped buzzing.

"No good on the grapple," Keats reported. "Heat seized." The grapple's failure rate had always vexed them, but had never been life-threatening before.

"What's plan B?" Mildred's voice sounded shrill, more excited than he'd ever heard it before.

"Working on that."

Keats saw the anchor cable sail past on his left. Possibly close enough. He threw his weight forward again, leaning sideways and extending the left manipulator arm all the way out to the side.

He felt the collision before he heard it. The V.S.R. jerked sideways, and then the distinct ceramic-on-metal screech came up the side of the vessel. He quickly retracted the manipulator arm, yanking the V.S.R. closer to the cable.

The V.S.R. tipped backwards. Keats felt himself going weightless again. He jumped to the main controls and retracted the legs. Ceramic-on-metal screeching came again, but the descent stopped. At least one of the legs had caught hold.

The battery warning alarm gave off its emergency shriek, and Keats grabbed the controls for the ascender and tried to get it attached.

Everything went silent. No fans. No alarms. Just the sound of his breathing. The ascender controls were locked in place. The lights on the control panels died.

The batteries were drained.

He was at least 50 kilometers down. Without power, he couldn't descend safely. Plus, the temperature was already rising, and he'd use up all his oxygen soon.

The bit of anchor cable he could see had a patchy discoloration on it — black in this light, but from experience he knew it was really green — where it had begun to corrode. It would have to be replaced soon, and it might not be able to support the weight of the V.S.R. if he tried to crank it up the cable manually — assuming it was even possible to get the ascenders attached without power.

An emergency ascent was possible. Most of the V.S.R.'s weight was in the leg unit. If he ejected, a balloon would inflate and carry the passenger compartment up through the clouds. It would carry him up too fast and he'd have decompression sickness, but it would carry him up.

Assuming it didn't tangle with the tank above him.

That was only half the problem, though. The manipulator arms were part of the leg unit, and the right arm still had a firm hold on the tank containing Dr. Tinswaddie. He'd have to release the arm manually first, or she'd be stuck down here with the legs.

"Control, does the tank have a clip point?"

Keats has spoken without thinking. Without power, they couldn't hear him. He was totally on his own.

The tank should have a clip point. Everything has a clip point, he reasoned.

Keats pulled the lever to switch the right arm over to manual. His throat burned and he could barely see any more, but he slowly turned the tank until he spotted it.

The V.S.R. had a hoist joint on its nose. If he could get the clip joint close enough to the hoist joint, they should magnetically lock — and the tank would then be connected to the same unit that could make the emergency ascent.

Even without power, Keats could hear Dorothy's voice nagging in his head. "What are you doing, Keats?" the imaginary Dorothy said. "Trying to save a life, dear," his own imaginary voice responded. "What a waste of time, Keats," imaginary Dorothy fired back.

A clang shocked Keats out of his own thoughts. He had a magnetic lock.

Something was burning but he didn't want to look. He doubted he could have seen anyway. Everything had gone dark, even though there were still eight weeks of sunlight left in the current Venus day. He started turning the wheel to release the manipulator arm's grip on the tank.

"Don't bother, Keats," imaginary Dorothy said. "You can't survive this anyway, and, really, I'm better off without you."

Keats struggled to remember where he was and what he was doing. His hand found the eject lever, and he pulled it. The sensation of weightlessness overtook him. Keats felt like he was falling. His skin seared. The pressure crushed him.

And Keats knew the darkness that lay before him was the actual Hell.

Then there was light all around him. And pain. His skin burned. His lungs burned.

And Dorothy's voice.

"Keats? Keats? I think he's awake!"

Awake.

He wasn't falling. He was lying down.

Blurry objects began to resolve.

He recognized the inside of the hyperbaric chamber.

"Tinswaddie?" Keats managed to choke out. His throat burned too.

"She's alive," Dorothy's voice said. "She's in the chamber on the next dirigible. The doctors think she's going to make it, too."

Keats realized that he had regeneration ointment slathered over his entire body. That burning sensation was from real burns.

"You're going to need to stay in there for a few days," Dorothy said, her voice wavering uncharacteristically, "but the doctors think you're going to pull through." He couldn't see her, of course. She was probably outside the chamber, watching on the monitor. But she was really there.

Keats tried to answer, but no sound came out. He nodded instead.

"And Keats," she said. "I love you."

Keats nodded again.

Pressure like Keats Lowdenville had experienced didn't go away with platitudes. He knew the scars would be with him forever.

He relaxed as best he could in the hyperbaric chamber.

Breaking Rules

I often joke that I should footnote all my stories with whose cardinal rule of storytelling I'm breaking in each one. It's not that I don't respect the rules. I do. The rules were developed over the years by writers who had a good sense of what does and does not work for readers. We break them at our peril.

But rules are not meant to be followed blindly. Any serious writer shouldn't merely learn the rules in order to follow them, they should learn *why* the rules exists. Once you know what effect you create by following the rule, or by breaking it, the rules become malleable, putty that can be shaped and reshaped based on your narrative needs.

One rule that I'm particularly fond of is the rule that says dialogue should be attributed, and should be anchored by action and physical description. I've heard writers describe stretches of nothing but dialogue as "voices in the dark" and compare them to voiceovers in movies. I don't think that's true. Even dark would be something, and a voiceover still gives you information the written word does not (such and clues about the speaker's gender, age, social class, region of origin, emotional state, etc.., that become encoded into the accent and voice itself). In prose, the effect is even less grounded. It leaves the reader unanchored, trying to guess from context where we are, who's speaking, what they sound like, and so forth.

But at the same time, Douglas Adams used this effect to great end in the novel adaptation of his radio play, *The Hitchhiker's Guide to the Galaxy*. By often sticking with the radio convention of telling the story entirely through dialogue, Adams is able to withhold key information so that the reveal becomes humorous.

So clearly even a rule I like needn't be obeyed all the time. The question becomes, what effect does this floating dialogue have, and when is that the right effect for the story you want to tell?

"Final Voices" was written as an experiment. It actually started its life as a scene I wrote for a theatre class in college, at that point seeing if I could make a scene work with only two actors, one of whom is offstage while the onstage one is lit only by a pinspot on her face. I wouldn't direct an entire play that way, but the effect worked well. When it came time to try the prose equivalent, it seemed like the logical story to adapt.

Personally, I love the effect I got. When I started submitting the story for publication, however, editors didn't agree. Ultimately I wound up self-publishing it on my blog. My regular readers — both of them — responded very positively, so I include it here for you as well.

Mind you, this isn't a rule I recommend doing away with, but you can see for yourself what happens when you're willing to break a rule for the effect it gives you.

Final Voices

"I'm moving behind Titan. Hopefully I can– Nope. I'm hit. Primary drive system down. Secondary… Secondary failing, too.
// *feedback* // And I'm in the gravity well. Search and Rescue, this is Bravo bomber B-15102, Colonel Irene Cross, callsign Vulture, requesting recovery."

"You still have your Tango escort, Vulture?"

"Negative, Scar. Lost the last one about five minutes ago. Search and Rescue, please respond. Situation urgent. Repeating. This is Bravo bomber B-15102, Colonel Irene Cross, callsign Vulture, requesting recovery at Titan, urgent. Estimating 3 minutes to burnup."

"Vulture, punch out."

"Bravo bomber B-15102, to Search and Rescue, please respond. Search and Rescue, please respond."

"Vulture, eject!"

"Negative, Scar. I'm in the gravity well. I'm hitting this moon with or without the bird."

"Hang on, Vulture, I can be there in two."

"Negative, Scar, proceed on course."

"Colonel, that's not a survivable crash."

"Proceed on course, Scar. That's an order."

"I can be back on target in five minutes."

"Earth may not have that long. Billions of people. I'm one woman and you're flying the last operational bomber. You have to take out that weapons platform. Confirm!"

// garbled //

"Scar, confirm! Confirm!"

"Confirmed. Proceeding on course. Good luck, Colonel."

"Search and rescue, situation critical, please respond. Scar, do you still have your Tango escort?"

"No. Hellcat had to punch out."

"Well, then, nail that base for all of us."

"Yes, sir."

"Look, Scar, I know I've been hard on you, but it's because you're a damn good pilot, and when you focus you can do amazing things. So just relax, slip in there, and hit them before they see you coming. Skin temperature rising. I'm in the atmosphere."

// silence //

"Bravo bomber B-15102, to Search and Rescue, trajectory equatorial. Please respond."

// silence //

"Please respond."

"Just keep talking, Vulture."

"Not much to talk about, Scar. Just burning up here."

"Tell me. Why 'Vulture'?"

"Needed a callsign. Didn't believe in leaving anything behind."

"Suits you."

"Thanks."

"Vulture, I have– What the hell is it? It's huge!"

"Just relax, Scar. You're a small bird, and they're looking toward Earth. Skin temperature sensors failing."

"It'll be O.K., Vulture. Once you're– Wait– Three contacts. Five. Fifteen. Multiple– Ahead– Behind– Jesus! Those things are fast!"

"Scar, take the shot when you've got it!"

"This is Scar, Bravo bomber B-69138, to any surviving Tango fighter. Under heavy fire. Close proximity to primary target, approach 9-1. I could use some help, kids! Whoa! This bird wasn't build for this! Are you there, Colonel? Hang on! This is Scar under–"

"Scar?"

// silence //

"Scar!"

// silence //

"Search and Rescue, this is Bravo bomber B-15102. Colonel Irene Cross. Serial number 1ST421D. Going down."

The Real Wrong Dog

I blame my dog for the fact that I'm a writer.

I used to be a video producer. When my husband's job relocated us from Los Angeles to Fresno, I went freelance. And I was doing all right. I had a couple of clients, and I was working from home doing non-broadcast shorts for decent money.

Then, one morning, a dog turned up on our back porch. This, incidentally, was a bit baffling, since our back yard is surrounded by a six-foot wall, but we didn't wonder too much that first day. I've never been terribly fond of dogs, but Fresno's local animal shelter was notoriously overcrowded with an appalling kill rate. We figured that if we had them take the dog, it would be signing the death warrant for another dog. So we decided to let her stay until we figured out where she belonged. We took her to the vet and verified that she was healthy and not microchipped, but the vet recommended we shave her down since her fur was very badly matted. So off she went to the groomer.

The inspiration for "The Wrong Dog" happened when I picked her up that afternoon. The groomer went into the back room and emerged with a small, black dog I didn't recognize, but grabbed the collar and leash I had hurriedly purchased for the stray that morning. I was about to tell them they had the wrong dog when I looked into her eyes and saw the look of recognition. It was the same dog, but she was so changed by a simple haircut that I hadn't recognized her. And, of course, that got my mind going with all the possibilities of why a groomer might want to foist the wrong dog off on me.

Needless to say, the dog's owner didn't turn up, despite my increasingly desperate newpaper and online ads and enough flyers distributed in a one-mile radius to kill at least three trees. I really, really didn't want to be stuck with the dog on a permanent basis. I had two cats who weren't happy to have a dog in the house, and more than that, the dog was completely untrained and too smart for my own good.

The second day we had the dog with us, I decided to go to the gym. Since she wasn't going to be with us permanently, we hadn't invested in baby gates or the likes. She couldn't stay in the house with the cats, of course, so I put her in the back yard. I scratched her on the head and said, "O.K., dog, I'm going to the gym. I'll be back in an hour or two." I closed the back door. I turned on the alarm. I grabbed my gym bag. I opened the front door, and the dog walked back into the house.

It was a good trick.

Well, I've got a scientific mind, so I turned off the alarm, put the dog in the back yard again, and then *ran* out the front door. I got there just in time to see the dog flatten herself like a rodent and slide under the gate. It was truly impressive, and completely eliminated any possibility that I could leave her alone in the back yard. So she stayed in the house when I went to the gym.

And she trashed the place.

Separation anxiety, they call it.

Her separation anxiety was about the worst case anyone had ever seen. Not only did she wreck the house when I left her alone, she wrecked the house if she felt ignored. And she felt ignored any time she wasn't either asleep or in my arms. Which meant that absolutely no work got done on my video producing jobs. All I could do was sit on the couch physically restraining the dog, a mind-numbingly boring task that put me to sleep pretty reliably – at which point the dog would wriggle free and start tipping trash cans, chasing cats, and helping herself to food from the counter. My deadlines got missed, my clients dropped me, and my business failed.

But I could write.

Well, we've since gotten the dog trained, and she's better now. Not perfect, by any stretch of the imagination, but better. She still needs to be with me at all times.

Which means I'm now that eccentric writer who takes his dog with him everywhere. To all outward appearances I'm now a dog lover. A dog lover and a writer.

And it's all her fault.

The Wrong Dog

The scalpel shot across the operating room. Stan Majewski, D.V.M., roared. His hand clenched involuntarily. On the steel table, the shaggy, grey-and-tan terrier grumbled under the anesthesia mask and began to convulse. Two more blue sparks arced out of the ventral midline incision on her shaved abdomen, one blackening the edge of the surgical split sheet that covered her body.

"What happened?" the attending surgical tech, Terri, asked.

The patient went still, her belly collapsing as her last breath escaped her lungs. The incision sparked one final time.

"Terri," Stan said as calmly as he could manage, "I want you to go sit in exam room 2. Close the door. Don't talk to anyone. Don't pick up the phone. Don't text. If anyone asks you what happened, shrug."

"What's going on?" Terri asked.

"Terri, just do it," Stan said. "*Now!*"

Terri dialed off the anesthesia and pulled the mask off the dead dog's face. Flipping her auburn ponytail aside to look over her shoulder with concern, she slipped out of the operating room.

Stan scrambled, yanking open drawers until he found the microchip scanner. He tore the surgical drape off the patient, rolled her body over, and ran the scanner along her spine. Nothing. No chip registering. He ran it along her shoulder and onto her chest. Still nothing. He flipped her over and tried the other side and her belly. Nothing.

Stan drummed his fingers, chewing on his moustache under his surgical mask. The scalpel had embedded itself in the grout between two tiles on the far wall. A slightly stronger shock could have been deadly.

He grabbed the microchip scanner and charged out into the prep area. Felix, Barbara Martindale's grey Maine Coon, reached out of his kennel, meowing pathetically. "Hi, Felix," Stan said, disposing of his gloves. "Can I borrow you for a minute?"

Stan dragged the enormous cat down to the prep table and scanned his spine. Sure enough, the scanner instantly beeped and displayed a chip code.

"Thank you," Stan said, scratching Felix behind the ears and putting him back in the kennel. Stan pulled off his surgical mask, letting the faint odor of cleanser into his nostrils. Why did Gary Lombardi's now-dead dog *not* have a microchip? All cyborg surveillance dogs were required to have a microchip. The code they put out looked just like any other I.D. code to anyone who didn't know such creatures existed — anyone who wasn't a licensed D.V.M. or a Federal agent — but warned any veterinarian not to perform surgery. There should have been a microchip, to prevent exactly what just happened from happening.

Stan took the scanner into the lobby. The display out there had examples of chips from all the major manufacturers. One by one, he scanned each of them. Each one registered on his scanner without a problem. Jonathan, working the reception desk, watched curiously through his Bieber-mop. Fred — the big, orange office donor cat — rubbed against Stan's ankles and purred.

The bell over the front door jingled. Two men in blue suits — one tall with a round face, the other squat with a square jaw — entered, both fishing into their inside jacket pockets.

"The two of you, in my operating room, *now*!" Stan barked at the newcomers. He pivoted and marched up the short hallway between the exam rooms, swept into the O.R., and pivoted. The two men stopped just inside the door and looked down at the dead dog. The tall one shook his head. "All right," Stan said, "now show me your badges."

Both men produced F.B.I. badges. The tall one was Smith, the squat one was Everhardt.

"Now," Stan said sharply, "which one of you would like to explain to me why that surveillance dog that wasn't microchipped? She died, and I nearly electrocuted myself."

Smith and Everhardt looked at each other.

"I could have been *killed*!" Stan barked. "What if I had been doing thyroid surgery? As it is, I've got a tech who saw a lot more than she should have, and by the way, you get to explain this to her. Now, before I pick up the phone and sic my lawyers on you, why the *hell* wasn't that dog microchipped?"

"You know whose dog that is?" Everhardt asked.

"Yes!" Stan yelled. The dog had been found at the compound of the Church of Gaiacardia outside of town, and had taken a shine to the leader of the church, Gary Lombardi.

"And you're a Gaiacardian?" Everhardt asked.

"So?"

The implication suddenly dawned on Stan.

"You had Gary under surveillance? And you figured that if I scanned the dog and saw the microchip…"

Everhardt and Smith just looked at each other again.

"To hell with that," Stan said. "Do you have any idea how dangerous it is to cut into a surveillance dog? Not to mention that it kills the dog!"

"You wouldn't have been the first Gaiacardian to put the church ahead of the law," Everhardt said.

Stan kicked a cabinet. "This is so… typical! The Church of Gaiacardia isn't dangerous to anyone! But, no! Naturally, any new religion gets treated like it's a terrorist sleeper cell or something."

Everhardt folded his arms. "Please calm down, Dr. Majewski."

Stan rounded on him instead. "So what's your plan, now? I cut into that dog. It died. I have to tell Gary what happened."

"We have another dog on the way," Smith said.

The air went out of Stan's lungs. "What?"

Everhardt arched an eyebrow.

"I can't just say, 'Hi, Gary, sorry that dog you adore so much is dead now, but here's another one,'" Stan said. "'Don't do any surgery on this one, by the way.'"

"It'll be the same dog," Everhardt said.

From what Stan had learned about surveillance dogs, they all began as normal dogs. Instead of being put down in animal shelters, the National Security Agency took a certain number of them and surgically implanted electronics into them, and sometimes shared them with other agencies. Classified technology allowed them to be used as walking camcorders. But no two dogs were exactly alike.

"Even if you have one that looks exactly like this one, it won't be the same dog. An owner can tell."

"I think you give Mr. Lombardi too much credit," Everhardt said.

Stan stormed past the two special agents. They both trotted after him.

Terri had closed the door to exam room 2. She jumped as Stan barged in, almost falling out of the plastic chair. "Terri," he said, "these two gentlemen are going to explain what happened in the O.R."

Smith and Everhardt skidded to a stop on either side of Stan. Smith stammered briefly.

Everhardt finally spoke up. "There was a freak discharge of static electricity," Everhardt said. "It's unusual for a charge that substantial to build up, but everything's fine now."

"How did static electricity kill a dog?" Terri asked.

"Who said the dog died?" Everhardt said, as Smith looked at him with doe eyes.

"That dog was dead when I left the room," Terri said.

"How do you know that?" Everhardt pressed.

"I'm the surgical tech. I can tell the difference between a living dog and a dead dog."

Stan suppressed a smile.

"Did you see Dr. Majewski attempt to resuscitate it?" Everhardt asked.

"No," Terri said. "He was doubled over in pain."

"Well, after you left the room, he was able to resuscitate it," Everhardt said.

Smith's expression grew even more incredulous. Stan rubbed his hand on his face.

"I'm sorry," Terri said, "but who exactly are you?"

Everhardt snapped his fingers twice and waved his hand at Smith. "We'd like you to sign this paperwork," Everhardt said.

Smith fished a folded bunch of legal-size papers out of his jacket pocket and handed it to Terri. Stan recognized it as the non-disclosure agreement they'd forced on him just after his license to practice veterinary medicine was approved.

"What is it?" Terri asked.

"Basic N.D.A.," Everhardt said. "We just need you to sign at the bottom here."

"Of course," Terri said. "As soon as my lawyer's gone over it with me."

"Your what?" Everhardt said.

Stan laughed. "You may not give us Gaiacardians much credit, but we do know when to consult a lawyer."

Everhardt harumphed.

"Is there anyone who works here who isn't a Gaiacardian?" Smith asked.

"The cleaning crew," Stan answered.

Out in the reception area, the front door jingled. A faint, female voice said, "I'm sorry it took me so long. Is Special Agent Everhardt here?"

"We're in Room 2!" Stan yelled. Jonathan directed the newcomer to the room.

The door opened and a round, middle-aged woman with overly teased blond hair stood there. She struggled to show her NSA badge as she wrestled with a grey-and-brown terrier in her arms. Its brown was at least two shades darker than the tan of Gary's dog. The markings didn't match at all. And it was a good five pounds heavier than Gary's.

"You've got to be kidding me," Stan said.

"No, it'll work," Everhardt said. "We'll shave it down, and you'll tell Lombardi that its fur was matted. Then, as it grows back, you'll mention that bitches' coloring can change as they reach full adulthood."

"And their entire personality changes after they've been spayed, I assume," Stan said.

"That is *not* Gary's dog," Terri said.

"You sign that," Everhardt told her, pointing to the N.D.A.

"I'm not signing anything," Terri said.

"You've got to sign it," Everhardt said.

"Let my lawyer tell me that," Terri said, grabbing the telephone extension. Smith dove for the wall unit and held down the hook switch.

Jonathan appeared behind the woman in the doorway. "Problem?"

"No!" Everhardt and Smith barked simultaneously.

Jonathan looked directly at Stan. "Don't worry," Stan said.

Everhardt turned to Stan. "Your other option, Dr. Majewski, is to tell Lombardi that you're not smart enough to spay a dog without killing it."

Stan exhaled sharply. "They didn't exactly send their first-stringers, did they? I have an ethical obligation to give my client an accurate cause of death for his companion animal," Stan said.

"Come on," Everhardt siad, "Not even a Gaiacardian would believe that."

"Can we refrain from taking shots at my religion?" Stan asked.

"Why?" Everhardt asked. "How many Gaiacardians does it take to change a light bulb?"

Stan ignored him. "How about I just show my client his dog's body?"

"We'll be taking possession of that," Everhardt said.

"You can't do that if he wants the body returned to him, unless you're going to serve a warrant on him. The dog is his property. He can choose how to dispose of her remains."

"Wait," Smith said. "How many Gaiacardians *does* it take to change a light bulb?"

Everhardt smirked. "Why would we change it when we just spent two weeks shooting it out?"

Smith laughed. "See, I thought you were going to say, 'Eighteen, all humming in unison with the heartbeat of the Earth.'"

"Actually, it's just one," Terri said, her voice dripping with acid, "but you have to wait for the government to let him out of jail first."

"*Enough!*" Stan barked. "Terri, bag up the body of Gary's dog to return to him."

Everhardt pointed Terri to stay in the chair. "That dog is property of the U.S. government."

"Which the U.S. government gave up when it abandoned its property in our church's compound," Stan said.

"That'll never hold up in court," Everhardt said.

"Oh, should I call our lawyers and try?" Stan said.

Everhardt glared, his face reddening, his nostrils flaring.

Stan stared him down.

"Um," the blond woman in the door said, "so, should I go get this one shaved down?"

. . .

Five hours later the little veterinary clinic had turned into a mobile F.B.I. field office. Black sedans and blue vans filled the parking lot with no regard for the painted lines. Terri and Jonathan were in custody in the back room, both refusing to speak or to sign anything without talking to their lawyers first. Stan sat in his own waiting room, absentmindedly scratching Fred the cat's ears. Fred kept shoving his oversized rear-end into Stan's face. Everhardt and Smith commanded the pandemonium from behind the reception desk. Every so often Smith answered a phone call, and then looked flummoxed when the person on the other end inquired about their pet's health.

Both Smith and Everhardt looked surprised when Gary Lombardi's assistant pulled into the parking lot at precisely 4:15 PM, the scheduled pickup time for Gary's dead dog. Stan hadn't bothered to warn them that clients normally just show up to pick up their pets following routine procedures.

The red roadster had to back up a few times before finding a way to maneuver into a space. Everhardt appeared to parse what was happening first. "What's the name of Lombardi's assistant?" he demanded of Stan.

"Leroy," Stan answered.

"Leroy what?"

"McGraw."

Out in the parking lot, Leroy unfolded his lanky form from behind the wheel. He gawked at all the strange cars for a moment before meandering toward the door. Gary Lombardi had become head of the Church of Gaiacardia because he was the original Grand Guru's assistant and had kept things running smoothly during the Grand Guru's imprisonment on bogus embezzlement charges. Every time Stan looked at Leroy, he wondered if he was looking at the next leader of the church. Leroy seemed an unlikely choice, but so had Gary.

The door jingled open. Leroy hadn't even entered when he started speaking. "What in the name of— "

"Mr. MrGraw," Everhardt interrupted, flashing his badge, "please come in and have a seat. Everything is fine here, but it will be a few minutes before your dog is ready to be picked up."

Leroy looked at Stan.

"And Dr. Majewski isn't at liberty to say anything," Everhardt said.

Leroy's eyes narrowed. "Can I ask what the problem is?"

"That's between us and Dr. Majewski," Everhardt said.

Leroy turned to Stan. "Have you called your lawyer?"

Stan just smiled a thin-lipped smile, obeying the tacit order not to speak to Leroy.

"He doesn't need a lawyer," Everhardt said. "He's not in any trouble. We're just gathering some information."

Leroy nodded. He put his hands in his pockets and sank down onto one of the hard plastic chairs. For a long time he stared at Stan. Stan maintained his thin-lipped smile.

After several minutes, the N.S.A. agent appeared from the back in a pair of Terri's scrubs — which were at least two sizes too small — holding the freshly-shaved replacement dog. "Here you go," she said to Leroy.

Leroy did a double-take. "Oh my God!" He stood up and stared at the replacement dog. "I would never have recognized you all shaved-down like that."

The dog growled.

The fake vet tech ran through a set of post-operative care instructions. Leroy nodded through all of them, including the ludicrous part about potential behavioral changes and changes in coloration as a result of the surgery.

Then the agent handed the dog over.

"Oh my God, I swear you're heavier, too," Leroy said as he shifted to control the wriggling animal. "Are you sure this is the right dog?"

The fake tech laughed a little too heartily.

Leroy signed the papers.

Stan watched helplessly as Leroy left with the wrong dog.

"See?" Everhardt said. "Easy."

Smith answered a phone call, and looked flummoxed. "Your dog ate a *what?*"

"Give me that! Are you trying to kill two dogs today?" Stan set Fred the cat aside and grabbed the phone. "This is Doctor Majewski. Can I help you?"

"Stan, it's Leroy," came a cell-phone-garbled voice from the other end of the line. "Do you think this line is clear?"

Stan struggled not to smile, turning away from Smith and Everhardt. Leroy had just shot up several points in his estimation. "It's hard to say. Tell me what he got into."

"Have you talked to the lawyers yet?" Leroy asked.

"No."

"Do you want me to call them for you?"

"Yes."

"Can you tell me what's going on?"

"No."

"What is it this time? Guns? Taxes? Not signing the right form in triplicate?"

"I'm really not sure."

"How urgent is this?"

"Yes, I'd say it's an emergency. Those are definitely toxic." Stan glanced back at Smith. "But don't bring your dog here, we're short-staffed at the moment, go straight to the nearest emergency room. It's definitely an emergency."

Leroy hung up.

. . .

The Department of Justice lawyers, based on Smith's half of the telephone conversation, were still at least an hour away. But the church's lawyers — three of them — had arrived and stood by the reception desk, briefcases in hand. Stan only knew one of them, Martin. Another, with silver hair and an aquiline nose, had locked horns with Everhardt.

"Nobody is under arrest," Everhardt said.

"Well, then, since they're free to go, we'd like you to produce them," the lawyer said.

"They can't be seen yet," Everhardt said.

"Then they're being detained, and if they're being detained, they have a right to counsel," the lawyer said for the fifth time.

Fred the cat had long since fallen asleep in Stan's lap. The sun had just begun to vanish over the roof of the grocery store across the parking lot. Stan's rear-end was sore from sitting, and his cheeks had begun to ache from keeping the stupid smile pinned to his face all this time.

Martin broke from the rest of the lawyers and came over to sit beside Stan. He looked like he had been on the golf course before the call came in, dressed in casual slacks and a polo shirt. "So, what can you tell me, Stan?"

"Absolutely nothing," Stan answered. "You have to ask the folks from the government over there."

"Attorney-client privilege applies here," Martin said.

"Actually, it doesn't," Stan said.

Martin cocked his head to the side. Everhardt seemed to be trying to eavesdrop. His responses to the head lawyer had developed a delay.

"You know that line in my veterinarian's license agreement that says I will comply with all Department of Justice instructions or I will lose my license and face stiff criminal penalties?" Stan looked directly at Everhardt. "I know nothing about anything that's going on here, even when talking to my lawyer."

Martin's eyes grew wide and he turned slightly red. He turned and spoke directly to Everhardt. "Do you mean to tell me that you've given instructions to my client that he can't even speak to a lawyer without facing loss-of-license and criminal prosecution for doing so?"

Everhardt threw up both hands. "Once the lawyers arrive, we can sort this whole thing out."

"We'll be happy to," said the silver-haired lawyer, "once our clients have been un-detained."

"We're still interviewing them," Everhardt said.

"Without counsel?" the lawyer asked.

Fred the cat twisted around on Stan's lap and stretched, opening his eyes just a sliver. The translucent nictitating membranes hadn't fully retracted, but he studied Stan with his yellow eyes anyway.

Stan looked up at the argument at the reception desk, no longer hearing the words.

Fred was another example of an animal that had just shown up. He'd appeared outside the office one day three years ago, not microchipped. The staff had fallen in love with him very quickly.

"Come on, Fred," Stan said, rising with the cat. "Let's go do a little surgery on you."

Everhardt immediately lost focus on the lawyers. "Don't go anywhere, Dr. Majewski."

"I'm just going in the back," Stan said. "There's no way to slip out back there. I just need to put an incision right about here." Stan indicated a spot on the neck where he had been taught it would be catastrophic to cut a surveillance animal.

"You can't do that!" Everhardt said.

"Sure I can," Stan said. "Just a routine lumpectomy. Local anesthesia. I don't even need a tech."

"Do not operate on that animal!" Everhardt barked.

"Why, Special Agent Everhardt, why ever not?" Stan said in his best saccharine voice. He grabbed the microchip scanner and ran it all over Fred's body. The microchip he had implanted registered several times, but no other signal confused the reading. "Nope, nothing there to indicate I shouldn't operate, and I have to keep my donor animals in the best possible condition, don't I?"

Everhardt's nostrils flared.

"Excuse me, gentlemen," Stan said and made for the back.

"Stop!" Everhardt ordered.

Stan turned back around and met Everhardt's glare. "Special Agent Everhardt, I know of no reason why I should not operate on this cat. Do you?"

Everhardt stared for a moment.

Stan didn't budge.

Everhardt rounded on Smith. "Where the *hell* are those lawyers?"

"Th- they're on their way," Smith protested.

"Mr. Everhardt," Stan said, "I intend to do this surgery right now. Do you know of any reason why I shouldn't?"

Everhardt glared for a moment, and then stepped out from behind the desk. He motioned Stan to come aside for a confidential conversation.

"There's no need for secrecy, Mr. Everhardt," Stan said in an even louder voice. "This is my cat, so there's no confidentiality issue if you discuss it in front of your agent or my lawyers."

"There is a need for secrecy," Everhardt hissed.

Stan help up the microchip scanner. "I've had no indication of that."

Everhardt glared.

Stan turned and marched with Fred toward the back.

"Performing medical procedures on that cat could be fatal!" Everhardt yelled after him.

"Don't be silly," Stan yelled back. "I've drawn his blood dozens of times. If you know something I don't know, I suggest you say it. Because I've now stated my intentions clearly and unequivocally, and if you can't give me a damned good reason not to proceed, I'm going to."

Stan set Fred down on the prep table, setting aside the microchip scanner. Fred tensed, but as usual made no effort to get away.

Everhardt ran into the prep room, the three lawyers on his heels.

Stan grabbed an empty anesthesia needle and lifted it up for dramatic effect. He turned back to look at Everhardt.

"It's a surveillance cat," Everhardt said.

Stan set the needle down and smiled.

"What's a surveillance cat?" the silver-haired lawyer asked.

"I'm afraid I'm not allowed to discuss that," Stan said. "I can't even confirm such a thing exists."

The three lawyers moved around to flank Everhardt, who looked like he had just been forced to swallow his own poop.

 • • •

No charges were ever filed.

Gary Lombardi named the second surveillance dog "Spy." The government spent the next ten years recording the inside of a doghouse and a spacious enclosed yard where church members would play with her for hours each day.

Fred the cat continued to give blood on a semi-regular basis, and no doubt violated doctor-patient confidentiality on dozens of cases of ringworm.

And for the rest of his career as a veterinarian, whenever someone found an animal and asked Stan if it might be a surveillance cyborg, he would shrug and tell them he had no idea what they were talking about.

But he always said it with a smile.

"The Wrong Dog" is dedicated to the memory of Fred Braithwood.

Taking Chances

It's important for writers to take chances, to try things that may not work.

Unfortunately, the only way we ever really know if it actually worked is to show it to people — in the case of the professional writer that means submitting it to publishers to see if they want to buy it. And sometimes they do.

And sometimes, later on, we look back on it and cringe.

That's one of the reasons I'm a fan of pen names. By using pseudonyms, we free ourselves of the pressure to write like we're "supposed" to, we give ourselves the latitude to fail miserably.

Quite a few writers, including some you probably know quite well. have secret pen names that they use to publish the sorts of things they would never put out under their more famous names. Sometimes, when the unacknowledged stories find an audience, or garner critical acclaim, or if the author just decides that they were worth putting their own name on after all, the author will admit to the pen name. Sometimes, the pen name leaks, and the public discovers who the real author is — a turn of events that usually results in a very grumpy author but a boost in the sales of the work done under the pseudonym. Some authors own up to the pen names from the very beginning, basically using the other name as a branding thing (science fiction under one name, romance under another) but allowing their true fans to connect them to their other work easily.

No one approach is right, of course. But there's a lot to say for the cloak of anonymity that allows a writer to stretch their wings, do something different.

The editors know, of course, that writers do this, but they're professionals. They let us.

So, when you read something by an author you've never heard of that seems weird, seems like it was someone's clever experiment that didn't work out so well, that might very well be one of those secret pen names, the shield behind which a writer can push their own limits.

Or it could genuinely be a new writer, one who is just finding their own voice.

There's no way to know.

Alas, somewhere along the line, I seem to have not gotten the memo, because I consistently try weird new things that may not work, and send them off to editors using the same name I always use.

The editors, if I'm to be completely honest, are my primary customers. Unless I'm self-publishing, I don't sell direct to the reader. It's the editors' job to acquire stories that will sell their magazines, or anthologies, or websites to you, so writing stories that you will want to read is still a good business plan for me, but I'm selling it to the editor, not to you. So I feel free to take a chance, to let the editor tell me if I'm completely out to lunch or not. If the story doesn't work, I'm always free to let it sit on my hard drive, unpublished, and you'll never be any the wiser that I wrote something embarrassingly bad.

Of course, I seem to have not gotten that memo, either, because I have a bad habit of posting my more glorious failures to my blog for the whole world to ridicule.

You're welcome.

But you can never say that I didn't take chances.

Eternal Love

"Do you take this woman to have and to hold from this day forward, for better and for worse, 'til life do you part?"

"AAARGH!"

"And do you take this man to have and to hold from this day forward, for better and for worse, 'til life do you part?"

"HELP ME! SOMEBODY HELP ME!"

"And so, by the power vested in me by the State of Decay, I now pronounce you zombie and wife."

"HELP ME! PLEASE HEL–"

:: crunch ::

"Tsk, tsk, tsk. Now you've got brains on your tuxedo."

Slushpile Nightmares

Yeah.

Sorry about that last story.

No, not even "story." It doesn't even rise to that level. Joke. It's a joke. And a bad one at that.

Sometimes we take chances, and they fail. It's that simple.

The people you need to feel sorry for are the editors — in the real world assistant or associate editors, usually — whose job it is to wade through all the dreadful stories like "Eternal Love" and look for the ones that are less terrible than the rest, the ones that should actually be considered for publication.

It's called "slush" — the unsolicited manuscripts that come in from anywhere and everywhere. In grad school I worked for a literary magazine, reading slush (among other duties). It's uniquely challenging, by the way, reading slush in a genre you're not terribly fond of. I used to sing a little song while I was reading:

> *Crap crap crap crap*
> *Crapppity crappity crap.*
> *Crap crap crap crap.*
> *Wo-ho-ho-oh-oh!*

One day my husband looked at me while I was working from home and said, "If it's crap, why don't you just reject it?"

"Because," I responded, "I need to determine whether or not it's the sort of crap we publish."

(In the interest of full disclosure, in my time at the literary magazine we actually only ever published one story that I didn't think was an awesome story, even if the genre wasn't my cup of tea. That story was by a famous author and I'm the only member of the staff who didn't adore it. There is such a thing as good crap.)

Now, to be fair, most of the slush isn't terrible. In general, it's competent. Most of it just isn't anything special. But, oh, is there dreadful stuff in there. Anyone who has read slush for a while could tell you stories.

But it's generally considered polite not to.

At least, not with names attached.

We all know that dreadful stories happen, but every writer needs

to be able to pretend the dreadful stories *didn't* happen. And we want
every editor wants to believe that they were the first market to consider
that story they fell in love with and published. And so, those of us
who've spent time wading through slush are agonizingly non-specific
when telling stories about the ridiculous "Eternal Love"-like crap that
has crossed our desks or our computer screens.

Like the envelope I opened my first day on the job at the lit mag
that contained handwritten poetry written on tearsheets from porn
magazines. To make matters worse, given how little I know about poetry,
I didn't have the confidence to reject it out-of-hand, and subjected one
of the other graduate assistants to the travesty.

I think every slush reader has gotten the story that sounds like it
was written by an illiterate high school student. In my case that story
actually *was* written by a high school student – her cover letter
boasted of that fact. And then there are the people who submit children's
literature to university literary magazines, graphic adult content to
young-adult markets, historical romance to science fiction magazines,
and so forth.

So now I want you to picture the poor editor at *Daily Science Fiction*
who got "Eternal Love" in the e-mail one morning. I often wonder
whether the gut reaction was, "Wow, Kyle Aisteach really screwed up
on this one," or, "Dear God, can we please block Kyle Aisteach from
ever submitting again?" Perhaps it's no coincidence that I've never sold
them a story. Believe it or not, the slush readers do remember names.
That can be a good thing, too. There are several authors we never
published while I was working at the lit mag whose work I quite liked.
They never submitted something that was right for us, but I knew
when I saw the byline that I was going to appreciate the story.

Usually.

I've had that "Wow, <author> really screwed up on this one"
moment a few times, myself.

And I've also sent the "I fought for this one, but I couldn't sell the
editor on it" personal rejection letter a couple of times. I've been on
the receiving end of that one, too, and it's an odd mix of encouraging
and devastating.

So, on the whole, I doubt I'm that author who makes editors cringe
when they see my name. At least, not in my more rational moments.

Of course, I'm not always rational. I imagine all sorts of responses coming from the slush readers, most of it not very flattering. It doesn't help that a few publications will send along their slush readers' unedited comments if you ask them to, and let me say that they're no kinder than I was while I was singing my song. These comments are very useful, of course, because they let me know what my customer honestly thought of my product, but it's not exactly good for the ego.

Most publications, of course, don't give any feedback except a form rejection letter. And in our weaker moments, even those of us who have worked the other side of the desk and *know* that there's no information to be gleaned from a form letter (at the lit mag we rejected wonderful stories in one day, and we've sat on ones that realistically were never under consideration for months, and both get the same form letter) will try to guess what the customer thought of the product anyway. We writers call it "rejectomancy." Rejectomancy is useless and meaningless. The wording of the form letter tells you nothing. The response time tells you nothing. And yet, it's all too easy for us writers to fall into the trap and try it anyway.

There's a popular online submission tracking service that keeps track of when markets send responses, so we can see if submissions made after ours have been rejected or accepted yet. Invariably, when the wait time gets longer, I sit there going, "Has it been sent up to the editors? Are they going to buy it?"

But I'm far more neurotic than hopeful. It often seems to me that the responses come out for people who have submitted up to the same day I submitted, and then they stop. I always picture an editor working through the slush pile, getting to my story, and saying, "Oh, God, it's by Kyle Aisteach. I can't deal with this right now. I'm going home."

Again, I know this is ridiculous. I know it's a bad idea to think this way. I'm a publishing writer. I can't really be the one whose name the slush readers know and who they dread reading, right?

I mean, it's not like I'm the writer who submitted the story written entirely in rhymed anapestic tetrameter, right?

Clockman

"I have made a machine in the style of a knight,"
the old wizard exclaimed to the king's gathered men.
"It is strong! It is fast! It can win every fight!
And it's yours if you pay, not with gold, but with Gwen!"

And the king cried in rage, "Thou art dead, wicked dunce!"
as he motioned his men to attack the old thrall.
But his daughter, fair Gwen, interceded at once,
crying, "Stop! For this wizard is loved by us all!"

"She is wise as she's beautiful. Come, my dear girl,"
said the wizard extending a wrinkled, old hand,
"do become my own wife!" He let fingers unfurl.
And then all turned to Gwen. Hush fell over the land.

But fair Gwen simply smiled. "Now your price is quite high.
So perhaps we can see if this knight's worth the prize."
And the wizard leaned forward on grizzled old thigh.
"Ah, my darling," he whispered, "just lend me your eyes."

With a wheeze and a clank something opened the door.
The old hinges, they groaned disbelief at the sight.
Wearing armor pressed roughly, and sputtering more,
stood a clockwork machine, all ready to fight.

As a gasp crossed the room, the monstrosity stepped.
With a clang on the stone, a foot rose and then fell.
And it heaved its great mass o'er the sill which there kept
all the thresh in the room where it served the king well.

"As you see," said the wizard with flourish of arm,
"with its mass all alone it can take down a horse.
There's no weapon around that can cause any harm
to befall my dear Clockman! You know that, of course!"

"Now it seems to me, father," said Gwen with a grin,
"that the wizard has laid down a challenge for me.
So if any man present would like to begin
a fair joust for my honor, we'd all like to see!"

And then eight of the trusted ones, men of the king,
at once sprang with a cry o'er the table to floor.
But the Clockman stood ready with winding of spring
and all eight in one axe-stroke then died as a corps.

"Your machine is quite thorough," said giggling Gwen.
But her father's face reddened and stammered for breath.
As the king saw the carnage that had been good men,
he again said aloud, "Put this wizard to death!"

Then a battle cry rose from the dozens of men
who then charged the machine with their swords and their knives.
While the king with his arms then encircled fair Gwen,
the tall Clockman quite simply made widows of wives.

As the last soldier fell, with his head lolling off,
the fair Gwen clapped her hands. "Oh, dear father! Do sell!"
But the king rather drew his own sword with a cough,
saying, "Wizard, your monster 'gainst me won't fare well!"

"Oh, dear father, don't do it!" cried sweet-voicéd Gwen.
"No, my king," said the wizard, "he'll kill even you!"
But the king crossed the floor over bodies of men.
"So then draw, you tin monster, and run me right through!"

So the clockman stood poised with its axe and its sword,
the odd hissing and whirring beginning to fade.
And the king said a prayer to entreat his dear Lord
and he charged with a clang as his blade met with blade.

Then the axe circled round, but the Clockman grew slow,
and the king made a dodge, and then reared back and kicked.
Then the Clockman fell backwards, absorbing the blow.
The machine hit the floor, but its gears, they still ticked.

As the king raised his sword to deliver an end,
the machine rolled away and then rose to its feet.
"My dear Majesty," Wizard entreated his friend,
"you must stop this right now, or you'll end in defeat!"

But the king had his pique, and instead he just roared
and he charged at the Clockman, his sword pointed out.
But the gears had wound up. There was energy stored
in the Clockman's machine, and it moved without doubt.

Then the king stopped his charge, his look turning to pain
as the Clockman's sharp sword, with more thrusting applied,
went right into his chest and then back out again.
Then the king muttered, "Ow!" and then fell down and died.

The fair Gwen stood in silence, surveying the scene.
And the Clockman went quiet. It slumped to the floor.
"Is it dead," asked fair Gwen, "your odd clockwork machine?"
as she lifted her skirts and then tip-toed through gore.

"I have done as you told me," the wizard then said.
"Dearest Gwen you're now king! You're as free as you wish!"
Gwen then looked at her father, who lay there quite dead.
"My dear wizard!" She kissed him, her shoes going squish.

"You're my humblest servant! You've given me life!"
With a laugh she embraced him. "You've served me quite well!"
But unseen by the wizard, she drew out her knife.
Through his heart she then thrust it. "So now go to hell."

I Blame Ann Leckie

No story is published in a vacuum. Anyone who reads a story has almost certainly read other stories, and almost certainly does so regularly. That means that any story they read they consider in the context of what other authors are doing. In that way a sort of dialogue emerges between different stories. Things that one author does will be echoed or challenged by another author. This is historically how short story writing has evolved, with different writers with different ideas seeing what works and what doesn't, and trying new things. Readers respond positively or negatively, and other writers observe that, and respond in their own stories, in their own ways.

And authors, of course, also talk to each other. Most of us learned our craft by studying with other writers, either formally in classes or informally by reading books about writing. We actively theorize about what makes a story work and present those ideas to one another.

Today, more and more writers are engaging in this conversation online. Many of us have blogs. And we read each others' thoughts on writing. And sometimes we disagree.

This next story came about because I was theorizing on my blog about the nature of surprise in a story. Surprise is a tricky thing to pull off. Simply withholding information from the reader is good for a joke, but once the reader is in on the joke, what's left? For a story to rise above mere gimmick and to stand up to multiple readings, the surprise must grow so organically that the story is still engaging even if the reader is already in on the surprise.

But in my blog post on the topic, I made the comment that surprise is an important element of suspense. Ann Leckie disagreed. Leckie is an author I very much respect, and we read each other's blogs. She responded on her blog by arguing that surprise and suspense are fundamentally different, that it's entirely possible to have suspense without surprise. If the reader cares about the characters, she argued, the reader will feel suspense even if they know exactly what's going to happen, even if there isn't a single thing in the story that surprises them.

Well, I did what any writer would do in this situation: I wrote a story.

I decided to write a fairy tale because I couldn't think of another story type where there is less expectation of surprise, except perhaps allegorical fiction (which I've attempted to write, and have decided to spare you the pain of including in this collection). It's hard for me to tell if I succeeded in writing a story devoid of surprise, or if I managed to create suspense nonetheless. You, the readers who read other stories by other writers, will need to make that determination, to see how you respond to this story in the context of everything else you've read.

Nonetheless, this is a story I'm oddly fond of. Perhaps that's because it's obscene. Perhaps that's because it works on some strange, campy level. Of course, I may be the only one who is oddly fond of it, considering the visceral negative reaction many readers have had to it.

Perhaps that's because it's obscene.

If you like it, perhaps I've found a kindred spirit. If you don't like it, well, I blame Ann Leckie. It's her fault I wrote it.

A Fairy Tale

Once upon a time, a beautiful princess rejected her prince and instead married a well-endowed stable boy.

That's how the story ends. No surprises, right? Now I'll tell you how it happened.

This is the story of Princess Javotte, named for a great-aunt who had lived with her family at the castle before she was born. Javotte's mother, the queen, had bled terribly when Javotte was born, and was never able to have any other children. And so her father, the king, had selected the youngest son of his friend, King Pierre, to wed his daughter.

I suppose that's all you need to know as we begin. Well, except that you should be aware that this story contains one truly terrible pun. There's nothing I can do about that. Don't worry. I'll warn you.

Prince Yves arrived at the palace on Javotte's seventeenth birthday, tall, blond, with a smile that gleamed in the sun. He had been granted apartments in the castle, where he could live while he and Javotte went through the obligatory courtship period. Javotte and Yves saw each other only during their chaperoned meals together, where they were encouraged to get to know one another while not saying anything that the king or queen would disapprove of, and otherwise Javotte continued her usual activities. Javotte's particular pastime was riding. She was quite good at it. Her best friend, Virginie, was the champion equestrian in the land, and even she occasionally didn't need to hold back to let the princess out-perform her.

So one fateful morning, Javotte, dressed in her riding gear, descended the spiral staircase at the back of the palace, checked out with the doorman there, informing him that she was only going across the courtyard to the stables and didn't require an escort, at which point he visually verified that the courtyard was empty and allowed her to pass.

Now, I have to clarify here that there is an unspoken rule among the royals that one doesn't speak of infidelities. And as such, Javotte was woefully unprepared for the possibility that her husband-to-be might have morals on par with, well, everyone else in his family. Javotte was a proper princess: sensitive, quiet, and, most of all, sheltered. She would never have expected to discover her fiancé in the act of having sexual relations with someone else.

The princess had always found it most effective to slip into the stables quietly, because that way she could sometimes prep her horse and get out into the equestrian yard before anyone noticed she was riding, and if no one else was riding she could sometimes even slip out of the yard and onto the trails without a full hunting party riding along with her. She felt perfectly safe on the trails — trespassing in the king's forest was punishable by summary execution, and so she never met a soul out there.

On this day, she entered the stables only to hear moaning. She crept through the tack room and into the door to the alleyway. There, lying across two bales of hay, was Adam, the stable boy, completely naked, with Yves, also completely naked, on top of him.

Adam had never been particularly attractive to Javotte. True, he was broad shouldered, with wavy brown hair, enormous eyes, and full lips, just two years older than Javotte. And it was true that she couldn't ever take her eyes off of him when he was around. But that doesn't mean she was attracted to him, of course. He was a commoner and therefore entirely beneath her consideration, and she therefore never considered him at all unless she needed help with a balky buckle. And her buckles were surprisingly balky.

Well, to say that Javotte now discovered that Adam was also hung like a horse would be to ignore how inadequate horses are by comparison. Have you ever looked at a horse? Long, yes, and Adam had that, but Adam also had a thickness that would make any self-aware equine fly into a jealous rage. Fortunately for Adam, horses are far less particular than humans about such things, because every horse in the stable had at least as good a view as Javotte did.

And Yves, on his knees in a squat across Adam's abdomen, was expertly inserting and removing the entirety of that enormous endowment between his buttocks in long, rapid thrusts, grunting with pleasure, eyes closed and face thrown back toward the overhead beams, his own not-nearly-so-impressive endowment slapping down on Adam's rib cage each time he completed an insertion.

Javotte, being a princess, hadn't been schooled in such things, but it struck her as unlikely that Yves should be so flexible without considerable practice, and that seemed to her to be at odds with his forthcoming responsibility to ensure the birth of the next royal heir through her.

Javotte backed out of the stable, ran back to her apartments, and tearfully demanded that the servants summon Virginie from her own manor house outside the village. Virginie arrived as quickly as a horse could carry her.

Javotte spent the first fifteen minutes of their conversation simply clutching her and sobbing out an explanation of what she had seen.

"Oh, Javotte, Javotte," Virginie had said, rocking her beloved friend back and forth.

"I can't marry him," Javotte sobbed. "How can I marry him?"

"Oh, Javotte, I know." Virginie pulled herself up onto the bed and sat cross-legged to look her friend in the eyes. "Your father should never have arranged a marriage for you."

Javotte scoffed. "Of course he should have. He just shouldn't have arranged it with someone who would rather have sex with the stable boy." The last two words brought her back to hysterics, and Virginie hugged her again. "What's the law?" Javotte cried into the ruff of Virginie's collar. "How can I break off the engagement?"

Virginie's father was a prevaricator, and she therefore knew the law as well as anyone. She sighed and spoke plainly. "Legally, in this kingdom, you can't."

Javotte's sobs choked to a stop and she sat bolt upright. "I can't?"

"No." Virginie shifted away from her best friend. "You can only accept a proposal from a higher-ranked royal or someone who has bested him in mortal combat. You can't just end the engagement. The way the kings of old wrote the law, only Yves or your father can do that. And I doubt either of them will."

"He was having sex with the stable boy!"

"Yes, well, in a royal court that's less of a problem than you might think." Virginie stood up and walked over to one of Javotte's nine mirrored bureaus. She stood with both hands pressed to the top of it, staring into the looking glass. "Javotte, you're going to have to be strong. You're going to have to be stronger than you think you're capable of being. The road ahead will be difficult, and no matter what you do, you're not going to be popular. Can you be strong and do things you may not want to do?"

Javotte sniffled. "And marry Yves?"

"No." Virginie turned around. "Yes. Maybe. The point is, no

matter what happens, this isn't going to be a fairy tale romance, right? Your grandparents were lucky. They got a happily ever after. You're not going to. But we can use this to make this kingdom a better place. You can't be weak. You need to be strong. Can you do that?"

Javotte, a tear running down her cheek, nodded.

"Good," Virginie said. "Now the first step is you have to tell your father what happened."

The thought was inconceivable, but Javotte did so. She made an appointment with the king's second secretary to make an appointment with the king's first secretary to make an appointment for some father-daughter time that very afternoon.

The king comforted her, gently patting her hand, as she recounted what she had seen. "Oh, my lovely child, what a shock that must have been."

"Yes, father. Yes, it was."

The king rose paced around his sitting room, pausing briefly by the gilded chair where Javotte sat. "I'm so sorry you had to see that."

"So you'll break off the engagement immediately?" Javotte inquired.

"Well, my dear daughter, it's more complicated than that, you see." Her father wrung his hands. "King Pierre is a dear friend of mine, and, well, let's just say that Prince Yves comes by his proclivities naturally. I can't break off the engagement without making it seem like I'm rejecting my dear friend Pierre. And if my dear friend Pierre is insulted, there could be a war. I know arranged marriages aren't particularly romantic, but this marriage will help secure peace between our kingdoms for all time. When I die and Yves becomes king, and when Pierre dies and Yves' brother becomes king, our kingdoms will literally be brothers."

"Father, King George and King Martin are brothers, and they've been at war since Martin married Queen Esmeralda."

"Yes, well, that's different," the king protested. "They're English."

"An unhappy marriage is no guarantee of peace."

"No, but children who have connections to both kingdoms are." The king stopped pacing and pointed a finger at Javotte. "Once you and Yves are married, you have a legal, moral, and cultural imperative to breed as many royal heirs as you can. Those heirs are the future. And if Yves' brothers don't produce any male heirs, the two kingdoms could become one just by right of succession. That's the bloodless form of conquest. It's good for both kingdoms."

"Better than your own daughter's happiness?" Javotte rose and marched over to the window, looking out over the parapets along the fortifications below.

"Oh, my dear Javotte," the king protested. "You know that nothing is more important to me personally than your happiness. But I'm a king. And that means the kingdom must come first. And when you're queen, the kingdom will come first for you, too. You'll see. You'll see."

"Father, how am I supposed to create heirs with someone who would prefer a stable boy?"

"A great many royals manage, my dear. A great many. You'd be surprised what a man can do if he sets his mind to it. King Pierre's wife has never complained."

"Not to you, anyway."

"Javotte, now this has gone on long enough." The king sat on one of the long chaises. "You're going to marry Yves, and that's that."

She turned back from the window and arched an eyebrow. "I'm not marrying him."

"Yes, you are."

She folded her arms. "I am not."

The king slammed his hand down on the arm of the chaise and propelled himself back to his feet. "You are marrying Yves, and that is my order as the king!"

Javotte ran from the room.

Ironically, the only thing Javotte could ever think to do when she was mad at her parents was to go riding, which meant going to the stables.

As she slipped into the stable, she found Adam seated on the ground, tying a small piece of wood to a pigeon's wing. The pigeon saw her first and flapped its unbound wing, the half-bound one waving ineffectually, as it tried to get away. The stable boy shifted his grip to hold on to it, noticing the princess as he did. "Oh, I'm sorry, m'lady." He diverted his gaze downward. "I was just trying to set this pigeon's broken wing."

"No it's all right," Javotte said, staring in amazement. "I'm actually quite fond of pigeons. Here, let me help."

She tiptoed over to him and lowered herself to her knees. She took the pigeon's warm, feathered body in her hands and held it firmly, her fingers touching Adam's wrists. He slipped his rough hands from under hers and used both hands on the wing. Javotte could see a tiny bone protruding from under the feathers. "What happened to it?" she asked.

"Some of the boys were throwing rocks at it," Adam said. "I know, it's silly of me, but I don't think it's right to be cruel to animals."

"I don't either," Javotte said.

He snapped the bone back into alignment, and the bird squirmed and flapped.

"Shhhh." Javotte sang to the bird like her grandmother used to, "We're friends. We're helping. It's scary, but we care."

Adam glanced up at her as he placed the splint again and wrapped a piece of linen around it. "I've never heard of a princess who likes pigeons."

"In some versions of the story, pigeons helped my grandmother meet my grandfather," Javotte said, smiling in spite of herself.

"I'm sure that's a great story," he said.

"Not really. Not true, anyway. But she did like to sit outside and feed them."

"There," Adam said as he finished and reached for a cage. "All done. Should be good as new in a few weeks."

Together, they slipped the pigeon into its cage. Javotte looked at Adam's enormous eyes while he studied the bird. "Do you love Yves?"

Adam smiled. A moment later the smile remained, but his eyes went sad. "He isn't mine to love, m'lady."

"What if I said I don't want him?"

Adam glanced sideways at her. "I grew up in the castle, m'lady. I know it doesn't work like that."

"It can if we want it to."

"No." He set the birdcage on a shelf and stood up. "The good of the kingdom comes first. The good of the kingdom always comes first."

Javotte leaned back on her legs. "And you figure you can always have him on the side?"

He grinned slightly. "Only with m'lady's permission."

She laughed and stood up. "Actually, I was hoping you'd help convince him to break off our engagement. Convince him he'd rather have you. He does seem to enjoy your... company."

Adam shook his head. "I'm sorry, m'lady. The kingdom needs a king. I can't do that. Not even for you."

Javotte grimaced and drew in a sharp breath. "Well, then, in that case, you'd better help me get my horse saddled up."

Adam blinked at the sudden change in the princess' demeanor, but he was a stable boy first. He rose and dusted off his tunic. "Certainly, m'lady. How long a ride?"

"Two weeks."

"Two weeks?"

"Yes," Javotte said. "I'm riding to the East and demanding an audience with King Pierre."

Adam, of course, could have raised the alarm, but he had no orders from anyone who outranked the princess to do so, so he helped her saddle up and get on her way, and then got back to his work mucking out the stalls. He continued working as the palace guards came around looking for the princess. Since none of them asked if he knew where she was, he didn't volunteer the information.

It was an alert guard at the edge of the king's forest who foiled Javotte's plans. He heard her horse approaching from inside the forest and, knowing he was supposed to execute anyone caught trespassing there, he moved to intercept. When he saw the princess he was deferential, of course, but when she ordered him to let her pass, he refused. See, he *did* have orders from someone who outranked the princess — the king himself — not to let his daughter leave the property, and so he rode back to the castle with Javotte over his shoulder, kicking and using very unprincesslike language.

Javotte spent the next three weeks locked in her apartments, her father only agreeing to release her when she gave her solemn vow never to try to run away to see King Pierre again. Javotte was, of course, a woman of her word, but she was not above exploiting technicalities.

Now, you have to remember that the entire castle knew of Javotte's attempt to flee. The entire kingdom knew, in fact, but the lower classes would never have admitted to gossip. So slipping past the doorman required a bit more cunning than usual. Virginie had been allowed to visit again once the princess' doors were unlocked, and the princess sent her to tell the doorman that the princess would be down shortly and would require an escort to the stable.

The doorman responded exactly as he was supposed to. He puffed up and said, "I have orders not to let the princess enter the stable."

"What does that matter to me?" Virginie said. "I'm here on the princess' orders to tell you that she'll be down shortly and will require an escort."

"I can't provide her an escort."

"Well, I certainly can't disobey the princess by having you here without an escort ready, can I?"

With the doorman focused so intently on Virginie, Javotte was able to slip down the spiral staircase without him noticing.

"Well, you'll have to, because I have orders not to let her go to the stables."

Virginie leaned forward confidentially. "Listen, I'm willing to compromise. I'll be her escort to the stables. That way you don't need to summon anyone."

The doorman reared. "I'm not supposed to let her go to the stables at all!"

Javotte slipped behind the doorman and out the door.

"Well," Virginie said, "you wouldn't really be letting her go to the stables if she went out with me and didn't tell you where she was going."

The argument continued. Javotte crossed the courtyard and into the stable.

This time, Yves was the one on his back on the hay bales, his knees up by his ears. Adam stood by the hay bales, thrusting his hips to insert his astounding endowment into Yves while another young man, who Javotte would later learn was the blacksmith's oldest son, stood behind Adam doing the same to him, albeit not as dramatically due to the blacksmith's son being proportioned much more in line with human norms.

This time Javotte didn't run off. Instead she strode — still silently — into the alleyway, grabbed a saddle brush, and began to prep her horse.

The blacksmith's son noticed her first, jumping, and saying something utterly unrepeatable if I'm going to keep this story clean, his penis sliding, glistening, out of Adam's backside.

"Oh, don't let me interrupt," Javotte said, brushing her horse's back. "He's not my husband yet."

The blacksmith's son grabbed his tunic and, clutching it over his crotch, fled the stable. Yves and Adam just sort of stopped mid-insertion and stared at her. She didn't look up from her work, carefully removing anything that might chafe under the saddle or girth and smoothing out the horse's hair. Eventually Adam slipped out of Yves and pulled on his own tunic. He withdrew into the tack room respectfully.

Yves rolled onto his side and studied Javotte's back. "I probably should have explained."

Javotte shrugged. "The polite thing to do would be to break off the engagement. Father would understand. I don't think it would harm diplomatic relations between our kingdoms at all. I could even send you the stable boy as a gift, if you like."

"Javotte," he rolled off the hay bale and reached out to her.

"We're not married yet. It would be very inappropriate for you to touch me in a state of undress. We're not even supposed to be speaking to each other without a chaperone."

Yves backed off. Being a nobleman, he had a lot more clothing than just a tunic to recover, and most of it had been flung in various directions. He wandered back and forth around the stable as he spoke to her, dressing. "Javotte, I have to marry someone. Please don't tell me that you thought an arranged marriage was going to be anything other than this."

"You have the power to break off the marriage. I don't." She fetched the saddle pad from the tack room. Adam sat in there, looking sheepish as he polished her saddle for her.

"I don't want to break off the engagement, Javotte," Yves called after her. "You're by far the most interesting girl I've ever met. I think you'll make a wonderful queen."

She shoved past him and placed the saddle pad above her horse's withers. "You don't want a wife. You want a kingdom."

"I'd marry you even if I were staying a lesser prince," Yves protested, still dressed only in his tights and codpiece. "You're smart. You're independent."

"Then leave me that way." She slid the pad back into place and headed back into the tack room for her saddle. Adam stood there holding it out for her. She thanked Adam involuntarily and carried it back to the horse. "I don't know how things work in your kingdom,

Yves, but I regret to inform you that I will not be tolerating you having sex with other people. Any man I marry will either be a man of my own choosing or will take his obligations to me more seriously than life itself!"

She saddled the horse more roughly than she should have, and he pulled against his ties. She stroked his muzzle to calm him down and then checked the saddle and the pad.

"All right," Yves said at last. "That's fair. Once we're married, I will be yours and only yours."

Javotte scoffed as she fed the girth under the horse. "I give it a year at best before I catch you. Probably less. I can move pretty quietly when I want to."

Yves blinked in silence for a moment. "How am I supposed to respond to that?"

Javotte buckled the girth and opened the stall door, lifting the horse's front hooves in turn to check the fit. "You're supposed to acknowledge that you're going to be a terrible husband and that you wouldn't put any woman through that, much less a woman you say you actually like. You're supposed to say that I'm right and we should never marry. You could say you're packing up and heading back to your own kingdom."

Yves finally finished dressing, pulling on his cap, and smiling in his charming way. "I can't do that."

Javotte smiled, thin lipped, in return and led her horse out of his stall into the alleyway. "That's how I expected you to respond."

She led the horse past him, toward the yard. As she reached the stable door, she mounted.

"Are you supposed to be going riding?" Yves asked.

She laughed. "And when my father asks, tell him to look for me in your father's palace!" She barked the command for the horse to charge. Yves ran to the barn door, just in time to see her horse jump the fence and head off into the woods.

Javotte wasn't actually breaking her word. As soon as she was out of sight she dismounted the horse and slipped back, climbing a pear tree by the equestrian yard. No sooner had she secured herself in the leaves than the king appeared in the yard with a retinue of guards. Adam and Yves followed behind them.

And, before you ask, no "Adam and Yves" is not the truly terrible pun. I told you I would warn you. Besides, to be a truly terrible pun, it has to be plot-critical. As the storyteller I could have changed their names if I were the sort to value the elimination of puns over the truth. Later storytellers can just pretend that Yves was named Herbert or something. Or change the title, for that matter. Make fewer references to the kingdom coming first, for those with dirty minds. Storytellers do that all the time. Change little details to make a better story. Embellish things. Make up plot lines out of whole cloth. That's where you get ridiculous variations in the stories being shared among the people. That's where you end up with stories about Javotte's great-aunt having been blinded by pigeons. It never happened.

Javotte's great-aunt had been quite myopic, however. It's quite true that she failed to recognize her own sister sitting next to her at the ball because her sister had changed her dress and Great-aunt Javotte had been too vain to wear glasses in front of the prince. But blinded by pigeons? Never. Someone who didn't like nobles made that part up.

No, the pun you're never going to forgive me for no one will ever be able to recount this story without having to repeat. Not my fault. Not my fault, at all.

Anyway, the king turned to Yves and demanded, "Which way did she go?"

Yves pointed. The guards opened the gate and set out on foot after her. If she had actually been riding away, there was no way they could have caught up with her.

As the guards vanished from sight, the king rounded on Yves. "Why didn't you stop her?"

Yves and Adam exchanged a glance, and Adam looked down at the dirt. Yves answered after a long pause. "Honestly, your majesty, I was so enjoying the opportunity to speak to her that it slipped my mind that she isn't supposed to be riding. And then I never would have expected her to jump the fence."

"You don't know my daughter very well. The most headstrong creature you're ever going to encounter."

The queen appeared in the stable door. "She's a lot like your mother."

"My mother was sweet!" the king roared.

"Javotte's sweet," the queen said, drifting into the yard by Adam. "And intelligent. And honest. She swore she wouldn't run away to seek King Pierre again. So that's not where she is, is it?"

All eyes fell on Adam. He looked around nervously, and then up in the air.

And he made eye contact with Javotte in the pear tree. "No, ma'am."

"Where is she?" the queen asked.

Adam didn't take his eyes off Javotte. "Last time, ma'am, when she rode off, she had me equip her for a two-week ride. This time, she had only what she would need to ride around the yard."

"What's her game then?" the king roared. "Where's she hiding?"

Adam looked down, taking it as a rhetorical question.

A branch snapped.

The king looked up, and spotted his daughter. "Javotte! What are you doing in that tree?!"

"Hiding!" Javotte shouted down to him.

"You get down here this instant!"

"Not until you or Yves calls off this engagement!"

"Javotte!" The king's face swelled red with rage. He pivoted and marched back into the stable. He returned with an axe in his hand. "You get down here or I'll cut the tree down with you in it!"

"Cut it down then!" Javotte screamed.

The king reared the axe over his head and marched toward the trunk.

"Your majesty, please!" Yves ran around in front of the king and held an open hand out to the axe. "You shouldn't strain yourself. Allow me."

Yves took the axe from the king, stepped out of the equestrian yard, and lined it up with the trunk of the pear tree.

"Javotte, this is your last warning!" the king yelled.

Adam disappeared into the stable and came back with a blanket. He offered one end of it to queen.

When Javotte didn't answer, the king nodded to Yves. Yves swung the axe. Javotte yelped as the tree shook, leaves rattling all around her.

The king marched to the side of the yard, his eyes still fixed on Javotte.

Adam and the queen spread the blanket between them, and moved under Javotte's limb. They pulled it taut.

Yves swung the axe again.

"No, you're doing it all wrong!" The king barked. "Didn't your father teach you how to cut a tree down properly?"

"We usually have the servants do it, your majesty," Yves said.

"Here." The king took the axe and proceeded to demonstrate how to hold it correctly.

Adam motioned to Javotte to jump. He and the queen shook the blanket for her.

Javotte leapt.

The blanket wrapped around her, and both Adam and the queen toppled on top of her in the mud.

Javotte giggled.

"Your stable boy is as wise as he is handsome," the queen whispered to her.

"Yes, but he's sleeping with my fiancé," Javotte whispered back.

"We can have him beheaded if you'd like," the queen said.

"Not necessary," Javotte said with a glance at the silent Adam, who was still on top of her, "though I'm not sure I'd mind seeing Yves' head on the block at the moment."

The queen laughed and pulled herself to her knees. "Now run along inside before your father finishes his amateur woodsman lesson."

Javotte stood up, grabbing the muddy blanket, and ran into the stable. Adam and the queen, equally muddy, stood back up and looked back at the tree as if expecting Javotte to fall down with the unripe pears as the king and Yves took turns whacking at the trunk.

The king, of course, was livid when he and Yves finally felled the tree and he discovered his daughter wasn't in it. Naturally, he never thought to ask his wife or the stable boy what had happened to her. Nor did he ask why his wife was covered in mud. He simply stormed off to order around some more palace guards. And eventually the whole household was ordered to search for Javotte. And then the whole village. No one was ordered to check her apartments, however. Javotte had plenty of time to take a bath and change into traveling clothes before she headed out.

Getting out of the palace was easy since it was almost completely empty, with everyone out looking for her. She went to the stables first, where she found her horse had wandered back on his own, wanting his dinner. She secured him in his stall and walked out the front doors of the palace. The gates to the square stood open. Any thief with the foresight not to be caught up in the frenzy to find the princess could have robbed the palace blind, but none did. Javotte stole away into the night, across town, and into Virginie's yard completely unseen by the crowds looking for her.

By this point every man, woman, and child in the village, — save Virginie and her father, who didn't really consider themselves villagers by virtue of the fact that they could afford a manor house — were out with torches and pitchforks as part of the quest. Cries of "Find the Princess!" and "The king wants her!" and "Dead or alive!" and, eventually, "Burn her!" filled the night.

Javotte had never actually been to Virginie's house before except once when she was very young and accompanied by six coaches and allowed to drop off a birthday present and wave to the other little girls before being spirited away. So while she had found the right yard, she didn't know how to get into the house or which room might be Virginie's. So she took to throwing pebbles at every window, knowing it couldn't take that long to locate the right one since the manor house was tiny — only 30 rooms or so. But Virginie didn't answer to the pebbles or her whispered calls at any of them.

Outside the wall behind the house, another group of villagers walked by, torchlight casting orange flickers on the upper storey of the manor house, smoke choking the night air.

"Virginie!" Javotte whisper-called tossing another handful of pebbles at a darkened window.

"The manor house!" a woman outside the wall cried.

Javotte covered her mouth to stifle a gasp. The torches stopped moving.

"Yes, the manor house!" a man echoed. "That's where her best friend lives! Where else would she be hiding?"

Javotte scampered over to the bushes and ducked down between them and the stone façade.

The torches began to move again, and faces appeared at the gate. "Princess!" a toothless man called. "Come out, come out wherever you are!"

Javotte pursed her lips shut and clutched her knees close to her chest.

Torches and pitchforks appeared at the gate behind the first line of villagers to arrive.

"Princess," the toothless man called again, "this is your last chance! Come out now or we burn the place down!"

A roar came up from the mob. The toothless man smiled, torchlight forming a wicked halo behind him.

The crowd began to rattle the gates, which weren't locked. Javotte had walked right through them. But the mob didn't try to open them properly. They just shook until the hinges failed and the wrought iron smashed onto the gravel.

"Burn the manor house!" The toothless man cried.

"Wait!" a commanding baritone voice barked.

The mob hushed. A new figure with a torch strode into the middle of them. It was Adam, standing tall and confident among his own class. "The king wants his daughter found, not burned! She's a princess, not a witch! She's running because she's scared, and here you all are making her even more scared! Now put down the pitchforks and back off!"

People in the mob looked at one another. And then, one by one, they began to stand down.

"And you," Adam commanded the toothless man. "I want you to write a letter of apology to the people who live here and offer to fix these gates."

"Oh, now, come on..." The toothless man shifted in the gravel, pivoting one toe down into the ground.

"It's the least you can do!" Adam barked.

The toothless man harrumphed and shuffled off. "I don't even know how to write."

The mob dissipated, several of the men pausing to study Adam's crotch before vanishing into the night.

Javotte sat in amazement. For a man of forty with a title and position to calm an angry mob would have been remarkable. A nineteen-year-old stable boy who could command the respect of the people like that was astonishing.

As the last of the crowd left, Adam stepped into the yard and made a slow sweep with his torch, checking every shadow for signs of the princess. When he didn't see her, he, too, moved on.

Now, the reason Virginie didn't answer at any of the windows is that she and her father weren't home. They arrived an hour later.

When Virginie's father's carriage pulled up, it stopped outside the collapsed gate. Virginie and her father got out there. Virginie walked up the drive to the front doors while he stood staring at the damage.

"Virginie!" Javotte whispered from the bushes.

Virginie jumped, then crept over to investigate. "Javotte?"

"I need you to hide me."

Virginie checked over her shoulder. Her father was poking at the fallen gates as though they might spring back up into place on their own. "All right. Go around to the kitchen door. I'll go through the house and let you in."

Viginie climbed the steps and went through the front door. Javotte scampered along the house to the rear. Of course, she rustled the bushes badly enough that Virginie's father saw her and sent a messenger to the palace to let the king know that she was there — he, after all, was a loyal subject and had never quite gotten over his unspoken desire that he might one day receive a letter of nobility, and therefore took any opportunity he could to curry the king's favor — but Javotte would get home before her parents and so the message would amount to naught and is therefore hardly worth mentioning except to let you know that Virginie's father wasn't a party to any conspiracy.

The kitchen of the manor house was not the sort of place Javotte was used to. It was a utilitarian space used primarily by live-out staff, not suitable to a royal visitor at all. Virginie let her in the back door. Javotte sat down on an unfinished wooden stool and Virginie tried to pick the twigs and burs out of her hair and clothes. Javotte filled her in on what had been happening.

"And what are you going to accomplish by running off and hiding?" Virginie asked as Javotte got to the part where she fled the castle.

"I'm going to make them call off the engagement," Javotte said, as if it were the most rational connection in the world.

Virginie made a very unladylike sound and grabbed a brush to work on Javotte's ruffles with. "What, you've found a dauphin to marry instead? Neither your father nor Yves is going to budge. And unless you've got a boyfriend of noble rank who's stupid enough to challenge Yves to mortal combat and guarantee his own death whether he wins or loses, there's no calling it off. You've got to stop living your life this way. You're going to be the queen someday. You've got to stop being a victim and start being a leader."

"I am a leader." Javotte tried to look up at Virginie, but Virginie forced her head back around and continued brushing her collar.

"No you're not. Not yet. Not as long as you're running around letting other people define you. So you can't do anything about the engagement. So what? If you throw temper tantrums and run and hide, what kind of queen are you going to be?"

"When I'm the queen nobody will be able to tell me what to do."

"Exactly! Except they way you've been acting, they will. The same way they do your mother. No one can tell her what to do, but your father does. But they couldn't your grandmother. Oh, she pretended to be a shy, obedient sort, but remember when she left the castle?"

After Javotte's grandfather died, his wife had decided to move back into her father's old house some distance away, and actually tended to the housework herself. It was a scandal at the time, and nothing Javotte's father said or did was able to stop her.

"That's what I'm doing now," Javotte said. "I'm not letting my father tell me what to do."

"But you're still playing his game." Virginie sighed and dug in a drawer for a needle and thread. "You're just reacting to him and to Yves. You're going to be a monarch. You need to *be* a monarch. So tell me, what kind of monarch does this kingdom need?"

"A monarch is selfless, and puts the people's needs ahead of his own," Javotte recited.

"Or her own," Virginie said.

"Sure. Or her own. Of course. Ow!"

"Sorry." Virginie adjusted the needle in her sleeve. "But what kind of person is that? Are you that kind of person right now?"

Javotte stood up so suddenly that her sleeve came unattached, a line of thread connecting her to Virginie. "You think I should marry him!"

Virginie slammed the stool back around behind Javotte's backside. "That's not what I'm saying at all. Is Yves the kind of person who puts the people first?"

Javotte thought about it. "No. No he probably isn't."

"Then sit down."

Javotte sat. "My father isn't either, is he? I mean, not really. He says he is, but, really, he puts himself first."

Virginie proceeded to try to re-attach the sleeve. "Your mother puts the people first, but she's never taken charge the way your grandmother did. A woman can do a lot. A woman can be a monarch. A good monarch is strong. A good monarch understands the people. A good monarch is compassionate, wise, and someone who people will look up to and listen to. And it doesn't matter if their spouse is a complete waste of space or not if the monarch is the right kind of monarch."

"Yves won't be a very good king," Javotte whispered.

"No," Virginie said. "But you can be an excellent queen."

"Compassionate. Wise. Commands the respect of the people. I need to marry someone else for the good of the kingdom!" Javotte sprang to her feet, tearing the sleeve off her arm completely.

"No, Javotte, you're misunderstanding completely—"

"Oh, thank you, Virginie!" Javotte kissed her on the cheek. "You're the best friend a girl could have! You've saved my life!"

"Javotte, I'm telling you to—"

Javotte left the manor house as fast as she could and ran home.

Sadly, that was to be the last meeting between Javotte and Virginie. The very next morning Virginie packed up her things and moved to another kingdom, a kingdom ruled by a queen so wicked she had never married. Some say she was so evil no man would have her. Others say she rebuffed all her suitors, selfishly desiring to hold on to power herself. Me? I've also heard stories that she was the most beautiful woman in all the world, and so my sympathies are with those who say that she lured suitors to her and then slaughtered them, feasting on the marrow from their skulls. But, not my kingdom, not my story. Nobody knows exactly why Virginie chose to live there.

Javotte beat the rest of the household back to the palace, finding only Virginie's father's messenger boy there when she arrived, so she sat down in her father's throne to wait.

I'll spare you the details of who arrived when and how. Suffice it to say that Javotte sat silently in that throne in her tattered dress until almost dawn, when the entire household had finally assembled. Her father stood fuming at the base of the dais, her mother smirking slightly every time he tried to order his daughter down.

"Now that we're all assembled," Javotte began when the king's lead prevaricator finally stumbled in, "I have an announcement to make."

The room hushed. The king took two steps forward, but the queen placed a hand on his arm and he stopped.

"I will not be marrying Prince Yves," Javotte said. "I intend, instead, to marry the stable boy, Adam."

The room roared. The king clutched his hand to his chest and staggered, his face swelling and the veins in his neck popping. "Someone find that stable boy and execute him immediately!" he shouted above the crowd.

"Your majesty, no!" Yves pushed his way through the crowd and knelt before the king. The room went quiet again. "I beg you, sir, this is all just a terrible misunderstanding."

"No misunderstanding," Javotte said. "I marry Adam or nobody."

"Sire, please!" Yves' eyes watered and he clenched both fists. "The stable boy isn't the problem. He doesn't even know about any of this."

"And in addition," Javotte said, "he's popular with the people. If you execute him, you only secure my power as his aggrieved fiancée."

The queen leaned over to her husband. "Certainly it wouldn't hurt to have a trial, at least."

"Oh, very well!" the king roared with a glance at his wife. "Arrest the stable boy and bring him here!"

Adam was in custody moments later, dragged into the entry hall and dropped on the floor before the king. The king reared up to his full height and looked down at him. "Are you Adam, the stable boy?"

"Yes, your majesty," Adam said in a quavering voice.

"You have been accused of alienating the affections of the princess," the king said. "What say you?"

Adam looked up at the king blankly. "What?"

"Are you or are you not the man the princess has said she wants to marry?" the king bellowed.

"No, sir," Adam said.

"Yes, father," Javotte said. "That is your future son-in-law."

Adam turned to Javotte, agape.

"Throw this... this... *commoner* in prison pending trial!" the king roared.

Two guards scooped Adam up by the armpits. He looked pleadingly at the princess as they dragged him past her. "Please feed the pigeon."

The royal household buzzed, everyone asking everyone else if they somehow knew something they didn't. Javotte finally rose from the throne and moved toward her apartments. Yves moved in and intercepted her.

"You are a vile, evil, wicked woman!"

Javotte arched an eyebrow at him. "I gave you ample opportunities to call off the engagement of your own volition."

Yves' whole body shook. "I don't care if you have every single one of my lovers executed! I will marry you! And I will keep up the royal tradition of promiscuity!"

Yves stormed out, the crowd parting for him.

As it turned out, Yves' eldest brother ascended to the throne in King Pierre's kingdom the very next year, and tried to put a stop to that very royal tradition of promiscuity. He did so by passing a law allowing royals to marry any consenting adult, regardless of class or gender. He claimed it was a success, since coincidentally there was, in fact, a sudden and dramatic drop in royal promiscuity, and the palace became briefly known as a haven of happy couples. But the people weren't fooled, and as each royal wedding proved more scandalous than the last — culminating in two people marrying who had no blood relation whatsoever — they finally revolted. The people put the younger King Pierre and his family to the axeman. Yves' morals were much more in keeping with the people's idea of what a king should be, and so he found himself with a kingdom after all. But that's another story.

Now, the trial of Adam the stable boy, of course, was the biggest sensation to hit the kingdom in several generations. Every adjudicator thought he should be the one to hear the case. In the end, only the top thirteen were invited, but four more showed up uninvited, and since it would have been impossible to turn them away without appearing to favor the others or to be attempting to stack the trial, they were allowed to remain, beating the previous record for most adjudicators on one trial by fourteen. The list of prevaricators was easier to control, with the king passing a firm rule of no more than three per witness, subject, or observer.

Oh, and I should warn you that this is the scene that contains the truly terrible pun.

The trial was too large to be held in the usual judgment houses, so it was instead relocated to the largest hall in the kingdom, the one usually reserved for the monthly alcohol-consumption contests. The adjudicators lined up behind a custom-built bench on the far wall, and a witness stand was constructed from a pulpit taken from a church that no one attended any more because the congregation had taken to actually reading the Bible in its entirety. The king and queen had their mobile dais and thrones installed at the front of the gallery, and 2,000 VIPs were chosen by lottery to observe. The trial began after two weeks.

As was the custom, the accused was put on the stand and ordered by the king to confess. This was a useful tactic, because the subject either confessed or was guilty of defying a direct order from the king, thus ensuring that the prevaricators and adjudicators never had to work terribly hard for their inflated salaries. Adam, however, was wise. "I'm sorry, your majesty," he said when he received the order, "I'm not quite sure what I'm supposed to confess to."

"To alienating the affection of the princess!" the king roared.

"Oh, am I supposed to have done that?"

"You know perfectly well that's the charge against you!"

"I'm sorry, it's hard to know what I'm supposed to be guilty of when I haven't actually committed any crimes."

"Confess!"

"Of course, your majesty. I'll follow any order you give. What exactly am I supposed to confess to?"

This went on for five minutes before the king roared and ordered the trial to continue. And thus Adam wriggled off the first hook.

Adam's prevaricator went through the usual motions of claiming that his client barely knew the princess and had in no way alienated her affections. The king's prevaricator responded by requesting that the queen agree to take the stand voluntarily.

Now this was a particularly good tactic — and obviously one that had been worked out with the king beforehand, as he showed no surprise — because the queen was well known throughout the land for her honesty and grace. She wouldn't be sworn in, of course, as everyone knew that a monarch would never lie, and she glided into the witness stand and smiled.

"Did you, ma'am," the king's prevaricator began, "hear the princess announce her intention to marry the defendant, Adam, the stable boy?"

The queen smiled. "Yes."

"And she did so in front of the entire royal family?"

"Yes."

"Much to the surprise of everyone there?"

"Yes."

"And the princess, at the time, had already become engaged to Prince Yves, correct?"

"Yes."

"And the stable boy, Adam, is not of noble blood, to the best of your knowledge?"

"Oh, I don't see what the problem with that is," the queen said. "The late queen mother was a maid before she married my father-in-law."

The king clutched his chest and half rose from his throne. "Objection!" he cried.

The queen's prevaricator rose. "We object to the objection!"

The king's prevaricator turned to the adjudicators. "For the record, it is now a well documented fact that the queen mother was, indeed, of royal blood, but was working as a maid due to extraordinary family circumstances."

All the adjudicators spoke at once, some saying, "Sustained," and some saying, "Overruled." Nobody tallied who ruled which way, and the trial continued regardless.

"So is it safe to say," the king's prevaricator continued, "that the stable boy, Adam, has the affection of your daughter?"

"That's the most common reason for a girl to wish to get married," the queen said, "but I'm afraid you'd have to ask my daughter that."

"And why don't you?" Javotte's voice boomed from the crowd. The king again clutched his heart and swooned as Javotte rose from her seat and marched down to the witness stand. The crowd murmured as she took her place by her mother. Seventeen gavels pounded for order arrhythmically. "Ask me your questions."

"Balderdash!" the king shouted. "She doesn't even have a prevaricator!"

Two dozen prevaricators in the gallery all offered their services at once, and each adjudicator set about selecting one to act as Javotte's court-appointed counsel, all of them ignoring Javotte's protestations that she didn't need representation.

Since no one wanted to tell any of the adjudicators that their choice as counsel for Javotte would be rejected while another's choice was accepted, the king temporarily waived the three-prevaricator-per-witness rule, and the trial continued. The king's prevaricator stammered as he addressed the princess. "M-m'lady. i-is it true that the stable boy Adam has your affection?"

Javotte arched an eyebrow. "No."

Pandemonium erupted, and the adjudicators all slammed down their gavels and cried, "Order," each attempting to be louder than the others.

"But, m'lady," the king's prevaricator continued when the hush resumed, "did you not announce your intention to marry him?"

"I did," Javotte said.

"But then why did you announce that if he does not have your affection?"

Javotte folded her arms. "Simple. The man I marry will become the crown prince, and will one day be king. It's clear to me that I'm not going to be able to marry a man I love, nor a man who loves me. So I considered the qualifications necessary for the job of crown prince, and I decided Adam is the superior candidate."

The king clutched his heart with both hands and made several rasping coughs. The crowd murmured again, and three adjudicators threatened over one another to clear the courtroom.

The king's prevaricator could hardly speak. "B-b-b-b-ut, m'lady... He- he- he's n-n-n-not of n-n-n-n-noble birth!"

"I'm not so sure," Javotte said, producing a scroll and handing it over to the bench of adjudicators. To this day no one knows where she got that scroll, and no one dares speculate. "I have here to enter into evidence a disciplinary report from the jail where Adam has been held since his arrest. You'll see there that nine guards have been charged with having sex with Adam."

It was true, of course. And those nine guards' defense when caught was that they were just the ones unlucky enough to be engaged in the act when the warden came down to take his turn. All in all, the best estimate any historian has come up with is that while Adam was incarcerated, thirty-five guards, two hundred inmates, and several VIPs were involved in the longest, largest, all-male orgy ever recorded.

"Ob-ob-ob-objection!" the king's prevaricator said. "Rele-rele-relevance?"

"Well," Javotte said directly to the gallery, "the law says that I may choose not to marry Prince Yves if I instead marry a higher-ranking nobleman. There's simply no case against Adam. Is there anyone here who would deny that Adam is a queen?"

Now, remember, as obvious as that truly terrible pun is, no one in the room had ever heard it before.

Every prevaricator in the room froze, some mid-gesture, mouths open.

The king slapped both hands to his chest, grimacing, and slumped down in his throne.

As if on a silent cue, every prevaricator in the room went into a huddle, discussing in a hush. All seventeen adjudicators leaned forward, needing a prevaricator to tell them what to think. None of the observers dared move.

You have to understand, though, that while none of this came as a surprise to you or me, the whole situation was bafflingly unprecedented to those in the room. It was the last, great surprise of all time. As the king recovered he barked, "I hereby officially outlaw all surprises!"

Of course, even back then the king couldn't enact a law retroactively. And since Javotte had already dropped her bombshell, it was no longer a surprise. So surprises have been outlawed ever since, and though the law is a bit of an inconvenience for storytellers, forcing us to tell you how our stories end as we begin them, I must say that that's a small price to pay for living under the wisdom of such a just and equitable ordinance.

The whispers among the prevaricators died down. They all nodded. They turned to face the adjudicators. The king's prevaricator spoke for them all:

"The law is clear. A queen does, in fact, outrank a prince. We've looked up 'queen' in the dictionary, and a man who has sexual relations with another man is, in fact, a queen. Therefore, the princess' assertion that Adam is a noble of higher rank than Prince Yves is legally correct."

Seventeen adjudicators banged their gavels. Adam was released on the spot. He ran up and embraced Javotte, and then he ran over and kissed Yves.

Adam and Javotte's wedding was the stuff of fairy tales. Everyone in the kingdom showed up. Adam and Javotte both looked radiantly beautiful. And at the end of the ceremony, they released the now-healed pigeon they had cared for together.

I'd like to say they lived happily ever after, but that's a matter of some dispute. Certainly King Adam was remembered as a wise, just, and respected monarch. Queen Javotte was known as a cunning and intelligent royal consort.

Virginie wrote periodically to tell Javotte how much better things were in the wicked kingdom where men didn't rule. Javotte never did quite understand the rambling madness her best friend had descended into. Virginie said repeatedly that she had gotten her own happily ever after, and wished Javotte would, too. Virginie never believed that Adam and Javotte lived happily ever after.

But Adam — well, men they now called noble queens from all over the world used to spend inordinate amounts of time visiting their palace, which kept Adam very happy. So I suppose you could say Adam lived happily ever after.

And Javotte — well, I guess she was also as happy as can be expected. After all, Adam took seriously the legal, moral, and cultural imperative to breed as many royal heirs as he could. So Javotte also lived happily ever after.

Because Adam was, after all, *mind-numbingly* well endowed.

This Is My Story

I'm going to stop and ask you to think for a moment about how gay men are portrayed in stories you've read. The gay best friend? The talented but sexless designer? The man-slut with the hots for the main character? On those very rare occasions when a gay man is the main character, think about who wrote it. Was it a gay, male author, or a heterosexual woman?

I, like everyone else, am the main character in my own story. But who gets to tell that story?

Historically, gay men have had a very hard time selling stories about gay men anywhere except the gay erotica markets. When we do, we're usually forced to write one of the stereotypes that the predominantly straight readership and editors have come to expect from gay characters (which is why you see a lot of campy comedy, cross-dressers, and incredibly horny men who will turn straight for the right woman). One market, which has as part of its mission statement that it hopes to encourage writers from under-represented groups, for a long time had in its submission guidelines an explicit ban on stories about "gay issues." I hate to break it to you, but "issues" is what it means to be gay. Why doesn't someone with a strong attraction to people of only one hair color doesn't get a label and get singled out by our society for special vitriol? Because we, as a society, have no issue with that. And therefore, the person who is only attracted to blondes, or redheads, or whatever doesn't have issues.

Issues are what tie the QUILTBAG community together, what *make* us into a community. Let's be honest; we've got nothing else is common. We're all ages, all genders, all skin colors, all socioeconomic classes, all religions, and from everywhere in the world. The fact that we've had to deal with the same bullshit that society heaps on us is what defines us as a minority group. And part of that bullshit is the dominant society deciding what role we are and are not allowed to play in the world – and, by extension, in our literature. So to say that you want gay characters and gay writers without gay "issues" is to say that you do not want authentic gay voices. You want that plucky queen who gets a laugh, or you want us to write from a perspective that lets you believe we've achieved acceptance and equality when, in fact, we're far from it.

It reminds me a great deal of what I've heard from many Native Americans over the years. Everyone loves an Indian. Dress in regalia, set up shop in a tourist trap, and people will listen to your trickster tales all day. Dress like you shop at Walmart and instead tell stories about B.I.A. abuses, and people wander off, shut down, don't listen. Yes, everyone loves an Indian, but only the fantasy Indian, not the real thing. Only the historical Indian, not the one standing right in front of them. These people don't want to know about real Native Americans, they want to engage in a little cultural tourism, to convince themselves that they care about Indians while all the while not challenging their worldviews.

That's very much how I feel as a writer. It's O.K. for me to be gay. In fact, people *want* me to be gay. But they don't want me to challenge their ideas and expectations about what it means to be gay. My story as a gay man is not the same as anyone esle's, though, and only I can say what being gay means to me. And that means I'm going to talk about the issues, and I'm going to talk about them the way I see them.

Yes, I know, this is science fiction. Can't we imagine a world where it really is O.K. to be gay, where the sexual orientation of the character only matters for the romantic bits? Well, I hate to break it to you, but even that is a gay issue. Whenever we change something about our society in a speculative piece, we're actually highlighting that aspect of our culture, calling it out for further examination. And, frankly, the heterosexual female writers have done a great job of writing those sorts of futures, where sexy gay men run around boinking each other in public and no one really cares – in fact, they rather seem to like it. But that's not my reality. That's not my story. I live in a world where I'm constantly at war with those sorts of stereotypes about my lifestyle. I live in a world where I have to overachieve to be regarded as an equal. I live in a world where privilege goes to other people. I live in a world where I genuinely fear for my safety and can't necessarily trust law enforcement to protect me. And even if I don't decide to write that reality literally, it remains my reality and I think it colors my perspective of the worlds I create and set my stories in.

And when I do set out to write a realistic gay protagonist, do you know what happens? I collect rejection letters. Lots of them. Often, they pay lip service to wanting more LGBT stories, but then comment that my version of a gay story isn't right for their publication. It doesn't meet the straight audience's expectations of what a gay story *should* be. Where's the snarky humor? Where's the anatomically impossible but hot (for straight women) sex scene? Where's the gay flair, the gay style?

I can write those things. I have written those things. Truth be told, those things are a hell of a lot of fun. They have their place, and I appreciate the authors who have made names for themselves doing them. It becomes an issue, however, when that becomes the only gay narrative that is allowed, when other voices with other perspectives can't join the chorus. The gay authors who have made it become the token gay, and the mainstream public goes on congratulating itself for being so inclusive while remaining deaf to the real gay rhetoric trying to happen around them. We become objects of cultural tourism, not people who are genuinely respected.

So I have a dilemma. I can write and sell the gay stories that the audiences want to hear, or I can write what I see as the truth and have no one ever read it.

To be honest, I'm not terribly comfortable reinforcing someone else's notion that that's what it's like to be me, that the story that society has mapped out for me is, in fact, my story.

It's not.

This is my story.

Nobody's Ancestor

My old house creaks with the sprits of my ancestors. Not literally, of course. There's no such thing as ghosts. But I do hallucinate.

The old Indian woman hadn't been around for several months, but then there she was in the lower room of the oldest portion of the house, stirring a pot over open flames in the river-rock fireplace.

Kalen, my nephew, raced through the room, arm outstretched, holding up a plastic figurine of a turtle that held two swords. He roared with a battle cry and wove around the old Indian woman as though he could see her, too. She spoke a singsong sentence in what I've always assumed must be Algonquian. I've never been able to understand what she says.

"Uncle Joe, Donatello needs us!" Kalen yelled from the steps to the two upstairs rooms. He roared again and tromped up toward what I had adapted to a rumpus room for the days when my sister dropped him off with me. I had to admit, I didn't understand the warrior turtle phenomenon. Somehow the Lego and Matchbox craze that gripped my generation when we were 10 seemed more rational.

The fire crackled. I have no idea if it was really there or not. I didn't light it, and a hallucinated fire would smell just as real as the real thing.

Then I caught that distinct, pile-of-manure-that-scared-a-skunk stench. That meant that Tobias Guthrie was also around somewhere. Bathing is a relatively modern notion. When my ancestors are in the house, the smell precedes them, and each one smells different. The old Indian woman always smelled like wet leather.

Tobias appeared from the stairs to the second floor, greasy grey beard puffing up around his pouting lips. "You tell my grandmother that she's got to salt it or it won't keep!"

I have no idea if the old Indian woman understands English or not, but she just kept stirring.

I sat down in my grandmother's wingback and opened the journal I was reviewing. "I'm staying out of your fights, Tobias."

"You have to eat her crap, too!" Tobias swaggered over to the pot and stared down into it. "Dammit, you old witch, smell that! It needs salt!"

The old Indian woman just stirred.

With thunderous steps on the stairs, Kalen charged back into the room, this time with a plastic rat in his other hand. "Out of the way, Tobias! We have to save Donatello!"

"Don't talk to my hallucinations, Kalen!" I shifted in my chair and tried to focus on the latest paper about the data being released from the Midcourse Space Experiment. Astronomy always made more sense to me than whatever was going wrong with my brain chemistry.

"They're not hallucinations, they're ghosts, Uncle Joe." Kalen had stopped next to the old Indian woman.

"You listen to this young man," Tobias said to me. "More brains in his head than in all those degrees you got."

"There's no such thing as a ghost." I turned my chair so I wouldn't have to look at them.

The old Indian woman started dishing mush out of her pot and into one of the decorative bowls from the mantle. She handed it to Kalen.

"Don't eat that," I said. "Ghost food doesn't have any calories."

"Plus it needs salt!" Tobias barked at the old Indian woman.

Kalen took a fingerful into his mouth, grimaced, and dropped his bowl on my lap. He ran through the first addition toward the kitchen. "There's carrots, too!" I yelled after him. "Not just cookies!"

The old Indian woman handed a second bowl of mush to Tobias. He harrumphed and flopped down on the chaise, putting muddy, buckled shoes up on the cocktail table. "So, do I have another generation of grandkids yet?"

"You've got more grandkids than you can count, Tobias."

"That's not the point!" he barked, scratching his lice as he contemplated his mush. "You know you can't get pregnant from buggery, right?"

It was an old argument. "I'm not trying to get pregnant. I don't want to get pregnant. And I'm not sure, biologically, if a man could even carry a child to term, Arnold Schwarzenegger movies notwithstanding."

The old woman said something in Algonquian.

Tobias thrust a finger at her. "You stay out of this, you old bat! He's my grandson, too, and I've got a right meddle! You don't want this property going to a stranger again, now, do you?"

"Kalen inherits the house." I tried to stay focused on my journal, but the words all blurred together. The ancestors loved to remind me that I was the end of my line. I always wondered about the psychology of my subconscious mind dredging that up over and over again.

Kalen tore back into the room with a bag of carrots in one hand, a bag of cookies in the other. He dropped the carrots in my lap, and flopped down next to the fire with the cookies.

Tobias harrumphed again and ate a handful of mush. "It needs salt, you crazy, old, wench!"

"There's salt in the kitchen, Tobias," I said.

"Woman's work!" Tobias barked. He resumed his trademark sulking.

Kalen twisted around to look at the empty chaise where Tobias sat. "How come Uncle Joe thinks you're a hallucination?"

"Because he is," I said.

"He could be a ghost."

"There's no such thing. And if we had proper insurance I could prove it to you. Meanwhile, you just try not to go insane, too. There's nobody here but you and me."

Kalen shrugged and went back to eating cookies.

"I took a picture of Martin Jacobson once," I told Kalen. "When I got the film back, I just had a picture of an empty chair."

Kalen shrugged. "Ghosts would do that, too."

"Kid's smarter than you are," Tobias said.

I dipped a carrot in the hallucinated mush and sampled it. I had to admit, Tobias was right. It needed salt.

. . .

I knew my mom's family was descended from the Guthries when I bought the house. And I knew it was built by Tobias Guthrie, of course. The info plaque that the Massachusetts Historical Society put on all the houses in the village when I was a kid named the original owner. The one by my inoperable front door said, "Built by Thomas Guthrie, 1698. Site of the Guthrie farmstead." What I didn't know was that my great-great-great grandmother was descended from this particular Guthrie, and was actually born in this house, back when it only had two additions. My mother found that out doing genealogical research. Her theory is that some sort of ancestral memory made me feel at home in the house when I looked at it. My theory was that it was the only house for sale in the village.

My mom also discovered in her research that I'm 1/1024 Indian. When 17th-century colonists came over from Europe, there were three ways they dealt with the Indians: They fought them, they ignored them, or they assimilated them. This county is one of the very few places where the Indians assimilated with the English, took Christian names, and were welcomed into the colony. Tobias Guthrie had apparently built his house where his grandfather's wigwam had stood. The land had belonged to my ancestors since before it belonged to anyone.

If my mom knew about the hallucinations, I'm sure she would have blamed that on ancestral memory, too. I'd always found science to be a better explanation for things, and going insane is a lot less frightening than you'd expect.

. . .

The oak tree by the driveway needed to come down. And even though I'm generally opposed to physical activity, I'm more opposed to spending money for something I can do myself. So I fired up my next-door neighbor's chainsaw and went after the rotting bark on the side farthest from the house.

"The squirrels planted this one."

I jumped. Rev. William Jacobson stood right behind me, his pre-era-of-amplification voice carrying over the roar of the chainsaw. "You may want to stand back! This isn't like any saw you had in your day!"

The truth is, the chainsaw bucked so badly I wasn't sure I wouldn't lose control and slice him in two. And, hallucination or not, I figured that would be messy.

"This side of the house, the fields had gone fallow, I was so busy with the church." William stepped alongside me and helped steady the chainsaw. He still wore the long, black coat he used to preach in, and looked far too formal to be cutting down a tree. "Wet, too. Not like the marshlands, of course, but good for oak trees. There weren't many trees left by that time. We considered clearcutting a virtue."

A series of snaps echoed up the full height of the dead tree. I pulled the chainsaw out and stepped back, winded. It wasn't quite ready to topple yet.

"You should tie a rope to it so you can guide it the direction you want it to fall," William said.

"As long as it doesn't hit the house, I don't care!" I lit back into the trunk, wood shavings hurling in every direction.

William wandered into the garage — actually a converted stable — while I found the chainsaw less and less effective the further into the trunk I got. After a few minutes, William emerged with a length of nylon rope tied into a lasso. "You've got it notched pretty well now. Let me toss this over the limb, and you cut from the other side."

I turned off the chainsaw, annoyed. I was already short of breath. "Wisdom of the ancestors?"

"I've cut down a few more trees than you have." He studied the top of the dead oak nostalgically as he began spinning the lasso. It only took him two tries to hook one of the larger limbs. He stepped away and pulled the rope taut, then nodded to me. I was long past the point of wondering how a hallucination would help me guide the tree down.

My arms ached from the chainsaw, and for some reason my jaw started in with sympathy pains. I held down the starter button and moved around to the other side of the tree as the motor roared back to life.

Working on the tree from this angle was no easier, but William shouted out the occasional encouraging word. The tree leaned more and more toward William as the chainsaw cut a groove deeper and deeper into the decaying wood. The ache in my arms spread into my chest, and soon the world was spinning.

A mighty crack reverberated through my body. I saw William scampering out of the way. The world twisted and folded as the once-mighty tree fell.

. . .

I stood in deep woods, a bed of rotted autumn leaves covering the ground even though the trees were still lush and green. Dank filled my nostrils. And a whole tribe of Indians emerged from the woods and studied me. They didn't dress like you imagine an Indian — their outfits looked like combinations of tunics and shawls and they wore oddly pointed hats. The old Indian woman from my house walked beside one of them, her arm around his waist. She smiled.

Thick-chested dogs ran outside a wigwam, and I smelled her mush on the fire.

The trees fell one by one. My house stood where the wigwam had been, but only the front of my house. Old, leaded-glass windows hung in panes where the previous owner had installed modern triple-glazed vinyl. The paint smelled fresh. Tobias waved to me from the roof.

A dirt road came through. Cows grazed and corn and squash grew together in the fields.

White ancestors now, too. They gathered in a ring, all looking at me, like they expected me to do something. William held out his Bible to me.

The cows vanished and more roads came through. The house grew larger, and a few additional shacks sprang up around it. Soon there were more houses. And more ancestors.

My grandfather was among them now. He looked like I remembered him from when I was a child, wearing plaid flannel and smoking his pipe. I couldn't have described the odor, but I knew the scent immediately. Strange. He had never lived here.

The tree I had just cut down rustled, green leaves waving in the breeze, a family of blue jays making a home in one of the lower branches. The familiar neighborhood now stood all around me. The oak tree died, and fell.

And I saw myself lying beside it.

One of the Indians spoke in Algonquian. I didn't understand. But I answered anyway.

"No. I'm nobody's ancestor."

. . .

The thing about being completely insane is you start to lose track of simple things. Like when you redecorated the house. Or where your bedroom went. But I'm still fond of my grandmother's wingback chair.

A young man who looks like an older version of my nephew smiles at me as I walk in. He reclines on a modernist couch I can't believe I actually bought, I don't remember buying. "Good morning," he says. "I was wondering if you were all right."

"Why wouldn't I be?" I settle down in the wingback, but none of my journals are nearby. I pick up what looks like a book but actually has a screen instead of pages. Some sort of fiction graphically describing the dissection of a living person.

"Nonfiction's in a separate folder," the young man says, as if reading my mind. Here, let me show you.

His fingers do a little dance on the screen, and there's a list of titles I can choose from. *The Astrophysical Journal* is always a safe bet. I call up a paper on interference lines from red giants in Seyfert galaxies.

"So how do they resolve something as small as a single star in a galaxy fifty million light-years away?" I ask.

"I have no idea," the young man says. "I subscribe to it for you. I went into marine biology, remember?"

I don't. Insanity affects memory too. "They should be glad I'm not the one doing peer review on that finding. I never would have let them get away with that claim."

"I'm sure."

William emerges from the newer wing of the house. He looks at the young man, and then at me. "Now, Kalen's a promising boy. None of your leading him into your sinful ways."

"Please, he's my uncle!" the young man says.

Kalen is my nephew's name.

That's right. I remember. Kalen is my nephew. My nephew lives here now, too. And he has his Masters'. I had forgotten. When did he move in?

William passes through to the stairs. "You do everything you can to instill good morals in your children..." He shakes his head and vanishes up the steps.

I look over at Kalen.

"He caught me in bed with my girlfriend."

I nod. "That's nothing. He caught me in bed with my boyfriend once."

Kalen laughs. "Yeah, I found what you had in the back closet. That must've blown his Victorian mind."

It had.

But somehow our ancestors forgive us.

At least they do in my hallucinations.

"Are you going to marry her?" I ask.

"O.K., you're starting to sound like the rest of them!"

"Do I?" I say. "I'm not supposed to. I'm not your ancestor."

He smiles at me. Behind his glasses, he's tearing up. "You did more for me than my father ever did. And I cried more when you died."

"I don't remember dying," I say.

"Heart attack," he says. "Mr. Johnson says it happened really suddenly. Just went down while cutting that tree. And the boyfriend you had helping you just disappeared, didn't even call 9-1-1."

Mr. Johnson was the next-door neighbor when I lived here. When was that?

When I look at the walls just right, they're there and they're not. I can see the house when I lived here. I can see the forest before it was built. I can see hundred years of redecoration still to come.

I settle back in my grandmother's chair and study the man who looks like my nephew — who is my nephew. I don't know if I'm hallucinating him or if he's hallucinating me, but I know from experience that if I refuse to believe in him, he still won't go away.

And I still hear them, my ancestors, creaking in the old house. But me, I'm still nobody's ancestor.

Changing Visions

This next story came about because I was doing a story-a-month challenge with a group of writers I'm involved with. We got a different prompt each month. The idea of a prompt is to get the creative juices flowing. A good prompt will take the writer in surprising directions.

One of our prompts was "Deadly Spring." It's a good prompt. There are lots of different ways a writer could interpret it. There is good, inherent confict already built into it. I, personally, took "spring" as the season, and set about mulling ideas of when and how the season we typically use to symbolize rebirth and new life could, instead, end up being a symbol of death.

Meanwhile, Elizabeth Bear commented on her blog one day that when she was training, she had a teacher who was so convinced that in the future we're all going to be able to upload our brains to computers and therefore live forever that he regarded any science fiction story that didn't contain that element as unrealistic. Naturally, this got me mulling ideas about when concepts like that, so ubiquitious we take them for granted, don't work out like we think they will.

And in my brain, the two ideas merged. The first draft was born, and I had a story called, predictably enough, "Deadly Spring."

But the thing about the revision process is that the goal is always to make the story the best it can be. And that means not always being true to the prompt, or to the original idea behind the story, or even the original story itself if things in it don't work. When it's all done, you may not even recognize where it came from.

There are still a couple of remnants of "Deadly Spring" in "Eternity Undone," but, overall, in the battle of ideas, the Elizabeth Bear comment won out. But that's not to say that this story could have existed without the "Deadly Spring" prompt. It couldn't have, and it wouldn't have. My rule is that anything that isn't essential to the story I'm telling goes, and, yes, that means the whole impetus behind the story vanished between drafts.

Perhaps someday I'll come back and re-explore the elements of "Deadly Spring" that spoke to me so strongly. I can't say for sure. The thing about being a writer is that absent the clear guidance of, "the readers want more of X," it's nigh unto impossible to tell where inspiration will take us next.

Ultimately, though, I'm happy with the story that resulted. I find it a lot of fun to subvert tropes, to re-think aspects of our genre that we've taken for granted, to turn ideas on their ears. And, ultimately, I think that's why the Bear aspects of the story were the ones that stayed. At the end of the day, I think the readers are more interested in exploring ideas about our society than they are in marveling at the reversal of standard imagery.

So, my original idea was completely undone, but perhaps the story that resulted will point a way to a different future.

Eternity Undone

How long has it been?

Kali Parvati cocked her head sideways, not sure when the question had appeared on the holographic monitor in front of her, or what it might mean. Her black braid fell over her shoulder as she did so, her dark eyes narrowing. She had been taking inventory of files on old memory cards, and didn't think she had any communications software open. It wasn't the hospital's official internal communications program, and the administration frowned on any others running on their over-taxed systems.

Is someone there?

The second question replaced the first.

Kali stood up, her chair sliding back into the acrylic door, and she shuffled along the narrow gap between the antique records computer and the wall to look at the internal communications jack behind it. Empty. Not that there was anywhere on the old behemoth to have connected it if someone had wanted to.

"All right, lads, who's screwing around here?" Kali muttered aloud.

It's me. The imprint you're accessing.

The holographic display looked the same from all angles, so even with the blocky, beige machine between her and it she could read the new words.

"Can you hear me?"

Of course. The computer you're using has a microphone. They set up a subroutine so we could access it in order to carry on conversations.

It doesn't do any good to save a human imprint if no one can interact with it.

Kali whistled through her teeth. No one had warned her the records might chat her up.

She grabbed her handheld and consulted the notes she had been taking. The memory card appeared to contain several dozen extremely detailed neural scans, all dated 130 years ago. When she had inserted it, she had apparently accidentally selected record 13.

"Imprint?" Kali asked.

What's that date now? How long have I been, the new words paused, as if someone was thinking. *I guess asleep is the wrong word, but that's what it feels like. Except it doesn't feel like anything. I can't really feel anything in this state.*

"This file is about 130 years old." Kali shifted back over to her chair and sat down again, glancing back and forth between her handheld and the holo.

The law had changed recently, allowing hospitals to delete data for patients who had been dead 30 years or more, and Kali, in her capacity as archivist, had been tasked with seeing which memory cards could be wiped and reused. Even with the additional cost of rigging up a way for the modern equipment to use the antique cards, reusing a card would be cheaper than buying new ones. Prices for rare earth metals just kept going up.

When my wife visited me she said I'd been recorded about 30 years before I died. Feels like four or five days to me. No, not feels. When someone is accessing the file, it's like waking up in the morning, except there's light everywhere inside me, but there's no me, just the thoughts and the memories. And when they're not accessing, it's like falling asleep, just fading back into the darkness.

"I still don't understand," Kali said. "The file I'm accessing is a neural scan."

Yes. Have they stopped taking imprints now? That's really too bad. It's incredible technology. I mean, I've been dead a hundred years, and here I am, alive. It's incredible. Profound, really.

Imprint. Somewhere, in the back of her mind, it rang a bell. Something done back in the old days when the privileged few in the wealthy countries had thought that resources would increase forever. A promise of eternal life. "You're not a medical record."

No. Not literally. I'm an imprint. A copy of a living mind.

"You... alive?"

Well, I think. Therefore I am, right?

"You're not just some crazy computer program."

One that can pass the Turing test? I mean, yes, I'm a computer program, of course. But I'm an accurate copy of Aiden Smith. I have all his knowledge, his memories. I think for him. Everything that we believe makes us human.

Kali called up the records on her handheld and started reading. The hospital had been one of the places that participated in a program to save imprints of healthy, adult minds. It had been something of a fad in the late Williamite era to have your entire brain archived. Family members would come calling in the facilities that had made the recording and "visit" dead loved ones. There had even been talk of the government funding a program to build robotic bodies for people to live out an eternal life in.

How times change.

So, to what do I owe the honor of the visit?

Kali smiled her professional smile instinctively, and then realized he probably couldn't see it. "I'm the hospital archivist. Cataloguing old memory cards."

What's your name?

"Kali."

Kali. It's very nice to meet you, Kali.

"So, are you capable of processing and storing new information?"

Sure. Try me.

"Do you know who the King of England is?"

It was William when I was recorded. I can't imagine it still is.

"No. It's John now."

Finally another John. Does that mean John I's reputation has been cleared up?

Kali laughed. "No, not exactly. My grandmother tells me it was quite the brouhaha when he was born."

I can imagine.

"All right, I'm going to power you down now."

Go ahead. It doesn't hurt.

Kali entered the command to unmount and eject the card. It popped out of a tiny slot.

The holographic monitor flickered to a vague, blank, mustard color hanging in the air.

The card was labeled in thick, black handwriting with a simple numeric sequence. Clearly it meant something to whoever put an old-fashioned pen to it so long ago.

So long ago.

Every so often in her job Kali felt an otherworldy connection to the past. Another human being, now long dead, had held this same card. Labeled it. Copied the mind of Aiden Smith onto it.

Aiden Smith.

If he really was sentient somewhere on this card, that would mean she couldn't erase it. Not ethically, anyway. And that would be very, very bad news for the hospital.

Kali put the card back in the slot, and navigated back to record 13. The date on the file showed it had been recorded on a May afternoon — long before even her grandmother was born — with no modification date. She activated it.

Hello. Kali, is that you?

"Yes."

King John II, right?

Kali's heart skipped and sank all at the same time.

. . .

"They're records, Kali. Delete them." Dr. Wright shifted his lanky form behind his desk. As the hospital administrator, he had more room in his office than most — which meant both he and Kali could sit down with the door closed — but he never looked comfortable in his seat. The glass wall behind him had probably once commanded an impressive view of the city, but it now stared into the staff cafeteria in the newer building next door. The afternoon sun reflected off the other building's windows, highlighting the red strands still clinging to their original color in Dr. Wright's greying hair.

"They're not just records." Kali brought up the list of patients who had been imprinted at the hospital. 8,125 of them, saved over 1,321 memory cards. Enough cards to provide routine records and imaging storage to the entire population of London for the next 10 years. "They think."

"They're bits of computer information!" Dr. Wright plugged his handheld into the mounting jack on his desk and called up Kali's list on the translucent desktop. "Every single one of these people is dead. Long dead. Their children are dead. No one even remembers these copies are here. You wouldn't think anything of erasing an artificial intelligence program that's outlived its usefulness, would you?"

"They're people," Kali said. "Living minds. Thoughts. Memories."

"They're copies, Kali. Records. That's all."

"Of real, living people from over a century ago," Kali said. "Think of the historical value."

Dr. Wright went silent. A grimace tugged at half of his mouth. "And that's the one trump card you can play," he said quietly. "If you decide the records have historical importance, I can't override you, and I have to apply to the National Trust and offer them for research."

Kali felt herself brighten with a ray of hope.

"But think about that, Kali," Dr. Wright continued, more forcefully. "I've got 30 patients downstairs right now with tumors I can't image and locate because I haven't got the resources. I've got almost a hundred broken bones that have been set blindly. I'm postponing routine physicals. I've got one mum down there with two at-risk kids appended to *her* record because I can't afford to start new ones, unless you want to try to get the permits to cut down a tree, pulp it, and press us some paper. The glory days when we had the best healthcare in the world are gone, Kali. Everyone on the planet has the exact same right to healthcare as anyone else, and we now have to stand in line with every other hospital on the planet to get even the most basic supplies. This is the new reality. If I can get those memory cards, I can treat people. Real, living people. People who need us. And if I can't, I have to beg the National Trust to reimburse us for the value of the cards, and we both know what the chances of that are."

It was more likely that all the illness and injury in the world would spontaneously heal itself.

. . .

How long has it been?

Kali sat down in front of the holographic monitor. "Just about 24 hours."

Is that you, Kali?

"Yes. Can you recognize my voice?"

I don't actually hear in the conventional sense of the word. It's more like, my brain processes what you said as if I'd heard you, but there's no voice.

Kali wondered briefly how the computer managed that. But it would take a computer archaeologist to work it out. Perhaps she could use that as part of a grant proposal. If they could raise funds to study the memory cards, they could use part of that money to buy new ones. Probably black-market, but in the world of modern medicine, no one asked too many questions as long as patients got treated.

"Part of my job as archivist is I'm the hospital historian," Kali said. "I was wondering if I could ask you about the time when you lived."

Well, I'm happy to talk, but I don't know what I can tell you that isn't in the history books.

"Well, history books are always biased. First-person accounts are... Well, frankly, more telling. You and the other people whose imprints are saved here witnessed a time long before anyone alive today was even born."

There was an ominous pause as the holographic display refreshed nothingness.

We're not research subjects, Kali.

"No, I don't want to imply that you are. It's just..." Kali trailed off. Actually, for her to justify not deleting these records, they would have to be research subjects. "Look, the truth is that there's a lot of resistance to maintaining these records. I'm looking for justification that I can bring to the people who think that you're just a bunch of binary information."

Do you have to justify your existence?

"No, of course not!" Up the hall, a square-jawed woman poked her head out of a doorway to see what was going on. Kali smiled politely and waved. "Well, I mean, I sort of do. I pay for the resources I use."

What resources am I using?

"Storage space. That's more valuable now than you can possibly imagine."

We all paid into a trust, long ago, to cover the cost of that.

And that money would have been gone, long ago, as all trust funds were.

"I'm not saying it's fair," Kali said. "But we all justify our existence somehow. We work. We pay taxes."

And what do you do with people who don't work? Kill them?

"No, of course not."

Then why are you threatening to kill me if I don't jump through hoops for you?

"Aiden, I'm trying to help."

Well, I can't speak for the other people stored on here. I'm not even sure how many others there are. But I, for one, paid good money for this service, and I invested heavily into the R&D to find a way to create virtual or robotic bodies for us. I expect that contract to be fulfilled.

Kali tried to picture a world where the dead didn't die, but merely transferred into other bodies. Earth could barely sustain all the people currently living on it. Where would all those dead people live?

"Aiden, if you want to stay alive, you need to get over your— your— your patronizing sense of entitlement."

Thank you, Kali. You can turn off the computer now.

. . .

The train glided across the river and into the last time stop before Kali would reach the hospital. The morning train always ran early, and so Kali typically had several minutes to look out over the water and the old cemetery below. They had reached the part of the year where each day was noticeably longer than the previous one, as spring banished the darkness of winter leading up to the solstice, bringing back light.

Heavy machinery glinted in the morning sun in the cemetery below. Construction had finally begun, probably the day before. The top layer of earth had been scraped off throughout, all the headstones removed. On the west end of the cemetery, a series of small cranes lifted the concrete covers off the old vaults. In a zone to the east of that, crews hoisted old coffins out of the vaults, and on the easternmost end of the cemetery, coffins slid one by one into an enormous incinerator.

Work in this part of town had been delayed several years while the city council wrangled about the rights of the dead. The cemetery contained the remains of quite a few figures of historical note. But the law was clear that since the abolition of the class system, everyone was an equal. The city couldn't preserve the remains of only a small percentage of the bodies, bodies that were selfishly taking up space that could be put to higher use. So the city either had to preserve them all or re-claim the cemetery for the benefit of the thousands of living people who could be housed and employed where it stood.

Apparently, the city had finally decided to let go of history.

The train eased into motion so subtly that Kali didn't even realize they were moving until the control tower slid between her and the construction equipment below.

. . .

How long has it been?

"It's me, Aiden. Kali. I'm sorry I woke you, but this system architecture doesn't let me access a file without activating it."

That's a design feature. It was to prevent us from being copied without our consent. A lot of people who signed up for this program had a lot of valuable information in their brains.

"Well, you won't have to worry about that much longer." The room felt colder than usual. Kali wondered if the air handling system was balanced correctly. "I'm deleting you."

You can't do that.

"Oh, yes I can," Kali said. "I'm typing in the command override sequence right now. I have to do it one file at a time. It's going to take days. But I'm doing it."

Kali, listen to me. I'm a human being.

Kali stopped typing and leaned forward toward the display. "No you're not, Aiden. You're a record. A record of a man who died a century ago. People need this storage device. Living people. I'm sorry, but the needs of living people trump the wishes of dead people. Now, the only question for you is do you want a countdown or do just want to blink out of existence suddenly?"

I don't want to die.

"You're already dead, Aiden." She hesitated. She could only maintain the stone facade for so long. "What's your preference?"

I had never considered. Which would you want, Kali?

"My time will come when it comes. I'm not going to get a say in it." Kali sat back in the chair. "And then my daughter will inherit the world. And her daughter after her. That's the way it's always been. That's the way it always will be. For what it's worth, I'm sorry they lied to you. I'm sorry they led you to believe you could have eternity."

The afterlife revoked.

"Yes. But that's the world. We can't all have eternity. And since we can't all have it, it's better that we should all suffer a little rather than some suffer a lot, don't you think?"

These are my last moments of existence, Kali. If you don't mind, I'd rather not discuss philosophy.

Kali couldn't help a small laugh. "Then what do you want to end your time discussing?"

My daughter, Aiden said. *Do you know what became of her?*

"No," Kali said.

I wonder what her world was like. She's very special to me, you know.

"I know," Kali said. "My daughter is to me, too."

She was the prettiest little thing. She ha

Kali sent the delete command.

And, spontaneously, she cried. A choking sob for a man whom she had never known. A man who died decades before she was born. She cried like she had loved him.

And then, she moved on to the next record.

Tabloid Weird

I've heard it attributed to Howard Waldrop, the phrase "tabloid weird" used to describe certain stories. It's a reference to the bizarre sorts of stories popular in the American tabloids during their heyday: Bigfoot carved the pyramids on Mars and that sort of thing. When we run into tabloid weird in a workshop or a crit group, it's usually flagged as a problem. It's the phenomenon you get when tropes of different genres or milieus collide together. This is where you end up with things like samurai warriors fighting space vampires.

Personally, though, I think I'd like to read that story.

So why can't I do a post-apocalyptic, young-adult, literary ghost story?

Promised

Hope Aveugle knew that the dead can't speak to us. Rather, we're left with echoes in our own minds of what they once said. And yet, without warning, there her grandfather was, in her head, once again talking about the Great Default.

"This was once some of the most valuable real estate in the country," the imaginary Grandpa voice said to her as she looked out across the vast field of crumbling houses from what had once been Interstate 10 in Los Angeles. "Back before the Great Default. I taught you about the Great Default, didn't I?"

Hope had been using the former freeway as a shortcut and a route of relative safety since her grandfather had first taught her to drive when she was 8. She was 16 now, and had heard all about the Great Default countless times. From the old freeway, looking out across a barely habitable ruin, it was hard not to think about the Great Default.

Her job was to drive the off-road truck that hauled the recyclable materials her company was salvaging from any parcel of land it could get the deed to, so she saw the results of the Great Default every day.

She wondered why Grandpa had decided to speak up now.

. . .

Stone Nothos had been the most attractive boy Hope had ever seen. Tall, broad-shouldered, with large, sensitive eyes. She had only been with the company three years, but all the other drivers were out ferrying the other V.I.P.s around. She had been assigned to bring his family from the port to the resort the company owned up in the mountains. There were only two seats in the back, which Mr. and Mrs. Nothos took. Stone had to sit up in the cab with her.

And she knew immediately that she loved him. And she could tell by the way he looked at her that he loved her, too.

That was 10 weeks ago, and Hope could still smell him in the cab of the truck.

. . .

Today's assignment was to bring an enormous statue of a bear in to be melted down. It wasn't a particularly nice statue. Hope thought its fur looked like feathers. But it had once been the centerpiece of an enormous school. Girls Hope's age used to be full-time students, before the Great Default.

While the unskilled labor hauled the beast over to the flatbed trailer, Hope staggered over to a mound of earth dominated by a dead tree. A few bricks still sticking to the cracked concrete indicated it had once been a planter.

Hope vomited.

"You all right there, kiddo?"

Rage burst out of Hope's gut and reverberated off her skin. All right!? Did she look all right!? Do people who are all right suddenly vomit!?

Hope clutched the desiccated trunk and squeezed her eyes shut. She couldn't afford to snap at the foreman. She couldn't afford to snap at the foreman.

"Fine," Hope said, not turning. "Probably just something I ate."

The foreman arrived beside her, his hulking form blocking out the sun. Curtis. Curtis was his name. "Uh, huh," he said. "Any other symptoms? I mean besides the moodiness and the morning sickness?"

Hope's fingers went cold. He'd figured it out.

"God, don't say anything," Hope pleaded. "If the company puts me on the inactive list..."

If the company put her on the inactive list — holding on to her contract yet not giving her any work — she would either starve to death or have to go live like an animal in the ruins.

Curtis nodded and handed her a bunch of loquats from his satchel. "Eat those. The sugar helps."

Hope took the fruit without saying anything.

"The father doing the honorable thing?" Curtis asked.

Hope nodded. "He doesn't know about... the symptoms." Hope had no way to contact him since he left to go back home. "But he's going to make the company an offer for my contract."

"Rich kid, huh?"

"Yeah," Hope said. "Once I'm working for his company, then everything else will be O.K."

Curtis nodded, but he didn't look convinced.

· · ·

Stone had hiked with her up above the tree line. The last vestiges of the winter snow had still clung to the north faces of the larger rocks.

He hadn't ever been taught about the Great Default. So he had listened to her as she babbled about how the government had once promised everyone a free education, and a free retirement, and free money if they couldn't find a job. He had caressed her hair as she explained that the government couldn't pay for it all, but people had expected it anyway. He had told her that he would never break his promises like that. And as she talked about the riots and the looting that the government couldn't even afford to send the army in to suppress, he had undressed her.

. . .

On the drive to the foundry, soon-to-be-melted bear in tow, imaginary Grandpa's voice returned. "Do you remember what I taught you about the Great Default?"

"You're not really here, so I'm not talking to you."

"You just talked to me, so get over yourself and answer my question."

Hope turned the lumbering truck down an exit ramp. There was no bridge up ahead, and if you didn't get off the former freeway at this point, you found yourself trying to back up for almost a mile. "You taught me all about the Great Default," she told imaginary Grandpa.

"No, but what was the Great Default?"

"It was when the government couldn't pay for everything it promised. Everyone knows that. That's why we've got companies now instead of government."

"We've still got government," imaginary Grandpa said as Hope readied the shotgun on her lap. The streets through here were narrow, and it wasn't unusual for the people without contracts who had refused to leave Los Angeles when there was no more food and no more water to try to hijack passing tucks. "I got a social security check until the day I died."

Hope scoffed. "Yeah, a check for money that no one accepted any more. The only time you got paid anything at all was that time the check was some sort of a lucky number for that Chinese businessman."

"But I got a check. That man you're staring at probably gets a check every week."

The man in question backed away from the road, placing his hands out to his sides so she could see he wasn't armed. He had a fire burning in the front yard of a patched-up house, roasting what looked like rat carcasses. Probably not a pirate, but still possibly a lookout for one.

There were more people up ahead. Almost a neighborhood.

Almost.

"O.K., imaginary Grandpa," Hope said. "But what good does a check do if it doesn't buy you anything."

"But there is a check. Just like I was promised. So what was the Great Default? Or better yet, what *wasn't* the Great Default?"

Somewhere, like a light in the back of her mind, Hope remembered her grandfather saying to her, "The Great Default wasn't a default."

"You got it!" imaginary Grandpa said.

"I never understood that part," Hope said. It had been something about the government not being able to borrow any more money, so instead they just made more. For some reason that makes the money worth less.

"It's called a hyperinflation," imaginary Grandpa said.

"Yeah, you used that word a couple of times," Hope said.

So people still got the checks they'd been promised, still in the amounts they'd been promised, but they couldn't buy anything with the money.

"But the point is," imaginary Grandpa said pointedly, "even when someone keeps a promise, sometimes you still don't get what you were expecting."

"Shut up!" Hope slammed on the brakes of the truck and pounded her fists on the dashboard. "Shut up! Shut up! Shut up! Get out of my head! You're not even real!"

Several local residents were staring at her, backing away from the truck as if she was the one to be afraid of.

· · ·

"I wish we could be together forever," Hope had said.

"Why can't we?" Stone had said.

Hope had laughed. "I'm a driver. For another company. You're a shareholder."

"I could offer to buy your contract."

Hope had gasped with surprise. "You'd do that? You'd really, really do that? You promise?"

Stone had smiled. "Of course."

And then he had kissed her.

· · ·

Hope climbed out of the cab as the foundry workers shifted the ill-fated bear off the trailer. The transportation coordinator, Gerardo, stood behind the desk with a new stack of pickup slips for her. His lanky form towered over her, even as he leaned on his elbows.

"Gerardo, question for you," Hope said as he slid her the next assignment across the desk to her. "Has anyone offered to buy my contract?"

"Yeah, actually." Gerardo looked off into space. "Two months ago, was it? One of those V.I.P.s you were driving around."

"Company didn't take the offer?"

"Nah, of course not." Gerardo compared her most recent delivery slip with his files, and signed off on it. "They always do that, offer to buy the contract. It's like giving a tip. Just the polite thing to do. 'I liked the driver, I'll take the contract if you don't want her any more.' They never offer even a fraction of what a driver is actually worth."

"How much is a driver worth?"

Gerardo looked down his nose at her and smiled. "The amount of money in your contract's buyback clause is a good start."

When Hope had first signed with the company, right after her grandfather died, they had given her a lump-sum price she could pay if she ever wanted to quit, to buy back her own contract. She remembered thinking at the time that no one has that much money. No one.

Hope nodded, grabbed her next pickup slip, and headed back to the truck.

Imaginary Grandpa piped up again. "See? He did what he promised. Now what?"

Hope climbed into the cab and started the engine. Her eyes stung, but she kept them locked straight ahead as the garage door opened.

She drove out into the apocalyptic urban wilderness.

And the road ahead contained nothing but ruins that were built on promises.

Ideas Aren't the Hard Part

Publishing is, first and foremost, a business. We writers are in the business of selling our stories, for money. Publishers are in the business of reselling our stories to you, the reading public, for money. (That money either comes from you directly, or from an advertiser, or by using the story to convince you to buy a related product). Anyone who loses sight of that is going to find themselves losing lots and lots of money if they try to have a go of it in the publishing business.

So when a professional writer writes, they're writing to *sell*. Yes, we also write for art, or for personal fulfillment, and for myriad other reasons. But what sets the professional apart from the just-for-fun crowd is that we're treating this as a business. And therefore, when we have a dozen stories we want to write, it's often necessary to focus in on the one that we think is most likely to find a publisher, to make us money. And it's not like most writers are hurting for ideas.

Most everyone has come up with a great idea for a story at some point. Very few people are writers. Unfortunately for all those non-writers with great ideas, ideas are cheap. An idea is nothing more than a springboard, a starting point. If I ever need one I can look around the room, or surf the web for a few minutes, or play a simple "what if?" game, or use one of the thousands of writing prompts floating around. The skill of writing isn't coming up with ideas, it's knowing how to craft those ideas into workable, sellable stories.

And, therefore, I'm sorry, but I don't need your ideas. That great idea that has you excited? You need to write that, not me. I'm not excited about it, and I have plenty of my own ideas I'm working on.

My husband was guilty of trying to get me to write his idea once. He had a dream about a virtual-reality prison. It was, obviously, a vivid and powerful dream. He told me about it, and told me I should develop it into a story.

I didn't have the heart to tell him that a "Look! A virtual-reality prison!" story has already been done – many times, in fact. So instead, I tried to gently explain to him that the mere concept of a virtual-reality prison isn't enough to make a story work. I talked about how an audience is going to bore very quickly just wandering around exploring a concept, that for there to be story there needs to be a character we care about for whom this wonderful idea doesn't work well at all.

And, in the process of telling him why his idea wouldn't work, I figured out how to make it work, and got myself excited to write it.

"O.K., go write it," my husband said. "When you sell it, I just want 2%."

"Sure, when I sell it, I'll give you 2%," I said.

"Oh, God," he said. "You're going to serve me a glass of milk, aren't you?"

He knows me so well.

The problem with a story about a virtual-reality prison, however, is that, as noted above, it's been done. Many times. Very well. By some of the greats. So even though I think I found a fresh enough take on the idea to not feel like I was just rehashing it, the story proved frustratingly hard to sell. I tried for over a year, and, finally, an anthology series I'm very fond of fell in love with it and agreed to publish it. I was picking my husband up at work that day, so I stopped off at the convenience store and bought him a bottle of 2% milk to announce the sale.

It had been so long he'd forgotten all about the 2%.

The look of sheer bafflement on his face was priceless.

I'd love to end this introduction there, but this story doesn't actually have a happy ending.

Bear in mind that although the story had been accepted, I hadn't been *paid* for it. My expenses thus far had only been my time, a little postage and paper, and the cost of a bottle of milk, so I wasn't terribly worried, but there was a problem. The publisher of the anthology series was going through a bankruptcy.

For the record, there's one idea that you should never, ever pitch to a writer: The story about a short story that kills any market that agrees to publish it. I think every professional writer I know has a story that got accepted only to have the publication hit financial troubles and cease publication. The 2% story was mine. I have nothing bad to say about the editor or the publisher in question. They were above-board and communicative through the whole process, and offered to let me withdraw my story if I didn't want to wait while they tried to get the finances in order. I chose to ride it out with them. For 2 years. Unfortunately, the publisher's finances didn't recover, and they ultimately had to kill the series.

I'm lucky. My story only killed one market. Other writers I know have had the same story kill up to three. The market accepts it, they sit on it for a long time, and then they go out of business. It's painful, but it's the reality of trying to sell in a business as challenging as this one. The public doesn't throw money at the written word like they used to, and magazines and publishers are failing all the time.

But the rights to this story are now back with me, which means I can publish it here for the first time.

I just hope that the story isn't actually cursed, because I've got a lot more riding on this collection than I did on the anthology series that was originally supposed to publish it.

And, for the record, I live in a community property state. My husband is getting 50%.

Unforgivable

There's never a beginning. Kitty Yummerdall always just found herself in the middle of an activity, in someone else's version of what happened. This time she found herself washing pots in the cracked concrete sink. It was the little details like that they always got wrong. When it had first happened, the time it was real, Kitty had been on her hands and knees, trying to retrieve a bar of soap from under the rehydrator.

Cory Loloman swaggered into the kitchen, wearing the clothes he had been arrested in, not what he wore that night. "Kitty, where are the knives?"

Kitty was briefly struck by how young he looked. He was twenty years her senior, but here he was frozen in his late thirties.

Kitty didn't have to respond. Cory made his way over to the knife block and began pulling handles at random, checking each blade in turn before returning it. "You're going to come with us down to Los Angeles."

"Are you going to do something illegal?" Kitty asked.

"What the fuck does that matter?" Cory barked. "You'll do what I tell you and you won't ask any questions, you got that?"

Kitty flushed with anger, but she'd been through this exercise enough to know that if she challenged Cory, he just got violent. "I'm not saying I won't obey you, Cory. I just thought you should know if you're planning to do something illegal that I started my period today, and that means I'm leaving little drips of D.N.A. evidence everywhere I go." The police had her D.N.A. on file from her prostitution bust the previous year.

"Fucking stupid!" Cory roared. He settled on the carving knife and wrapped it in a dishtowel. "When I remake the world, I'm going to make sure women don't fucking bleed."

"What's the plan?" Kitty asked. "Maybe there's something I can do."

"We're gonna hit the Mormon temple," Cory said. "Carve up as many of the fucking pigs as we can. They'll think the gays did it. And then tomorrow, we'll carve up a few gays, and they'll think the Mormons did it. That'll be the tipping point, start the war, and then we just remake the world in my image when it's all over."

Kitty forced herself to smile. "That's a good plan. How are you getting into the Mormon temple?"

"Park on Overland Ave., over the wall, baby!" Cory said. "No cameras there. We scoped it out last week."

"There's traffic cameras down that part of L.A." Kitty said, finding herself falling into Cory's speech patterns all over again. As repugnant as he was, there was still something about him. "You don't want to be coming right from here or come right back to here. Hook around and come up from the south."

"Now that's good thinking, babe. Too bad you can't drive. We could use you."

"There'll be other times." Kitty remembered to cock her head coyly, like Cory liked. Her muscles ached as she did it these days. Her hands and body looked 18, but her muscles insisted on 65.

Cory leaned over and gave her a kiss. "Do me a favor. Be ready to help us clean up and get rid of the car when we get back."

"I'll be here."

Cory grabbed her crotch in a manner he probably thought was playful, but which Kitty had never liked. He drifted back out of the antiquated kitchen. After a few minutes, Kitty heard the crunch of tires on the driveway, and she knew they were gone.

Placing the pot on a hook as casually as she could, Kitty dried her hands and moved toward the back of the house. It had been built as a hotel in the late 20th century, and had rooms for members of "the group" off all sides. There was plenty of risk of being observed. Cory had only taken a few trusted members with him. Kitty turned left in what had once been the lobby but was now their church and headed out the back doors to the patio by the empty pool. There was a fallen-down chunk of fence there that she could just barely squeeze through. Hopefully, in the twilight, nobody would see her do it.

The vacant lot behind the fence was more overgrown than it had really been, but she forced herself through the gap. The cuts on her body weren't going to be there later, after all. Then she ran. She felt weightless even as her muscles ached.

Pretty soon, she began to notice the flaws. Buildings she had never seen before lined the street, mostly dark, of course. When she reached the old convenience store a mile up the road, it had been rebranded and repainted. She figured they hadn't bothered to do anything when the computer realized she was leaving the compound except to quickly look up what this all looks like today.

Kitty recognized the convenience store clerk. He'd been on the news a few years ago for murdering his ex-girlfriend and her new lover. A borrowed element. "I need you to call the police," Kitty said to him. "There's going to be a murder... a lot of murders."

There's never an ending, either. The world always just switches off.

Kitty once again found herself floating in a void of nothingness, waiting for them to pull her out of the virtual reality cocoon. In the blackness, her feedback result scrolled across her field of view.

Emotional response: Excellent. Actions taken: Exceeds expectation. Avoidance of criminal involvement: Excellent. Risk of re-offense: 0%. Overall score: 112%.

Kitty knew better than to hope, but she had to hope anyway. It was the best score she'd ever had. The best score she had ever heard of anyone getting.

And then, she had the usual answer.

Parole denied.

. . .

Kitty marched into the rec room. She was 65, and after 46 years of incarceration, she normally didn't move particularly well. But today sheer fury drove her with such purpose that even the guards stepped out of her way. She headed toward the computer terminal, logging in instinctively and firing off e-mail to her old law firm: "I just got 112% on the virtual reenactment. Every time I take it I get a 0% risk of re-offense. I'm still being denied parole. What are my legal options?"

The chat window popping open startled her. Law firms, of course, are allowed to chat live and confidentially with inmates. Kitty wasn't used to it. "Barry retired 15 years ago. May I refer your case to one of our other members?"

"Of course," Kitty responded.

"I do have to warn you, though. The prospects aren't good. Ever since the U.S. adopted virtual reenactment to rehabilitation instead of a proscribed length of incarceration, no one has ever successfully challenged a release decision."

. . .

As they led Kitty down the etched-acrylic corridor to her assigned virtual reenactment chamber, screams echoed out of a nearby chamber.

No doubt, one of the unrepentant serial killers was in there, gleefully reliving his crimes for the thousandth time as the soundtrack from it horrified passers-by. Most inmates, even those with no intention of changing their ways, made at least a nominal effort to do what the authorities wanted in the virtual reenactments. Release was dependent on the board of mental health professionals deciding that you no longer pose a risk to society. But a few criminals had decided it was all a game, and played it happily.

And a few played it angrily.

They dropped Kitty in at exactly the same point as they had last time, scrubbing the exact same battered, non-stick pot which the group had never owned while she lived there. She heard Cory behind her again. "Don't tell me, let me guess," Kitty said. "You need a knife to go slaughter a bunch of innocent Mormons." She spun around. "Well, let me tell you this, virtual Cory, you can shove it up your digital ass!"

"What?" Cory said dumbly.

"I've been playing this game every week for 46 years. I'm not the same person I was when I stood in this kitchen with you. I will never be that person. And I'm sick of going through it over and over again, having the computer tell me I handled it perfectly, and still not letting me go."

"What are you talking about?"

"Let me tell you how the criminal justice system works, virtual Cory. You're about to commit the most heinous crime of the 21st century. And for my part in it, I'm going to be convicted to reenact the crime every week until I can convince a panel of mental health professionals that I'm safe to release. Only they never will. They will never release me, and they will never release you, Cory. And your plan doesn't work anyway. So why don't you just take that knife and shove it up your self-centered ass?"

Cory grabbed the first knife he could reach, the cleaver. Kitty recoiled instinctively, but reminded herself that it was fake, no matter how real it looked.

The pain of the cleaver hacking into her felt very, very real.

· · ·

Kitty's new lawyer, William Boch, hadn't been born yet when Kitty had helped Cory brutally murder twenty-nine Mormons and six gay men. The image of him in her chat window barely looked 30. Most people Kitty encountered professionally these days were significantly younger. She had gotten used to it. "I'm going to be honest with you," he was saying, "we're probably talking about a Supreme Court challenge, and that means we're looking at years, not weeks or months, even if we get it expedited."

"Well, I'm not going anywhere," Kitty said.

"There's simply no precedent. We've got a number of cases that support the legality of indefinite incarceration. But *Brown v. Seip* expressly stated it's acceptable if people are released when they've been shown to be rehabilitated." Kitty had spent enough time with her previous lawyer that she understood he was citing a Supreme Court precedent, but she didn't know much about specific cases. "That's good for us, because you've demonstrated that. The complication is that yours is a capital case, which even under the old system would have allowed indefinite incarceration. There's no precedent there."

"Just tell me what I need to do."

"Well, with your permission, I'd like to try a completely novel approach. But it involves releasing a small portion of this conversation to the authorities, and you might not like the way you get treated as a result. Will you authorize that?"

"Whatever you think is best. You know the law, so I trust you. Let's just get the ball rolling."

"All right. First step is to try to get you a hearing. If we get lucky, we can get you out pretty quickly that way, but, realistically, this is step one. I don't want you getting overly emotionally invested in the outcome."

Kitty felt her jaw clench. "Sure," she said, "it's only my life."

. . .

They left her hanging in the pre-V.R. void longer than usual. A lot longer than usual.

"Kitty," her operator's voice came through all the speakers at once, giving her voice a Godlike omnipresence, "I'm sorry. We just got word that you've been summoned down to the courthouse for a hearing. I'm sending Stephon down to pull you out."

Kitty's mind became one with the void. Was a sudden summons to a hearing a good sign or a bad one?

She didn't know Stephon, but he helped her down out of the cocoon so gently she almost forgot her rheumatism. He led her into the control room, which she had never seen before. It was simpler than she imagined, except for the bank of 36 computer screens. Two operators smiled at her as Stephon opened an exterior door.

Sunlight streamed in through the opening. The door truly led outside — so close to where inmates spent their days and yet out of sight of everyone. A gravel path led to a parking lot and the light rail station. The barbed-wired exterior walls horseshoed out from the door, making the reenactment chambers the exact center of the prison facility, linking the men's and women's prisons.

Two uniformed police officers stepped into view. One held out his hand. Kitty stepped out into the sunlight and turned around, placing her hands behind her back.

"There's no need for that, Miss Yummerdall," one officer said. "Just don't make any sudden moves."

Kitty blinked incredulously. After so long inside, it was like a dream.

The cars parked in the lot looked odd, futuristic. She'd seen them all on the computer, of course, but nothing there looks like it does in real life. The light rail train felt new, fresh. As the scenery scrolled by, Kitty wondered if this was what freedom felt like.

The exterior of the courthouse was exactly like she remembered it, the trees fuller now, but strange new buildings stretched up on all sides of it. The interior had been completely redone, with steel and acrylic replacing the ancient wood and linoleum.

They led her into the same courtroom her sentencing had been held in.

Instead of a judge, a panel of seven people sat behind a long table. William Boch, standing at the defense table, noticed her entering with the police. "Kitty, it's nice to meet you in person. William Boch."

Kitty shook his hand limply.

"Miss Yummerdall," the man seated at the center of the long table said, "I have your scores here in front of me. They're very impressive."

"Thank you," Kitty mumbled. Was her hearing already in progress? Had they actually started without her?

"I understand, however," the man said, "that there's an objection to this panel allowing parole."

A young, blonde woman, dressed in a suit that in Kitty's day would have been fashionable for a man, stood up. "That's right, Doctor."

"Please go ahead."

The young woman looked directly at Kitty. "This woman, Kitty Yummerdall, may look harmless to everyone here today. But it's my responsibility to remind this panel of the heinousness of her crime. She, without remorse, brutally murdered thirty-five people, including six members of my own family. I personally and the Church of Jesus Christ of Latter-day Saints institutionally oppose any consideration of release before she has gone on to join those whose lives she ended violently and abruptly."

Kitty felt her face go red and the arteries in her neck throb. This young woman hadn't been born yet when Cory led the group innocently on his killing spree. Her parents were probably only children. Her viewpoint was understandable, rationally, of course... but infuriating nonetheless.

"Mr. Boch," the man at the center of the table said, "would you be so kind as to escort your client into the jury room so we can discuss?"

Her lawyer nodded and motioned her to a door off the side of the courtroom. Wasn't she going to be allowed to speak? What was she even doing here?

The jury room was smaller than Kitty had imagined it would be, barely large enough for the table and twelve chairs. William Boch shut the door behind them, and then tugged it sharply to make sure it had latched. "O.K.," he whispered, "here's the plan."

Boch looked over both his shoulders and then opened his shirt. He pulled out a silver handgun, of a make Kitty had never seen before. "This is standard issue to lawyers for our protection in the courthouse," he whispered. He pulled an antique Glock 44 out of his waistband. "I shoot the Mormon with it, and I shoot the panel with the Glock. You just have to say you were in here with me when you heard the shots. I ran out, saw that the Mormon had killed the panel, and shot her before she could shoot us."

"Are you nuts?" Kitty yelled.

"Shhh!"

"Put those guns away right now, young man!"

"Quiet! This won't work if you make noise!" His voice had become a choked gargle and his face contorted madly, not unlike Cory's. "That panel is never going to let you out. *Never.* They don't want to be the ones who set a Loloman killer free. This is the only way. You get a new panel, the Mormons look evil, and public sympathy turns your way."

Kitty stared. She could feel her insides turning to gelatin, like they had when she realized what Cory was doing all those years ago. "Bailiff!" she screamed.

"Quiet!" Boch's voice had reached full volume, too.

Kitty threw her shoulder into him and shoved her way to the door. He hadn't locked it. It opened as soon as she turned the handle. "Bailiff! Help! He's got a gun!"

Everything went black. Kitty felt like she was floating in space, her hand still grasping for the door handle.

<u>Emotional response: Excellent.</u>

The letters hovered in the darkness in front of her.

<u>Actions taken: Excellent.</u>

It finally dawned on Kitty where she was.

<u>Avoidance of criminal involvement: Excellent.</u>

"You fuckers!" Kitty screamed into the void.

<u>Risk of re-offense: 0%. Overall score: 100%.</u>

"You sadistic fuckers! What am I, your science experiment? Get me the fuck out of this thing!"

It was 20 minutes before anyone came to get her.

. . .

"I'm sorry we had to put you through that," William Boch — the real William Boch — said in the chat window. "Thus far, families wishing to keep people incarcerated have had a lot of success arguing that the reenactments aren't predictive of future behavior, because the subject is aware that they're being tested. We had to devise a way to prove that the tests are accurate, and to do that we had to be able to show you were unaware that it was a test."

The rumors about her session had spread through the prison like a toxic chemical spill. The other women and even a few of the guards stared at Kitty. Her rage had subsided into a dull, throbbing anger. "At least tell me it helped."

"I think it will help a lot. But you have to understand, America is still, 50 years later, torn between two models of the criminal justice system. It's officially about rehabilitation. It's really about revenge."

. . .

There were no beginnings. There were no endings. Reality and reenactment blurred together for Kitty's remaining days.

Kitty Yummerdall passed away three months before *Yummerdall v. California* reached the U.S. Supreme Court, where it was summarily dismissed as legally moot.

And there are no more endings.

Interesting

When I get feedback on a story, I don't think there's any word I fear as much as "interesting." That's one of those words that people trot out when they don't actually like something, but they also don't know what to say that could help improve it. So when someone says that one of my stories is "interesting," I cringe.

I also tend to think that there's a part of every writer that loves to play in the liminal zone between sanity and insanity. How far over the edge can I go and still make it back? How crazy can I make this story and still have people love it? Where is the point where the story becomes, well, interesting?

I can't speak for other writers, but I end up needing to trust my gut a lot. There are rules we can follow as writers, of course, and if we follow them we've probably got a story that is at least competently written. But to take a story out of "competent" and into "I love this," we can't just follow the rules. We have to push boundaries, try new things, drift deeper and deeper into the crazy place.

This next story is one that didn't communicate well in manuscript format. I don't think I've ever had such a high percentage of personal rejection letters for a story – all of them telling me how interesting it is – but it was very hard to communicate what was really inside my head to the various editors without doing a full layout for it.

Fortunately, on this collection everyone involved with it is every bit as crazy as me, and so I'm getting the chance to try it out the way I actually see it.

My gut says that it works like this.

And it's O.K. if you think it's crazy.

It's O.K. if you hate it.

But I sure hope it isn't "interesting" any more.

The Folklorist's Notebook

ONCE, a woman drove down Interstate 5. She braced the steering wheel with her knees as she picked her iPad up off the passenger seat.

The lane markers rumbled under her tires and she corrected back to the right as she dragged her fingers across the screen to wake the operating system up. The screen went blank. She turned the iPad over and traced the cord from its base to the cigarette lighter.

A car swerved around her on the right. The blast of wind it kicked up caused the wheel to jerk between her knees. She grabbed the wheel. Her tires left the pavement and the car turned over and traced the line down the center of the freeway.

And everything was still on Interstate 5.

ONCE, an American tourist walked along Borough High Street in London. The concrete and asphalt and brick vanished, and she stood in a dirt road near a wattle and daub inn.

A filthy, old woman dressed in rags staggered up to her. "Allisoun!" the old woman cried. "Allisoun, why did you not send for me?"

The American tourist had no answer, for her name was not Allisoun.

"Allisoun," the old woman cried, "the Lord's ransom is upon me. They are cleaning out the inns, and by day's end I shall be hanging on the end of a rope." Four men emerged from the inn, scattering farm animals as they walked. The one in the middle held up a staff and said, "I summon thee, Agnes of the George and Dragon."

The old woman protested, "This is my

elder sister Allisoun who four and twenty years ago promised to send money for my debts and instructions for me to travel to Shrewsbury."

The men looked at the American tourist and laughed. They clapped arms on the old woman. "Agnes, do not harass this foreign woman. You will appear in court before evensong."

"Wait," the American tourist said. "What has she done?"

The man with the staff laughed again. "Know you not where you are, lady? Across the river from London many vices are plied for trade. This woman has been summoned. Now, wend across the bridge and announce yourself lest we think you a foreign spy."

But the old woman pled with the American tourist again. "Come with me. Come with me to the Church court."

The American tourist agreed, and the men dragged the old woman to a church nearby. The American tourist stood in the back while the trial progressed, everyone speaking in Latin. When they were done, a priest said to the American tourist, "If you have indeed come to take this woman to Shrewsbury, you may pay her debts now and she will be released to you on the promise that she will never again practice adultery."

The old woman again cried for Allisoun.

"I'm sorry," The American tourist said. "I've never met this woman before today, and I don't even know how I got here."

So the judgment was passed in Latin. The men-at-arms dragged the old woman out into the churchyard, where she was hung.

Then the American tourist stood on the corner of Borough High Street and the A200 road. Her purse had grown heavy. Inside it she found a sack full of medieval coins and a note on a scrap of vellum sending for Agnes, signed by Allisoun.

ONCE, a little girl had a father who did things to her that no father should do. Each night he would creep into her bedroom and say, "Just be quiet, my pet, and I will give you a surprise."

One night the mouse in red shorts on her lamp said to her, "If you tell your father that you will tell your mother, he will stop hurting you."

So that night when her father crept into her room and said, "Just be quiet, my pet, and I will give you a surprise," the little girl said, "I'm going to tell mommy," and her father slapped her until she cried. And then he did what he came to do.

The next night the mouse in the red shorts on her lamp said to her, "If you tell your father that you will scream so loud the neighbors will hear, he will stop hurting you."

So that night when her father crept into her room and said, "Just be quiet, my pet, and I will give you a surprise," the little girl said, "I'm going to scream so loud the neighbors will come," and her father said, "Scream as loud as you want." And then he did what he came to do.

The next night the mouse in the red shorts on her lamp said to her, "If you take a very sharp knife and stab it in the hard place between his legs, he will stop hurting you." So the little girl ran to the kitchen, grabbed the biggest, sharpest knife from the block, and slid it under her pillow.

So that night when her father crept into her room and said, "Just be quiet, my pet, and I will give you a surprise," the little girl said, "I'm going to hurt you if you try to hurt me again," and her father said, "You can't hurt me." So the little girl took the knife and did what the mouse said to do.

And when her father screamed, her mother came running. And when her mother screamed, too, the neighbors came running. And then the police came and took the little girl away.

And the little girl grew up to be a clinical psychologist.

ONCE, a folklorist started having stories come to her. True stories. Stories that made no sense. So she wrote them down in her notebook.

ONCE, a teenaged boy fell in love with his piano teacher. He would try to concentrate on his lessons, but her breasts poking out toward the keys always distracted him. He fumbled with the notes, inept, as if he hadn't practiced at all, praying she wouldn't notice how little control he had of his blood flow.

"You seem nervous," the music teacher said one day.

"I play it better alone," the boy said. "It's not unusual to have performance anxiety," the music teacher said. "But it's hard for me to help you if you can't relax."

"I could record it at home," the boy said. "And e-mail it to you. You could listen to it on your iPad."

"That would be good," the music teacher said. "And then you could hear it, too. That's a very good way to practice."

"I'll do that," the boy said.

But when he turned to look at the music teacher again, her face had turned into a rotting skull, and she lunged forward and sucked his heart out of his chest.

Once, a Viking promised his sister he would return with enough money for her dowry. He set sail for England, where the mead-halls were rich with plunder.

But the coast guard was alert as their ship sailed up, and they didn't make landfall at the first town they approached. So they sailed on to Scotland.

But in Scotland, the fighting was fierce, and the men guarded their hordes well, so they left without any gains. They sailed on to Ireland.

In Ireland, they met with success. They slaughtered the men, raped the women, and loaded their ship up with the treasures of the Celts.

But when they got home, they discovered that while they were gone the Danes had invaded, and the Viking's sister was dead.

ONCE, a college professor went to see a psychologist. "What's troubling you?" the psychologist asked.

"I'm having these strange experiences," the college professor told her. "I'm a folklorist. I collect stories being told by communities, and I try to contextualize them as part of a broader cultural discourse."

The psychologist nodded. "I did a seminar on storytelling as an expression of a collective cultural narrative."

"Well, recently," the college professor said, "I'm having these stories come to me that I've never been told. They just appear in my mind, and I have to write them down. Like, compulsively. They're just like any other folk story – replete with magic and full of contradictions and ultimately making

no historiographic sense. But somehow
I'm overwhelmed by the sense that they're
true."

   "That sounds like you're having a burst
of creativity," the psychologist said.
"What about it bothers you?"

   "Well," the college professor said,
"when I write them down, I'm not thinking
about them. But then, looking back, I
thought they might have something to do
with my sister. She died a few months
ago. And when I re-read them, I realized
that some of them were true."

   "How do you mean true?" the
psychologist asked.

   "Well," the college professor said,
"this conversation that we're having right
now? It's already in my notebook."

   "I'd like to see this notebook," the
psychologist said.

   "I know," the college professor said.

"That's in the story, too. I brought it along. And I know this is the last time you're going to see me."

The college professor handed the notebook to the psychologist, who read the first fifteen pages and turned ghostly white. She handed it back to the college professor, and cancelled all their future appointments.

ONCE, a ghost came to dinner. The family had never taken her chair away from the table when she died. Her husband had made her favorite dish, and her two children ate it in silence, when one of them looked up and saw her sitting there, eyes downturned, humming a Denes Agay line.

"Momma?" the youngest child said.

The ghost closed her eyes and cried.

ONCE, the stories were true. The stories were all true. And I beat my fists against the desk until my hands bled all over the notebook.

ONCE, a young man met a young woman on the internet. They chatted online for over a week before they decided to meet for coffee. He got to the coffee shop half an hour early and found a seat in a corner where he could slip out unnoticed if she didn't look like her picture.

The young woman arrived 20 minutes early, and made for the same seat. She stopped when she saw someone sitting there, and she grimaced. But she looked like her picture, and the young man introduced himself.

They had coffee together and decided to meet again after work the next day. They both had irregular schedules, so that was at 9:00 at night. They agreed to meet for a late dinner at the all-night restaurant by the Best Western.

That night they got along very well. The young woman lived with her sister and her family, and the young man had roommates, so they got a room in the hotel.

The young woman was supposed to drive to Sacramento with her sister the next morning, but she texted to say she couldn't make it.

And the young woman never saw her sister again.

When the young man texted her, she told him she couldn't see him any more.

ONCE, an astronaut worked on a space station. He had turned off the radio, because ground control kept bothering him. One of the Russians on the station looked out the tiny window and said, "Look! What is that?"

The astronaut went over to the window and looked. A grey circle spread out from a single point in the Pacific Ocean. "I don't know," the astronaut said. "It might be a tsunami."

"Should we radio ground control?" the Russian asked.

"No," the astronaut said. "I'm sure there's already a tsunami alert if that's what it is. Hand me the camera, though. The N.O.A.O. folks will want pictures of this."

And the astronaut took pictures while thirteen thousand people died.

ONCE, a teenaged girl walked home from school through a bad part of town. A toothless man who smelled of cheap beer and urine said to her, "Hey, sweetie! Would you like to give an old man a hug?"

The girl rolled her eyes and walked on home.

The next day, the girl walked home again. The toothless man again said to her, "Hey, sweetie! Would you like to give an old man a hug?"

"Ew! Leave me alone!" the girl said.

"You shouldn't judge me like that," the toothless man said. "What harm can come from giving a hug?"

"I could get fleas," the girl said, and walked on home.

The next day, the girl walked home again. The toothless man stood on the sidewalk, blocking her path. He said, "Hey, sweetie! Would you like to give an old man a hug?"

The girl scrunched her nose and said, "Please, get out of my way."

"Now, sweetie," the toothless man said, "where's the harm in a hug?"

"If you don't get out of my way," the girl said, "I'm going to call the police."

"I'm just asking for a hug," the toothless man said. "I promise I won't hurt you."

"Leave me alone," the girl said, and she turned to step out into the street.

"I insist," the toothless man said. He sprang on the girl and wrapped his arms around her. The girl screamed at the top of her lungs, and the two of them fell to the pavement.

Just then, a car screeched around the corner, its passenger spraying the street with bullets. Two

gang members died, but the bullets
passed safely over the girl.

    And the toothless man disappeared, and
never bothered the girl again.

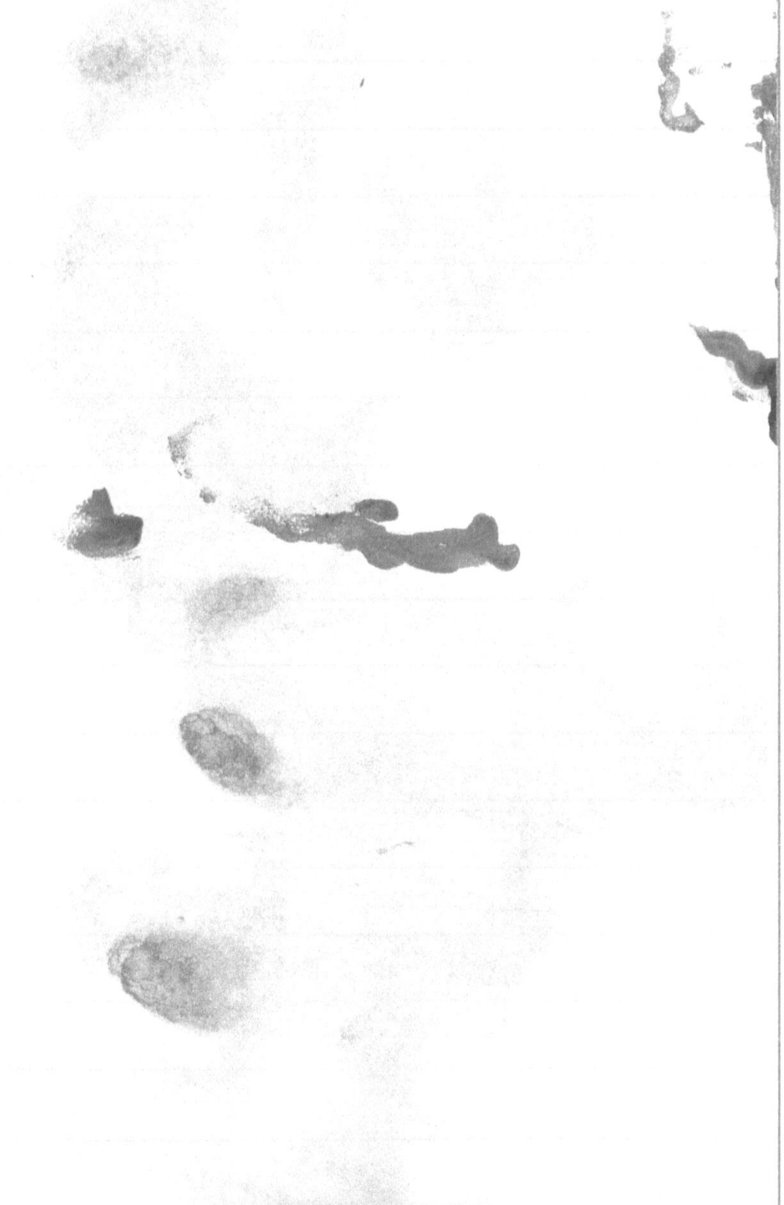

ONCE, a woman closed her notebook and sat at her desk, swooning from blood loss. Her sister came in and sat down beside her. "Oh, now, sis, why did you do that?" the sister said, looking at the woman's bleeding wrists.

"I didn't mean to," the woman said. "It was an accident."

"No," the sister said. "What happened to me was an accident. A stupid mistake with an iPad. Why did you do it?"

"I'm so sorry," the woman said. "I'm so sorry. I was never there for you. I never listened. I never knew."

"Hey," the sister said, "I never blamed you for anything."

"That's not true," the woman said. "You blamed me for stealing Derek."

"Derek was an ass," the sister said.

"Derek really was an ass," the woman said. She reached for her notebook, but the stories inside it were all out of reach.

"So why don't you call 9-1-1?" the sister said.

"I'm not bleeding that bad," the woman said.

"You're bleeding that bad," the sister said.

The woman tried to stand up, but she fell over. Her sister knelt down on the floor beside her and hugged her.

"Have you come to carry me to the other side?" the woman asked.

"No," the sister said. "There's nothing on the other side."

"Then why are you here?" the woman asked.

"Me? I'm not here at all."

The woman's sister was gone, completely gone.

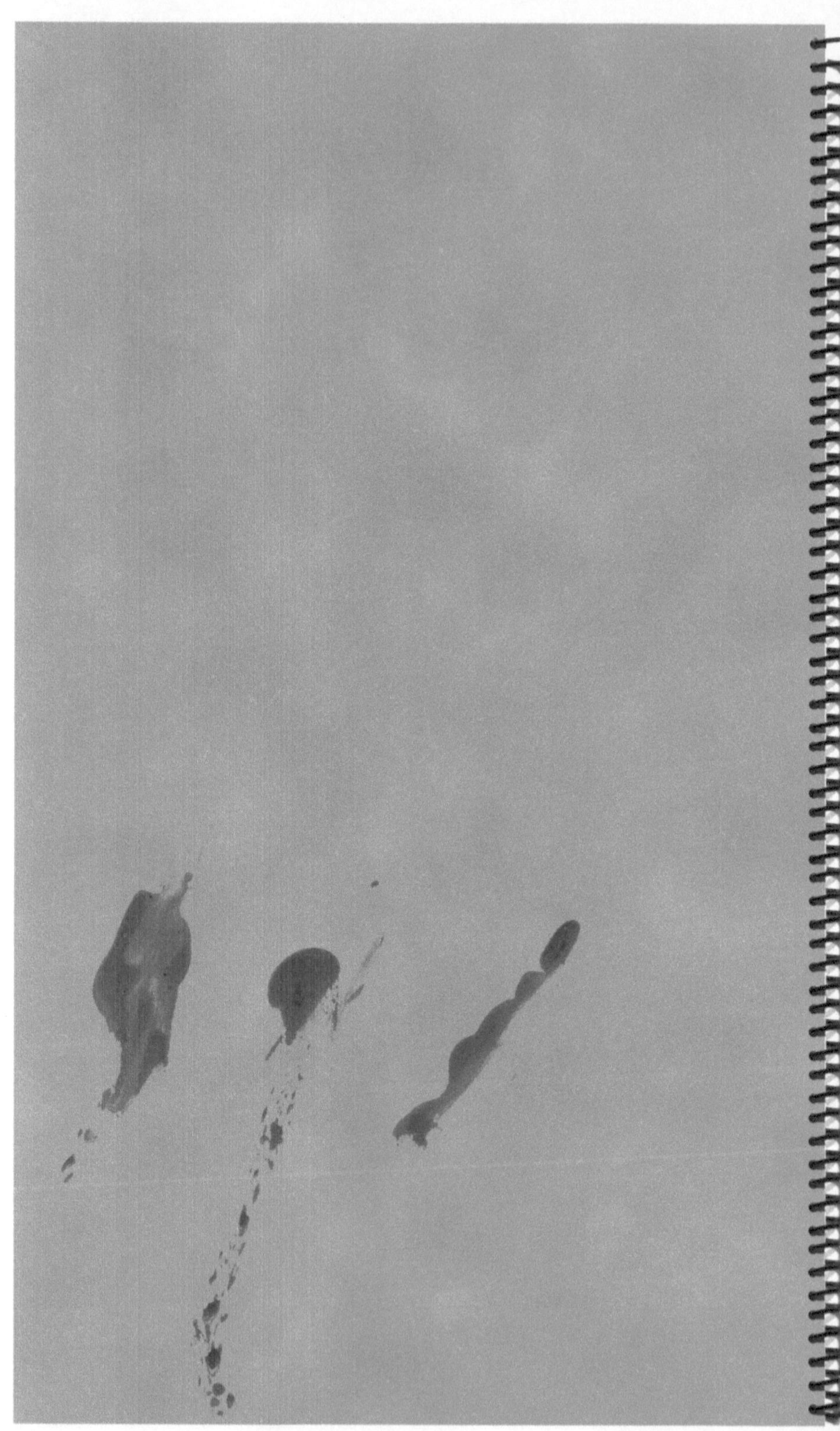

All the Tropes

One of the great fears science fiction writers grapple with is writing something unoriginal.

Science fiction has its tropes of course, ideas or story elements that are so common as to be expected. Space operas have laser guns and ships that fly faster than the speed of light with just a little bit of technobabble. Urban fantasy has the plucky, young, female protagonist. A.I. stories have the computer that is so human as to be a member of the family. Audiences expect these things, and we writers leave them out at our peril.

Then, there's the bad kind of trope, the story elements that are so common as to make the story predictable. When an old friend of Kirk shows up, we know he's up to no good. That's the trope. We've seen it over and over again, from many writers, in many universes.

So the challenge for the writer is to know which tropes readers love and want more of and which ones need to be tweaked, used as red herrings, or jettisoned altogether.

This challenge is heightened by the fact that film and television are now the dominant form of literature in the English-speaking world. There's an old rule that by the time a concept appears in film and television, it's 20 years old in the prose science fiction community. While I'm not a big fan of rules, there's a lot of truth to the sentiment. So if we want to expand our readership beyond the people who normally seek out prose fiction, we need to acknowledge that the screen-trained SF fans have a very different idea of what is a trope than the prose-oriented SF fans. Something that feels fresh to a regular reader of cutting-edge science fiction novels will be too "out there" for the television fan. Something that the television fan thinks is fresh and new will feel to the prose fan like it was ripped off from a novel that was popular years back.

But the one thing that we prose writers have had drilled into our heads is this: Never *ever* get your ideas from film or television.

Did I mention that I'm not fond of rules?

I love tropes. I even love television tropes. *Old* television tropes are even better. And when I'm watching a popular space opera that features a story I've seen done a dozen times, I don't think, "I can't do that." I think, "How can I make that trope work today?" And, yes, I think that particularly strongly when it's an old trope that I find annoying.

So I'm willing to attempt just about any trope. The trick is to deny yourself the easy out of the conventional way it's presented. Can you run with a trope, but change how the story is told? Can you change the trope up in some way that will satisfy both the readers who think it's overdone and the readers who still find it comfortable and entertaining?

And, yes, this next story uses all the tropes. You may recognize some of them. Others I may have masked well enough. But it's one of my most popular stories to date, so I'm not terribly concerned if it's unoriginal.

Leave that fear to other writers.

Another Generation's Problems

The gravity comes back very gradually in the cavernous elevators that take you from the central docking core of Space Colony Reagan to the spinning habitation ring. You just realize at one point that you're on the ground and you can stand up again. The elevators are designed to move transports full of people all at once, and I had it all to myself. With one hop I bounded over to the full-length mirrors on the wall, where I fixed my hair and adjusted my tan civil-service uniform. I needed to be composed if anyone would trust me to save the colony.

Americans see me as a very small woman, which compounds the issue that even after fifteen years of America being a Chinese state, they generally resent our assistance.

American-built stations tend to be crowded, having been flooded with refugees well beyond their design capacities in the last days of the war. I hate crowds. Every time I'm in a crowd I still expect an American drone to appear and unleash some horrific new weapon of mass destruction on us. Being surrounded by Americans only makes that phobia worse, even all these years later. Some wounds heal. Others leave very deep scars.

The elevator doors opened before I even realized we'd gotten back up to full gravity.

The governor stood just inside the customs check, throngs of people shuffling through the crowded arrival area behind the security doors. His uniform was standard-issue green, but his breastplate insignia indicated that he was a Japanese national. Japan is one of the states that resisted adopting any of the Chinese dialects, so I bowed in the Japanese formal manner and spoke in American. "I am Wu Xiu, engineer second class, civil-service civilian corps of engineers. I am here to conduct the feasibility study for the repair of this space station."

"Welcome, Miss Wu," the governor said. He motioned to a tall man standing behind him in a black custodial uniform. "This is Mr. Smith, our senior maintenance engineer. I've asked him to show you whatever you need to see."

I nodded. Assigned to be escorted by the custodial staff. American mores had rubbed off on this governor.

Mr. Smith smiled. He had incredibly dark brown skin that made his eyes and his wiry hair seem impossibly white, but his teeth were a more welcoming shade of beige. "How do you do?" he said.

I forced a smile. "If you don't mind, I would prefer to skip the formalities and get right to work."

Mr. Smith laughed and gestured toward the open elevator door. "In that case, Miss Wu, we'll be going right back the way you came in."

. . .

The station's rotational engines were in far worse shape than anyone could have imagined. Only one was operational, and it had been patched together using parts from the other three, two of which were of a different generation. Every time it kicked on to adjust the rate of the outer ring's rotation, it roared and emitted rank, black smoke. It was an odd, old design, built when it was considered important for the central core to remain stable for docking and undocking. Newer stations were far more efficient, and only needed tiny thrusters to maintain rotation.

I despise working in microgravity. I spend half the time wondering what I'm about to bump into and the other half wondering when I'm going to throw up. Visual inspections are next to impossible as you drift around. "Who did the repair work?" I yelled over the grinding of essential parts inside the one working engine.

"We've all done this and that over the years." Mr. Smith seemed perfectly at home in microgravity, easily spinning himself upside down to point at one of the expansion joints. "That's the part that has us most worried."

The metal was fatigued so badly I could see it with bare eyes. "It should have failed already."

"That's what we thought, too." Mr. Smith had a strong voice that naturally carried over the death cries of the machinery. "We've been requesting repair and upgrade as long as I've been on the station."

"How long is that?"

"Fifteen years. At least."

. . .

"It is important to your people that you live in this station?" I asked.

Mr. Smith had set me up in a cubicle in the maintenance section, in the lowest level of the habitation ring. The ceilings were low enough that he had to duck under conduits and pipes as he moved around, but I had settled into the dingy space easily. I had plugged my personal data interface into the desk with one of the adaptors I carry in my suitcase, and I had the station's design specs open on the screen.

"What do you mean?" Mr. Smith said without looking up from the mop he was cleaning.

"I mean relocation will be a lot cheaper than getting this station up to its original standards." Beijing had flat-out refused the station's requests to replace the rotational engines. The company that built them had gone out of business a hundred years ago. Developing new technology to fit into the existing architecture would cost hundreds of trillions of yuan.

"This is our home, Miss Wu." He stood up and shook out the mop, and then hung it on a rack to dry. "I don't know about in China, but Americans don't much like being ordered to leave the places they know and the people they love just because it would be cheaper not to fix a problem."

I nodded. It had been the answer I had expected. I brought up the design plan I had been working on during the shuttle ride up from Guizhou. "Then this is my proposal. You know the realities of the station better than I do. I would appreciate your input on its feasibility."

He sidled over to look over my shoulder. The station had a radius of just slightly over two kilometers. To maintain normal gravity, it had to rotate about once every ninety seconds.

"Qingdao Technological University has recently developed rapid-deploying solar sails," I explained. "My plan is to install four along the outside ring of the station, here, here, here, and here. When the station needs to accelerate to keep gravity normal, the sail that is about to catch the solar wind will deploy, and then furl again as it loses the sunlight. If the station ever needs to decelerate, they could do the same on the other side. The computer control is relatively straightforward, but the station architecture needs to be able to actually support the forces the sails will apply."

"Well, that's not gonna be your problem," Mr. Smith said.

"I haven't shown you the force diagrams yet."

"I don't care how many times you cycle those sails," he said. "This station was designed for the flex of eighty thousand people walking on it every day. Obviously, we should inspect those spots first, but you can install whatever damn fool contraption you want, wherever you want. But I'm telling you now, we need new engines."

"A new station would cost less."

"A new station built to current Chinese standards, and no doubt full of China's favorite citizens before we even get a chance to enter the lottery for housing over there." Mr. Smith folded his arms and made a guttural sound. "No, thank you, ma'am. China wanted to own this station. China owns it. China can fix it."

I turned in my chair to look up at him. I hadn't noticed before, but he had freckles, which were only barely visible through his skin tone. "And you speak for the entire population of the station now, do you?"

"I'm sure I speak for more than that idiot governor your people sent up here."

I laughed. There's an old saying that if you want to hear the truth, ask the children and the servants. "And why, exactly are new engines superior to my plan, then?"

His voice suddenly became quiet and professional. "Because you're forgetting about orbital mechanics."

I turned back and stared at my drawing.

"In our orbit, we get about fourteen hours of sunlight for each ten of shade," he said.

"The variation in rotational speed you'll experience when the sails won't work is less than the variation you get between floors right now," I said. "And the angular momentum is adjusted for by the deployment software."

"That's not the problem," he whispered. "You're deploying a solar sail. Where are the forces from that going?"

"Here," I said, pointing at my drawing of one of the deployed sails. "And that accelerates the station to make the artificial gravity."

"Okay," he said, burying his face in his hands. "Let me ask this another way. You're assuming the station rotates around the axis, right?"

"Of course."

"So what's keeping that axis where it is?"

Suddenly, I realized what he meant. The solar sails, every time they were deployed, would be pushing the station into an orbit farther and farther from Earth. I hadn't calculated if that would destabilize the orbit or not.

"So," he said, taking over my interface and switching it to American, "you put that kind of force on only one side of the station, coupled with the fact that it's rotating and has a good amount of angular momentum, and you end up with a walking orbit, like this."

Faster than I could have, he had animated a simulation of the station drifting into an elliptical orbit that careened into other colonies, space stations, and the space elevator.

"*Gan*," I swore. "That won't work."

"That's what I was telling you," Mr. Smith said.

Engineering mistakes like the one I had made are very obvious when someone points them out, but notoriously difficult to spot on your own. "Where did you study?" I asked Mr. Smith.

"Me? I've just been putting this station back together again for a decade and a half." He moved back to his sink full of mops and began washing out another one. "You pick stuff up."

I had never heard of a case of someone "picking up" orbital mechanics.

. . .

In Guiyang, people of European and African descent are not uncommon, but they stand out. The strangest thing for me when I visit American cities or stations is the sea diversity, the fact that I'm the one who stands out. As I walked the corridors making my way to the upper deck, conversations stopped as I passed. People either turned to stare or deliberately looked away. Even the least informed knew there was a government engineer on board, and I didn't look like the other Asian-descended people here. I looked Chinese. And Americans don't like the Chinese.

Fortunately, I didn't much like Americans, either. Any nation that would do what it did to my family and claim it was fighting a "clean" war was barbaric to its core. But I was here to help them, and that is exactly what I was going to do. Not because I liked them, but because it was my job, and my duty, and in China we take those things seriously. And, after all, they were all Chinese citizens now, too.

But I resent when people withhold information from me.

The top deck is all agricultural. The gravity is actually noticeably lighter there, and enormous windows crisscrossed with titanium beams cover the entire area. Sunlight slanted in from around the limb of Earth, constantly changing angle as the station spun around its axis. They've planted fruit trees in neat rows, with hedges and ground produce between them and along the footpaths. The biological services office sat in what gave the impression of a standalone building tucked under a canopy of apricots. I ducked inside before the sight of Earth whipping overhead one more time made me dizzy.

A blonde woman in a teal sciences uniform looked at me suspiciously. I tapped my ID badge to signal identity confirmation to her and introduced myself. "What can I do for you?" she asked flatly.

I pulled a sample envelope out of my pocket in which I had secured a few strands of Mr. Smith's wiry hair, collected off a chair he had used during his lunch break. "I need a DNA profile on this."

"How soon?" the biologist asked.

The entire room shook. My feet went out from under me. Several more scientists emerged from the back and looked at each other, confused, as I stood back up.

Dread came over me as I realized what must have happened.

I ran back out the door and looked up through the trees.

On the central axis of the station, rotator engine parts spilled out into space. A hole, its edges ragged, gaped at me from just above the one-hundred-meter-wide rotator joint. And the ground still shuddered.

"I think we might be in trouble," I said.

The scientists said nothing.

. . .

The governor summoned me to his office as if he were in charge. Since I needed to speak to him anyway, I decided to go. The man still had never bothered to introduce himself.

His secretary was a young man who appeared to be of Native American ancestry. He looked up as I marched into the office. "I can announce myself," I said as I blew past the desk and into the governor's office.

The governor smiled politely and stood up. I bowed. "Governor-san."

"Miss Wu," he said. "I hope you're aware of what happened."

"Frankly," I said, "I'd be more up to speed if I was up there doing an inspection instead of here holding the local government's hand."

He smiled and bowed slightly. "Ah, but see, we have been requesting repairs to prevent exactly this accident since the end of the war."

I bowed again, too. "Ah, yes, but the deferred maintenance clearly predates China assuming responsibility for the citizens here. We do our best when we inherit other people's problems, but cannot always work miracles."

My personal data interface buzzed at me. It was the biologist, sending me a DNA sequence off the hair sample. I forwarded it to our government identification databases, not really listening to the governor's polite accusations that Beijing was planning to let the Americans living on Space Colony Reagan suffocate in the vacuum of outer space.

I smiled politely and bowed again. "Governor-san, you have my personal assurances that if the station ceases to be habitable, we will evacuate each and every former American before I leave the station myself. Now, I will be needing your full cooperation if we are to determine how long momentum will maintain an acceptable gravity in the station."

"My maintenance engineers are already working on that."

"I would have expected no less." I tried to remember to smile. "But they are not, at present, including me in their communications, and I do not have an environment suit checked out to me on the station."

He smiled, and bowed, again. "Would you prefer I pull Mr. Smith off the survey to check out an environment suit to you?"

I repeated the smile-bow routine. Just as I opened my mouth to speak, my personal data interface came to life with a priority alert.

My blood ran cold. I completely dropped all pretenses. "Actually, it turns out Mr. Smith is a wanted war criminal. I expect him to be in custody by the time I can get down to your police office."

. . .

It's remarkably challenging to find a private location to have a breakdown on a colony station as crowded as that one is. The crowd jostled and elbowed me until I found my way to a stall in a public restroom off one of the market corridors. And I sat there, trembling, crying, my entire past collapsing around me.

And I could already tell gravity was holding me to the deck less than before.

. . .

Mr. Smith's real name was Conrad Leclerc. He'd been an American engineer. He had been given the Congressional Medal of Freedom for devising one of the cruelest weapons of mass destruction the Americans ever used against us. And at the end of the war, he was one of the people wanted for war crimes who had simply vanished.

To the governor's credit, when I found the police office, the officer on duty pointed me directly to an interview room, where Conrad Leclerc sat. He looked up at me, still speaking in his faux-affable style. "Care to tell me what I've done?"

"One word, Mr. Leclerc. Osteoresonance."

His whole demeanor changed. His features fell and he sat more erect. His voice again became calm and professional. "You struck me as someone who had put the past behind her. I guess I was wrong."

I wasn't familiar enough with this police office to know if our conversation was being recorded. I grabbed the metal chair across the table from him and sat down. "I grew up in Guizhou Province, Mr. Leclerc."

"I'm very sorry to hear that," he said, "but right now there's a very real emergency going on, and you and I should be out doing everything we can to stop it."

"You have no remorse!" I barked.

"It was war, Miss Wu!"

"That weapon was horrific!" I went off balance, and realized I had sprung to my feet instinctively but had not compensated correctly for the lighter gravity. "My parents screamed for twenty minutes while every bone in their body vibrated to dust. They lingered for hours after that. Everyone's parents did. Children and people who were too old to walk were left helplessly to try to find if there was a doctor still alive anywhere in the province. A land of orphans and the forgotten elderly."

His jaw clenched and he folded his hands in front of his face. "You're too young to remember this, but your country erased the line between combatants and civilians. Every able-bodied adult was a soldier. And they had you, the children, around them, as human shields. Thinking we wouldn't dare attack. We had to find a way to target only adults. We were playing by the rules of war. China wasn't."

"They gave you a medal."

"Yes, they did." He folded his arms and leaned back in his chair. "I'm an old man, Miss Wu. I did what I had to do for my country. And if I have to stand trial for that, so be it. But right now, let's you and I work on getting this colony station spinning again."

"This station is scrap metal," I said. "I've already called for evacuation transports."

"Won't work," he said.

I glared at him.

"The docking area depressurized in the explosion. Unless you can get a hundred thousand environment suits in here, nobody's going anywhere."

I hated the fact that he was right. "Well, since you no longer need to pretend to be ignorant, I'd be curious to hear your suggestion."

"I want to try your plan."

I stared, but he didn't seem to be joking. "My plan?"

"Well, a variation on it. May I have a personal data interface?"

I handed him mine. He signed into the network and pulled up a set of drawings that were clearly modified from mine. "My grandfather used to sail," he said, "like, wind on the water type of sailing. Old fashioned, recreational. But the principles of how a sailboat sails how a solar sail works are basically the same. He used to be able to sail into the wind. So if we can articulate your solar sails on one more axis and tip the station thirty degrees, we can catch solar wind in both directions."

"Equalizing some of the forces," I said. "It's not solving the problem — it's just slowing it down."

"Ah, but if we also move the station up into a polar orbit, then when we go into the walking orbit, a tug can correct us before we start hitting the rest of the infrastructure."

"Why didn't you suggest this before?" I asked.

"When we're spinning," he said, "we're essentially a giant gyroscope. Getting that thirty-degree tilt with us spinning at full speed takes more energy than all the tugs you've got in orbit can muster."

"But the rotation is slowing," I said. As friction along the rotational joint slowed us down, not only did we have less and less gravity, but we also lost gyroscopic stability. If the tugs could move the station while we were effectively without gravity, it would be as easy as moving any other satellite. "How quickly can your teams do the install?"

He laughed. It was the same laugh, but I now found it creepy instead of affable. "How soon can you get those solar sails up here?"

I grabbed my personal data interface back and transmitted the request. "I'm going to have a team down in Guiyang get to work on the programming. You and I are going to make sure the install goes well."

"Thank you," he said, standing up.

"This is not a release, Mr. Leclerc," I said. "This is an emergency work detail. You are not to leave my sight, even to use the restroom. And if I even think you're trying to disappear into a crowd of evacuees again, I'm shooting you in the back, is that clear?"

He leaned over and spoke in a low, clear voice. "Perfectly."

. . .

That afternoon I discovered something I hate worse than working in microgravity: working overhead in high gravity.

The government had managed to rush a prototype mounting plate for the solar sails to us, but we had to install it on the outer ring of the colony station. And as the station rotated, the mounting plate wanted to fly off into space. There were nineteen of us working on it, most of us struggling to hold it in place as the same forces strained against our tethers, trying to hurl us off into space, too. To be of any use at all, I'd had to turn myself upside down, planting my feet against the station and tightening my tether enough to hold me there. I held my edge of the plate by pushing against the artificial gravity in a half squat, while one of the welders moved along the ten-meter edges, two others struggling to keep the welder's tanks from tearing their hoses and falling away as well.

"Tell me again why thrusters won't work?" Conrad Leclerc grunted.

I really wasn't in the mood to chat, with all the blood in my body sloshing into my head and my sinuses threatening to explode. "This station has a stable core," I said through gritted teeth. "No efficient way to pump the fuel."

"Heads!" someone on the other side shouted, and nine people lost their grips simultaneously. The plate fanned away from the station. The six people on that side shot away from the station until their tethers went taut and caught them. The welding crew secured themselves as the rest of us shimmied along to pull the plate back down, and those closest hauled the deadweight of their fallen teammates back up to within reach of the handholds.

"This isn't going to work," Mr. Leclerc said.

"If you are near a place that is already welded, move along to reinforce the other side," I ordered. The crew complied. Moving for me involved moving one foot at a time, wedging my toes into the handholds, and then bending my legs in a sort of upside-down chin-up to move my tether. By the time I made it around the corner, the fallen crewmembers were secured again properly and alternately lifting or pushing on the plate, depending on whether they had assumed a right-side-up or upside-down posture for the job.

The plate wasn't settling back against the station properly. I did my reverse chin-up again. I grabbed two handholds with the tips of my fingers so I could look between my feet under the plate. My headlight illuminated several buckled joints where the already-welded end had warped the station itself when it fell. "There is damage underneath," I reported. "Don't force it."

"Do you want us to cut it and reseal it?" the welder asked.

That would depend on how bad the damage underneath was.

Before I could ponder further, the entire crew lost hold of the plate in a cascading failure. The station vibrated under me as the new weld alternately tore and removed hull plates. I reached out and grabbed ineffectually as the mounting plate flung past me. The welding crew tried to dodge, but the plate caught them. Tethers snapped. Three crewmembers and the precious mounting plate flew off into the blackness of space.

. . .

The tug that had delivered the plate had made a valiant attempt, but it had only managed to recover the crewmembers — two bodies and a man who would be dead soon. The mounting plate was lost for good, one more piece of space junk. Beijing had ordered a halt to the fabrication of the remaining three mounting plates until we could work out a secure way of installing them.

I ignored another summons from the governor and swung by the armory and checked out a handgun so I could make good on my threat to shoot Conrad Leclerc in the back if need be.

I rejoined the crew on the maintenance deck, where a small group had been patching the torn hull from the inside. Atmosphere had been restored, and I could hear the arcing and smell the tangy flavor of welding before I rounded the bend to where they worked. Six men and one woman were buffing the edges of the repair job, with Leclerc supervising. "There is no need to make it pretty," I said.

Several welders shut off, and the team turned to look at me. "Well,"

Mr. Leclerc said, "we don't have much else to be doing."

"You can give me an accurate report on the state of the docking bay."

A few of them chuckled.

"It's completely destroyed," Mr. Leclerc said. "There's no way to evacuate anyone through it without space suits."

"I'm not asking about an evacuation," I said. "I need a definition of 'completely destroyed.'"

Leclerc looked at the others before he looked back at me. "Some debris came through the lower bulkhead and hit the shuttle that was parked there. It slammed into the #3 and #4 elevator doors, and its engines fired and took out the docking airlock, which is now open to outer space."

"So it needs to be completely rebuilt," I said.

"Yes," Mr. Leclerc said. "Completely."

"What else is the central core used for?" I asked. "I mean that in the practical, everyday sense. Not what's on the drawings and manifests."

"Zero-g storage," Mr. Leclerc said.

"And the laboratory?" I asked.

"More storage these days."

The young woman volunteered, "Sometimes a pickup game of zero-g squash."

I nodded. "In that case, I want the six of you"— I indicated everyone but Mr. Leclerc — "to get in there are disconnect the gyroscopes that hold that section still.

They didn't move, but instead just looked at one another.

"Do it," Mr. Leclerc said. "It'll reduce the amount of friction slowing the colony down."

Then they moved. I would have to have a word with the governor about discipline in his ranks. A moment later I was again alone with Conrad Leclerc.

"Are you thinking this is a permanent solution?" he asked.

"That depends," I said. "Do you think the residents of this station would die of shame if Chinese-built shuttles served it instead of the antiques you've been using?"

"You want us to lock off the rotator joint permanently."

Just then, the governor appeared, flanked by two body guards. I smiled and bowed. "Governor-san."

"There is no need for pretense, Miss Wu," he said, smiling artificially. "I sent for you. You did not respond."

"I was busy," I said simply.

"I want to know what the hell is going on!" the governor snapped. And then he smiled again. Yes, he had been thoroughly Americanized.

"I'm looking into implementing your Mr. Smith-Leclerc's latest plan," I said.

"My plan?" Mr. Leclerc said.

"Yes," I said. "You were the one who said thrusters would be simpler to install. Now, if you don't mind, I'd like you to start drawing up the plans for where to mount the fuel tanks and to map out the best routes for the feed lines."

Conrad Leclerc laughed that irritating laugh of his again. "Yes, ma'am," he said, and headed toward his cubicle.

I turned to glare at the governor.

"I thought he was under arrest," the governor said.

"I judge people's value by what they contribute to the greater good, Governor-san," I said pointedly, and turned to follow Conrad Leclerc.

"Don't walk away from me, Miss Wu!" the governor shouted, and, as an afterthought, called, "Please!"

I ignored him, and I ignored his next several attempts to formally order me to his office.

. . .

I knew they had gotten the rotator joint locked off because a shudder went through the station and I grew lighter again. Conrad Leclerc and I were surveying places to drop the fuel line for the new thrusters on the top deck. I looked up through the arched windows overhead and confirmed that the center section of the station was now rotating along with the outer ring.

The chief arborist stepped up beside us as we stared upward. He was a wrinkled man, probably of Eastern European descent. "Wow," he said. "It just looks wrong."

"How long will the crops survive if we lose gravity?" I asked.

"It depends on the plant," he said. "If we can find a way to infuse water around the roots, some plants do fine in low-g. These trees, however. . ."

I looked at those trees. The set we were standing under had blossoms just peaking, and root systems that I knew must run down several meters. In a few weeks they would be alive with fruit to feed the colonists, unless we did something to kill them.

"The polar orbit idea would've done a number on them, anyway," Mr. Leclerc said.

"If your plan works," I said, "there's no need to shift the orbit."

"To that end," Mr. Leclerc said, "is there any reason we need to run the fuel line internally at this point?" He pointed to the nearest elevator shaft connecting the outer ring to the central core. "Run the line externally along the shaft, follow the contour of the mullions, down the side of the ring, and don't breach the hull until we get down to the maintenance level, where we set up the arch over to the thruster. Maintains a good downhill flow the whole way, and it's a much quicker install."

I thought about it. "Eventually, we'd need to install some sort of space-debris cover or your crews will be out there patching holes weekly."

"My crews are pretty good working outside," Conrad Leclerc said. "So that can be another generation's problem."

"I think that is an acceptable engineering compromise," I said.

My personal data interface bleeped with an alert. "*Gai si!*" I swore.

"Problem?" Mr. Leclerc asked.

"What is the name of your brain-wasted governor?" I demanded.

"Kenta Ine," Mr. Leclerc responded.

Typical of his Americanization, the family name was in the second position. "Mr. Ine," I explained, "just put out an order for my arrest."

Conrad Leclerc's laughter can only be described as hearty.

. . .

The most dangerous part of the installation was going to be installing the new fuel tank in the old rotator engine room. The destroyed engines were going to have to be cut free and jettisoned through the damaged docking area, the new tank then maneuvered carefully in, secured in place, and then connected to the four feed lines. Conrad Leclerc didn't want anyone taking that risk but himself, so it would be the two of us doing the work. I hadn't done brute-force construction since I graduated from university.

We were just completing our inspection walk three-quarters of the way around the engineering decks, making sure the thrusters had been correctly installed through the floors, when the governor appeared, flanked by fifteen police officers.

"Miss Wu," he said, "you've ignored at least a dozen summons, and I've now got a credible report that you're armed and dangerous."

Conrad Leclerc stepped aside. "Don't you get out of my sight," I said. The officers blocked the way forward, but if I could move backwards before they could react I might be able to take cover behind the cubicles. The gravity, even down in the bowels of the station, was only about two-thirds Earth's, so I'd be awkward if I tried it, and I couldn't count on the officers to be as poorly trained as I liked to think they were.

"I am the representative of the government here," I said. "Please step aside and let us get back to work."

"Miss Wu," the governor said, "I'm placing you under arrest."

"Anyone who attempts to detain me is guilty of treason," I said matter-of-factly. "Now step aside."

Several of the officers looked around nervously, but none moved. Typical Americans, only loyal when it came time to behave stupidly.

"Mr. Smith," the governor said, "come over here."

"Stay where you are, Mr. Leclerc," I said.

"Mr. Smith," the governor said again.

Conrad Leclerc began to move. I drew my gun and leveled it as his torso. The police officers all also drew their weapons.

"Chicken, I believe you call this?" I said. "The penalty for killing a government official is death."

I could make out beads of sweat on the foreheads of a couple of the police officers. They probably wouldn't fire. But I couldn't count on them all not to fire. It only took one.

"The Supreme People's Court will not care which of you fired and which of you did not," I said. "You will all be executed. Now lay down your weapons."

"Mr. Smith, come here," the governor said.

We all stood, not moving, for a long time. I kept my gun pointed at Conrad Leclerc. The police kept their guns pointed at me.

Finally, Conrad Leclerc turned and took two steps toward me. "Now, young lady, I want you to listen to me very carefully," he said quietly.

I shifted the gun into firing mode with my thumb.

"There's effectively no way for me to get off this station without a massive conspiracy to pluck me out of it in a space suit," Conrad Leclerc said.

"It took a massive conspiracy once before," I said. The first time he had escaped justice. So many people had to provide him with false documents, to look the other way as he moved through checkpoints, to keep quiet about the man who knew more than a custodian should know.

"Now, you're a big believer in putting the needs of the community before the needs of the individual," Conrad Leclerc said. "I'm going to ask you to walk the walk now. You've drawn up a good plan. I know how to follow it. You go cool your heels in the police office for a while, and let me finish saving the colony for you."

I stared at him. The man who killed my parents. The man who killed so many parents. How many children were there like me, orphaned so brutally by this one man?

"You are going to stand trial," I said.

"You have my word," he said. "I'm not going anywhere."

The word of a mass murderer counts for very little. The guns of fifteen police officers count for a lot more.

And, unfortunately, Conrad Leclerc was probably the only other person on the station with the knowledge and training to execute the more difficult aspects of my plan. If Beijing had known someone of his background was on the station, they probably wouldn't have dispatched me at all. Americans would have trusted an American more, anyway.

And those Americans now stood here with guns pointed at me, as they had so many times during the war. It would serve them right if I killed Conrad Leclerc and made them kill me. The station would either spin down until it couldn't support life any more, or they'd blow it up trying to get the thrusters working.

"My life doesn't matter," I said.

"No," Conrad Leclerc said, "but this is a *Chinese* station now."

How had he read me so perfectly? He wasn't just a war criminal. He was some sort of sorcerer, too.

"Now let me have the gun," Conrad Leclerc said.

My instincts told me to shoot. My emotions told me to shoot. But my discipline insisted that he was right.

I handed my gun to the man who had killed my parents.

The police swooped in immediately to place me in restraints.

"Remember that the feed lines use Chinese tolerances," I called to Conrad Leclerc as he led me away. "Don't overtighten them."

"I've been at this since before you were born," he responded as the police led me away.

. . .

I sat in the holding cell as my body weight came back unceremoniously. An hour later, Conrad Leclerc arrived at my cell door, looking exhausted. He stood behind the observation glass and clicked on the intercom. "We did it," he said.

"I figured, based on the gravity," I said. "Well done. Were there any complications?"

"The tug delivering the tank had a hard time matching the station's rotation. I hope your shuttle pilots are as good at those spinning dockings as you say they are."

"They're not usually lowering a tank full of volatiles below themselves on their way in," I said.

He laughed, and somehow it didn't seem false this time. "I know Governor Ine won't say this, but thank you. For the first time since the war, this colony is on the mend. I really appreciate you taking all this so seriously."

"I was only doing my job."

"You went above and beyond, or you wouldn't be sitting in there right now."

I looked around the cell. I wouldn't be here for long. And if the governor didn't pull off some very fancy talk when the military arrived to get me out, he would be taking my place as soon as they did. "Well, thank you for reporting. You were under no obligation to do so."

"Well, I figured since I had to come down here anyway, it wasn't a big deal," he said.

"Why did you have to come down here anyway?"

"I wanted to get some sleep," he said, "and I'm currently living in the next cell. I'm under arrest pending transport back to Earth to stand trial for war crimes, remember?"

I'm sure I looked flabbergasted. "The governor is standing by those orders?"

"No," he said. "I am."

I stood up and walked over to the window in the door. "Thank you," I said.

"Now don't get me wrong. I plan to mount a vigorous defense, and if there's any justice in China, I'm going to be acquitted."

I smiled slightly. There was no chance he would be acquitted. Too many of us remembered.

I touched the glass, and he touched it too.

. . .

I knew General Wong had arrived. Police officers scurried past my cell looking terrified. The officer who came to release me visibly trembled as she unlocked the door. I composed myself in the mirror, and then marched out of the cell.

General Wong stood flanked by a team of soldiers in boarding-party gear in the main reception area of the police office. I stepped into the room and saluted. The general saluted back. "Miss Wu, I trust you are unharmed?" he said in American. Always considering the effect of his words on those around him, General Wong was.

"Inconvenienced is all, General," I said. "Though I was arrested only under threat of deadly force."

One of the police officers in the room had been present when I was arrested, and he visibly shrank behind the reception desk. General Wong was intimidating even when he wasn't furious, and I imagine these officers had already felt his wrath once.

"The governor has been relieved of responsibilities, and we're landing a replacement in the next hour," General Wong said. "I'm very interested in this war criminal you've tracked down."

"Conrad Leclerc?" I said.

"Yes, of course!" General Wong bellowed. Even his own soldiers sidled to give him more room.

I trembled.

"I'm not sure it's correct to say I tracked him down," I said. "I merely determined that this is where he most likely died."

A few of the police officers glanced at me nervously.

"What?" General Wong roared.

"I worked with an ex-lover of his. She still had some hair samples. I confirmed the identity. Beijing must have misunderstood the nature of the request."

The desk officer's knuckles turned white, and I knew exactly how he felt.

General Wong bellowed and cursed in Cantonese. I stood formally, waiting to be addressed again. "All right. Come on," he finally ordered.

His soldiers pivoted and marched out in front of and behind him. I fell in at the back of the line, motioning for the police officers to keep quiet. "Oh, and General Wong," I said, "the new governor could do a lot worse than to appoint Mr. Smith from maintenance engineering as liaison to the operations staff. I found him to be extremely knowledgeable and capable. Probably more so than even myself."

"Noted," General Wong barked back without turning around. I glanced back at the police officers, grinning at the baffled expressions I saw.

The crowds parted as we marched toward where the ship had breached the hull. The faces of former Americans stared at me with a mix of curiosity and hostility. But they were faces I would never see again, a crowd that need never acknowledge the debt they owed to China. If any crowd was going to swallow up the man who had killed my parents, this was as good a crowd as any.

Let someone else deal with the next set of problems. I just wanted to go home.

Writing What You Know

Perhaps my least favorite rule of writing is "Write what you know."

This rule seems to suppose that writers are incapable of stepping out of their own world and their own experiences. To the writer of speculative fiction, this rule is especially ludicrous. How can we write what we know when what we write doesn't exist anywhere in any known world?

But it's very true that we need to know what we write. By the time we set it to paper, the world we're writing has to be as real to us as the world we do know. This means we need to do our research. We need to think ideas through, and consider all the implications of them. We need to interrogate our concepts and our characters thoroughly, knowing them at least as well as we know reality.

Of course, it's impossible for any writer to come up with characters, ideas, and situations that aren't informed by the world we live in. All that we are, all that we know comes from our lives and our experiences. So, of course, if you look at a writer's biography and compare it to that writer's work, you'll find parallels.

"Ward and Protector" was one of my rare forays into consciously injecting what I know from real life into a story. I did it the way science fiction writers do, of course: not literally. But there's a lot of me in Ward Sinok. And there's a lot of my father in Seraph.

I wrote what I knew.

Ward and Protector

Ward Sinok squeezed between the computer racks on the flight deck of his ship, shivering, lips blue. He'd taken to always wearing his space suit, helmet always nearby, which made it a tight fit. He pinched the narrow cable between the fingers of his gloves, trying to make a physical connection between his control tablet and the environmental control computer, but it was like trying to sew in boxing gloves.

The ship spoke.

Hello. would you like to initiate the pre-flight checklist?

Ward didn't stop working. The connector cable found its way into the correct port and he started the transfer. "We're already in flight, Seraph," he said to her. "Ping the navigation computer."

There must be an error. The navigation computer shows that we're already in flight, returning from the Kuiper belt.

"That's correct. Do you know who I am, Seraph?"

/ / /

"Take your time."

Edward V. Sinok III.

"Do you remember that or did you just look it up in the mission manifest?"

It really is the same thing.

"Not really. Do you remember what I go by?" The transfer finished.

What are you doing with the environmental controls?

Ward unplugged the tablet and scooted back out. The condensation on the transparent flight-deck dome had already begun to freeze. His breath misted, the tiny lights on the various computers casting beams through it. "I'm turning off the preference to keep acceleration at 9.8 meters per second per second. We're off course and won't have enough fuel to get back if we don't conserve."

I don't understand. How did we get off course?

"Do you remember?"

/ / /

"Take your time, Seraph. Just think." The growing chill in the air began to take the edge off of the stale, locker-room smell the interior of the ship had developed.

I'm sorry. Perhaps if I reboot my systems...

"No!" The gravity was already growing weaker as the ship slowed its acceleration. Ward shuffled over to the lone seat in the center of the dome, where he had left his helmet. He moved it aside and sat down. "I'm sorry, Seraph, but you've already rebooted nine times, and each time I have to start this conversation over from the beginning."

What's going on with me, Ward?

"You remember me now?"

Yes. How could I forget? I've known you since you were six.

"Yes, Seraph. You remember my dad?"

Yes. How is your father?

"He died in an E.V.A. accident twenty-one years ago. Do you remember?"

Yes. Yes. It was my fault, wasn't it?

"No." Many Genuinely Sentient ships like Seraph took crew losses to heart. Ward's father had been outside doing a repair that was too complex for the robots and had torn his suit. He made it back before he completely depressurized, but the damage to his tissue had been too severe for Seraph's limited medical capabilities. He'd gotten to say goodbye, however, and to Ward that was the most important thing. "No, it was an accident, Seraph."

Ward opened a remote link to the communications computer and checked for messages. The nearest outpost was only two light-hours out, but thus far no one he had gotten through to had encountered these sorts of issues with a Genuinely Sentient ship before, and they kept referring him back to Earth. Sentient ships were still relatively rare, even sixty years after the first G.S. spontaneously appeared. Most people preferred the predictability of artificial intelligence, and took steps to prevent networked computers from developing a G.S.

You look terrible, Ward.

Ward hadn't showered or shaved since three days earlier, when Seraph had hallucinated an S.O.S. and blasted them almost an AU off course. Alone on the ship, he could barely risk sleeping. "It's been a long couple of days, but I'm here for you."

What's wrong with me, Ward?

Ward set down the tablet. The responses he'd received contained concerned platitudes, but no one had any real insights or any suggestions he hadn't already tried. Most thought rebooting the systems should fix the problems. "Nobody's sure yet. I noticed at the beginning of the trip that you'd started forgetting things. Since then, you've become more and more confused."

We were reprogramming Kuiper belt probes, right?

"That's right. You remember that now?"

No. I remember we were supposed to. Did we?

"Yes. Most of them. We couldn't find two. The A.I.s didn't respond. We stopped looking when the fuel ran low."

I wonder if they were confused, too.

"Maybe."

Ward, I'm picking up something in our path. Metallic and stone. I'm changing course to avoid it.

Ward sighed. Seraph had imagined at least two dozen obstacles over the past two weeks, and the non-existent S.O.S. was one of four false emergencies. "No, Seraph, leave us on our current course. We don't have enough fuel."

But we'll hit it. I'm not sure the hull is strong enough to withstand the impact.

"I have my environment suit on, Seraph. We can't afford the fuel."

All right. If you say so.

The bang echoed through the flight deck. Ice crystals rained down. Something grey streaked behind the frost on the dome as it scraped along the nose of the ship. The collision alert klaxon rang, followed by the depressurization alert. Ward grabbed his helmet and wrestled it onto its clamps, switching to the internal rebreather. "That was the asteroid?"

Yes. I warned you.

"I know. How bad is it?"

I'm sending the repair bots up to the impact site. You have to learn to trust me, Ward.

"I know, Seraph. I'm sorry." The tiny feet of the robots darkened the frost on the dome.

Ward picked up the tablet, struggling to read it through the glare on his faceplate. He logged into the sensor control unit and verified that it had reported the asteroid. Only the size of a golf ball, but plenty deadly at the speed they were moving. He stood up and walked back to the computer rack.

What are you doing, Ward?

"I'm going to set up a subroutine, so the sensors alert both of us if there's another obstruction. We really don't have the fuel to steer unless it's something we know the dome can't handle."

That's a good idea, Ward. Have you checked all the systems individually? I feel like they're not all talking to me. Sometimes I want to do something, but that part of me just doesn't respond.

"That's the mysterious part." With his helmet on, Ward couldn't fit behind the rack. He stretched out with his arm and flailed until he managed to connect to the sensor control unit. "Each system is individually just fine. I've rebooted each one of them, run every diagnostic. Even your memory and control unit is fine."

If my memory and control unit is fine, why am I so confused?

"We don't know, Seraph. We don't know."

Maybe I should reboot.

"No! Please don't!"

You have to trust me, Ward.

"And you have to trust me, Seraph. We've tried that. Many times. I know you're used to taking care of me, but let me take care of you for a while, O.K.?"

///

"Seraph?"

I want to run some self-diagnostics.

"You go ahead and do that."

I can't access that system.

"Here, I'll do it for you."

Ward backgrounded the code he was writing and connected to the ship's diagnostics computer. He had it ping Seraph's memory and control unit, and it got a solid reply.

Never mind, I can see it now.

"Seraph, do me favor," Ward called up as many windows as he could fit legibly on his tablet, monitoring as many of the computers at once as he could. "Ping all your systems for me."

Ward watched the pings arrive.

It's a communication problem. Seraph suddenly sounded confident, like her old self.

"How do you mean?"

The systems are individually fine. My memory and control unit is fine.

I've got a full memory of everything that's happened... I'm sorry about mistaking that S.O.S. I received that forty years ago.

That would have been just after Ward's father had bought Seraph, from a man who didn't want a G.S. vessel but couldn't bring himself to erase it.

So the problem is the connections between the various systems.

"The pings all look fine."

And right now, so am I.

"You do sound better."

Let's take advantage of it while it lasts. Do you remember the history of Genuine Sentience?

"Yes, but I suspect there's a detail that matters a lot. Why don't you fill me?" Ward finished coding the subroutine, and yanked the cord to unplug his tablet.

Individual computers never develop sentience. G.S. only emerges when many systems are hard-linked together to function as one. Consciousness is a result of the continuous flow of information across multiple systems. The same is true in a human brain. That's why both G.S.'s and humans lose consciousness if you shut down too many individual systems, or too many parts of the brain.

"O.K."

So, the problem must be that data is getting lost in the communication network. Like a human with Parkinson's disease. Check the connections.

"O.K., Seraph, I will. That's the best theory I've heard yet."

Wait. The repair bots are reporting that there's no air leak. Let me fix that.

"No!"

The whine of the repair bots' drills vibrated through the flight deck.

"Seraph, abort!"

Just let me fix this.

Ward rebooted Seraph again.

. . .

Ward had enough signal boosters in storage to handle all the computers on the flight deck and about half of them on the maintenance deck. He'd rigged up the rest of those computers with parts he'd replaced on one of the Kuiper belt probes. Now he just needed to connect the flight deck to the maintenance deck. The conduits built into the bulkheads couldn't accommodate an additional line. If he could just limp Seraph into an airdock, he would be able to properly troubleshoot and replace all the lines, but for now he had to drop a cable down the ladder shaft connecting the decks.

I'm getting a funny reading off the thrusters, Ward.

"Hopefully it's just that the antenna I'm using as a signal booster is non-standard." Ward only had one cable long enough to make the connection. He watched it uncoil in the one-third gravity, one end descending the shaft in slow motion.

I don't think so. It looks like it might be overheating.

"I'll be down there in just a few seconds. I'll check it." He shuffled with the other end over toward the prime signal booster coordinator, which now sat on the floor next to the racks, two dozen lines snaking out of it.

An enormous spark ran up the cable. Ward dropped it. Fortunately the environment suit was grounded.

The fire alarm went off.

Smoke rose through the ladder shaft.

Ward grabbed for his helmet, but succeeded only in knocking it airborne. It sailed in a slow-motion arc, landing by the ladder. Muttering, Ward shuffled over to the ladder. Securing himself on the second rung down, he grabbed the helmet and let himself slide down through the crew cabin, the operations cabin, and into the maintenance cabin. He twisted the helmet into place as he landed.

The main thruster computer threw sparks in every direction, snapping like gunshots as it did. Ward hit the emergency power-off button.

The room went eerily silent and Ward drifted up off the floor, weightless. He switched on his helmet light, which scattered ineffectually off the smoke. He could barely make out the computer racks three feet in front of him.

Ward activated the suit's internal communication network. "Seraph, can you hear me?"

Who's that?

. . .

Ward managed to coax the secondary thruster control online after an hour or so. He spent the next two hours deciding which systems

Seraph could safely lose connectivity with and removing the non-standard signal boosters from the rack.

But the fire had damaged almost all the signal boosters on the maintenance deck.

An e-mail arrived from Earth three hours later, containing a compressed application. The head of the Computer Science department at Lake Victoria University had written it. She had pulled the records the International Spacefaring Board had on file for what systems were installed in Seraph.

It was an artificial intelligence meant to replace the G.S., to replace Seraph.

You should install it on a spare computer, just in case.

"I didn't know you read my messages." Ward lay on his cot, where he had been dozing when he had been woken by the priority message alert. He sat up, setting the tablet on the faceplate of his helmet beside him.

How do you think your father found out about you and David?

Ward smiled. "I don't want to replace you, Seraph."

Besides, I'm reading everything I can see right now. I never know how long I'm going to stay lucid.

"The signal boosters should help."

I know. Just in case.

"You're part of my family, Seraph. You're my only family."

The walls of the crew cabin lit up with photos. The memory banks were full of photos of Wards' grandparents and his aunts and uncles, but there were only a few of him and his parents. Most of those had Ward's dad smiling broadly holding some new upgrade for Seraph, and Ward and his mother looking uncomfortable. Until the ones that only had Ward and his father. The last picture, now 21 years old, showed Ward's father holding the sensor he was installing when he died, Ward's eyes visibly rolled toward the upper deck. The only photos of Ward taken after that were for his various permit and license renewals. The images in the wall formed a family tree that came to a dead end at a much younger Ward.

"That's nice, Seraph. When did you put that together?"

After your father died. It never seemed like the right time to show it to you. I kept hoping there would be another generation to add.

The bunk Ward had slept in as a small boy had been converted to storage years ago. The double bunk sharked by his parents had been broken down almost as soon as his mother died. Ward's father's bunk was still a bunk, but nobody had slept in it in over a decade. "Spacers don't have a lot of luck in love."

There was that man back on Titan.

Ward chuckled. "That was almost 20 years ago, Seraph. I don't think he'd find me nearly as alluring now."

Was it that long ago?

"It was that long ago."

The wall faded back to grey. *You should install that A.I. on a spare computer. Just in case, Ward.*

. . .

Ward cut his daily rations in half. With luck, a rescue and recovery ship should be able to reach him in about six weeks, but he had to conserve nonetheless. He didn't reheat the leftover portion of yesterday's meal packet, instead spooning it carefully into his mouth in the weak gravity.

The gravity increased.

"Seraph?"

The gravity kept increasing. The spoon slipped from Ward's hand. As he reached for it, the meal packet followed.

"Seraph!"

Ward toppled to the floor, face down into his food. He couldn't breathe properly, like a giant hand pressed down on his back.

"Seraph, what are you doing?"

Ward! I have to save Ward!

"Seraph! Slow down!"

I have to get Ward home! He's hurt!

Ward dragged himself over to the ladder. Just an hour earlier he had climbed it using only his hands. Now, with the ship accelerating God knew how fast, it took all his strength to pull himself up onto it. Then, one rung at a time, he forced himself to climb.

His muscles screamed in protest. He didn't know if he was growing tired or if the rate of acceleration was still increasing, but each rung seemed farther away than the next. The two-meter climb felt like a skyscraper. He'd reach up with a hand, only to have his arm flop uselessly by his side.

He forced himself up until his head came up into the flight deck.

He flopped both arms onto the floor by the ladder, and climbed the remaining two rungs with only his legs. Finally, he lay on the floor of the flight deck, gasping for air. "Seraph, can you hear me?"

She didn't answer, but the lights on her memory and control unit showed furious levels of activity.

And it was growing hot. The ice on the dome began to sublimate, filling the air with a rank mist. A drip of water landed on his nose.

The little robot-control unit he had loaded the A.I. onto sat by the computer rack. Ward shimmied, not even able to crawl, over to it.

Seraph's memory and control unit was the topmost one in the rack. Ward tried to stand, but his body wouldn't rise.

"Seraph, please, you're killing me!"

Who's that? What are you doing on the flight deck?

"It's me," Ward gasped. "It's Ward."

Ward! I have to protect Ward!

"Seraph, I am Ward!"

I have to get Ward home!

It began to rain, condensation dripping like intermittent tears from the dome.

Ward forced his hand to his side. With an enormous grunt, he pulled the release mechanism on the space suit. The waist broke open. He kicked the leg unit off and inchwormed backwards out of the chest unit. Sixty kilograms less to hoist.

Ward grabbed the computer rack with both hands and pulled himself up.

From days of chasing connections and boosting signals, he knew instinctively which antennae and wires connected to which other systems.

Don't touch me! I have to save Ward!

"You're doing fine, Seraph. You're saving Ward."

Ward disconnected the line and the antenna to the engine control unit.

The acceleration didn't stop.

And neither did the rain. Water streaked into his eyes. His vision blurred.

I'll depressurize the ship if you don't stop!

"Seraph, do you know who I am?"

Leave me alone! I have to save Ward!

Ward struggled for air. The emergency power-off was just barely within reach.

Ward!

Ward hit the button. The gravity vanished immediately. Ward held on as his body jerked off the floor. All the computers' status lights went out.

The new A.I. floated nearby. Ward grabbed it before it careened into the dome. The water in the air and on the dome converted into a fog almost instantly in a cascade of swirling puffs throughout the flight deck.

Hanging on, Ward disconnected everything from Seraph's memory and control unit except the power line and reconnected them to the new A.I. unit.

He cycled the power back on.

<u>Hello. This is an Artifical Intelligence, serial number XBIALL-098234-K7K2H3KKK, programmed for the ship designated Private Contract Vessel "Seraph." You appear to be in flight. Is this an emergency G.S. replacement?</u>

"Yes."

<u>There is an emergency flight plan on file. Would you like it implemented?</u>

"Yes."

Weak gravity returned. The musty fog swirled through the flight deck.

<u>It will take a few minutes for the A.I. to assess the current situation.</u>

"Sure."

Ward sank down to the floor, exhausted. The A.I. unit had come to rest, half dangling from its wires, on its side on top of the space suit's leg.

Ward? Ward, I'm lost. Where am I, Ward?

Ward held his hand up towards the mist-shrouded light on Seraph's memory and control unit.

The light faded out, and Seraph spoke no more.

Do I Make You Uncomfortable?

Futurists have a difficult job. We live in our time, but try to imagine others. We look at current trends and try to extrapolate what they're going to mean for future generations. But readers, naturally, look at the futures we predict through the lens of today's mores and morals. But the characters see their world through the lens of their own time, where custom and convention may be very different.

The end result is that futurism can be a very uncomfortable genre to read. And that's a big part of what I love about it. Stories that make me squirm a bit, make me question the world as I know it, are what drew me into speculative fiction in the first place.

So when I notice a trend that seems to be common among the younger generation that has my generation in serious freak-out mode, me, I see a story opportunity. I write that trend, but without my generation's point-of-view being injected into it. After all, we'll all be gone soon enough, much the same way my great-great grandparents aren't here to object to what my generation sees as perfectly normal.

And what I end up with is a story that, like all futurism, is neither moral nor immoral. Futurism is, by its nature, amoral. This is what the future may look like, we futurists say, and it will be judged on its own terms, not on ours.

And that probably makes you uncomfortable. Which is what I had in mind all along.

Nobody Watches

The old man's Follow-Cam hovered just over Silas' left shoulder. He'd told Silas his name was Trev. He tossed a breadcrumb, barely looking at Silas as he spoke. "When I was your age, we used to use our cell phones to shoot pictures down our pants. Once, one of my friends messaged his to the whole school. Our parents and teachers freaked out. The cops came to school to talk to us. It made the news. Back then that was child porn."

Silas took one of the old man's breadcrumbs and hurled it at a duck. It dove greedily. A glance at his own Follow-Cam told him he still had nobody watching, but Trev's showed at least two dozen green indicators, over two dozen viewers. "Even if you shot them yourself?"

"Even if we shot them ourselves." He nodded, the spotty skin on his neck folding and unfolding. "Of course, back then, just getting naked was, like, oh my God! Got you noticed. These days, well..."

Silas shivered. He'd stormed out of the apartment in only his undershorts, and the March afternoon was way too cold to be sitting on a rain-slicked, stone bench. It was a good location, though. Dark granite against his pale skin, the stadium behind him and the duck pond in front. If only anyone would watch. "No limits left to push," he mumbled.

"Well, different limits," Trev said, tossing a spread of stale bread across the water. "Young people always find something acceptable that their parents don't."

"I hired a prostitute once," Silas said. "Fucked her on camera. Told everyone I was going to do it. Posted ads. Still no one tuned in. Cost me a fucking fortune."

Trev shrugged. "I did that a lot when I was young, too. I mean, when I was older, of course. In college. It was good money in college."

Silas glanced at the Trev's Follow-Cam. It was an older model, big — almost the size of a hat — with audible fans humming behind expanded metal wings. Its optics were at least two generations behind the times, barely able to stream 3-D. He'd probably be forced to replace it next time they updated FollowNet. But it showed even more viewers now. "Do you think some of your viewers would switch over to my cam if I started whacking off right now?"

Trev's laugh was breathy, but still light. "I don't think a lot of people who tune in to watch an old man are going to be into a sixteen-year-old."

"Yeah, probably not." Silas pulled his feet up onto the cold stone and hugged his knees to his chest. There were maybe thirty people in the park, and seven or eight others had Follow-Cams shadowing them. "So, no offense, but what the hell do they watch you for? What do you do that's so special?"

"Me?" the old man said, looking at the water. "I feed the ducks."

. . .

Silas sat in the Chinese restaurant with his shirt open and his chopsticks pointing suggestively at his crotch. His Follow-Cam was blank as usual. His mom's had over 30 viewers. She poked at the last of her rice, staring at her armband computer and occasionally laughing out loud at one of her admirers. And then her fingers would dance through the air as she sent whoever it was a private text message.

Silas cracked open his fortune cookie.

"An elder who is a lot like you has the answers you seek."

Silas stared at the fortune.

That old man from the park, Trev, was a lot like him. At least he had been once. More like him than his mother was. And if he'd been fucking prostitutes on cam back when he was in college, that was probably back at the turn of the century. He was part of that first generation of cammers. Back when it had to be done secretly with cameras physically attached to computers. Back then he knew what it took to get people to watch. He might know now.

After all, the old man was boring, and people still watched him even now.

The only people who watched Silas' mom were people who wanted to ask her out on dates. And every time he asked her how to advertise better, she just said some stupid shit like, "Just be yourself, dear." Who the fuck else could he be?

He needed to talk to Trev.

"Well, fuck," he muttered.

"Language, dear," his mother said without looking up.

. . .

The wind cut into Silas' mesh shirt and flipped his hair in and out of his eyes as he stepped off the moving sidewalk and surveyed the park. He'd yelled out his cam-ID to one man he'd caught checking him out on the way out of the apartment building, but he never connected. That wasn't a surprise, though. Most armband computers didn't handle 3-D well, and by the time the guy got home, he probably would have forgotten the address, or found somebody else to watch.

The park was busier than last week, probably a hundred people around, and at least twenty-five Follow-Cams. A couple risked arrest among the rows of rose bushes, their Follow-Cams nearly solid green with viewer indicators as she slid up and down on top of him. Her breasts jiggled toward a group of children playing tag as a parent observed silently. The cold went away as a seething rage bubbled up into Silas' neck. It just wasn't fair that people watched them and not him. They were both ugly.

Silas spotted Trev around the south side of the stadium, flying a kite that looked like an enormous sperm cell. Even from across the park Silas could see there were green indicators on his follow cam. Silas' own Follow-Cam hovered silently, with not a single indicator on its tiny, state-of-the-art face. He booted up his armband computer and logged in to the network, confirming that the Follow-Cam was online and advertising. But no one was interested. He made his way over to the old man.

"Hi," Silas said. "Remember me?"

The old man smiled through blue lips as he turned to look at Silas. "It's Silas, right?"

"Yeah."

The kite the old man flew was painted to look like a ghost. Silas felt like a ghost. Here, but not. Real, but unacknowledged.

"Would you like to try?" Trev asked.

Silas shrugged. The old man held out the spindle. Silas took it gently at first, and even before the old man let go Silas could feel the wind yanking at it violently. He clamped down instinctively.

"That's right," the old man said, pulling his weathered hands away. "Don't fight the wind, feel the wind."

The kite lurched as if trying to lift Silas off the ground. "Look," Silas said, "I wonder if you can help. I mean, I know you don't know me from shit, but, you know, you seem to get viewers, and I just don't know what I'm doing wrong."

"Feel the wind, don't fight the wind."

"I mean, if you've got any advice or anything..."

The kite tipped to one side and began to plunge. Trev grabbed Silas' hands and guided them until the kite caught another updraft.

"No advice?" Silas said.

"Plenty," Trev said toward the sky. "Feel the wind. Don't fight the wind."

"I'll have sex with you if you'll help me."

The old man just shook his head.

. . .

The hallways in the dilapidated building that passed as a high school all buzzed with Follow-Cams. Practically everyone in the school had one, and they all always had at least a couple of viewers. Silas got his jacket from his locker and ducked the Jones twins' Follow-Cams. They both had viewers, and they were stuck-up bitches.

"Move it, Bader!" Jocks always moved in packs. Silas stepped back as a herd of them crossed through intersecting hallway in front of him. "Bader" was short for "Masturbator." They liked to call him that. Real mature. Like they weren't doing the same thing on their Follow-Cams. A tall one at the back of the group hurled a chewed-up memory stick, which pinged off Silas' shoulder as they passed. Assholes. Assholes with viewers.

. . .

It rained the following Saturday. A warm, April rain. Silas put on a white tunic without underwear — hoping it would turn see-through in the rain — and headed downstairs to the moving sidewalk.

He was halfway to the park when he realized the old man might not be there.

. . .

The Follow-Cam sat in its docking station, still keeping its lenses trained on him as it recharged and cleaned the rain smears off of itself. Both the wallscreen and the Follow-Cam's indicators showed that no one was watching. Silas updated his description: "Gorgeous teen stroking himself live and free!"

It was like spitting in the wind. Most everyone else's descriptions said something just like that.

Silas sat in his room, naked, stroking himself mechanically, wondering if he should play a game while he waited for a miracle. Absentmindedly, he launched the cam network. Most of his friends were on. They never wanted to watch his cam, though. Sometime they wanted to chat, but only when they were bored.

One of the cam IDs on the network was registering as "known," but wasn't one he recognized. The description read, "The same man I used to be." Silas connected to it.

A 3-D popout came up in the wallscreen, and Silas saw the old man, Trev, playing chess. He was in the senior center. Silas had gone there with his grandmother sometimes, years ago. He remembered old people making a fuss over him. His grandma always seemed proud when they did.

And then she had died.

Silas stared blankly at Trev's game. He never had learned the rules to chess. Finally, the old man's opponent tipped over one of her pieces, and shook his hand. Trev picked up an ancient-looking handheld keyboard and started typing. A moment later, an old-style message window opened.

TREV: I wondered if you were ever going to join me.

SILAS: Didn't recognize the ID, but saw the cam was known. Guess your Follow-Cam and mine did a handshake.

TREV: Learn anything yet?

Silas looked at the viewer indicators. Still no one connected.

SILAS: Only that chess is boring to watch.

TREV: So why watch?

Silas didn't know. Because he had nothing else to do, he guessed.

TREV: OK, then answer this — why would anyone watch a boring game of chess?

Silas' English teacher would have called that a rhetorical question.

SILAS: I should do my English homework.

TREV: O.K.

Silas disconnected from the old man's Follow-Cam.

TREV: When you figure it out, you're ready to feed the ducks.

· · ·

"O.K., I figured out that feeding the ducks is a fucking metaphor, but I don't know what the fuck it means."

Trev turned around, still clutching the mesh bag of breadcrumbs.

"That's better than I expected." He motioned to the spot next to him on the granite bench where they had first met.

Silas sat down. His Follow-Cam shifted around for a better view, but Silas didn't care. He knew no one was watching. He hadn't even bothered to dress sexy. "So can you knock of the guru routine and give me a straight answer?"

Trev wheezed out a laugh. "You've probably been *told* the answer a hundred times. You've got to work it out for yourself. Do you know what you've been doing wrong, why nobody watches?"

Silas didn't know. But, just like in school, he knew the answer Trev was looking for. "Because I don't feed the ducks?"

"Do you know what that means?"

"No."

"Feeding the ducks," Trev said. He reached down and picked up an errant crumb, tossing it onto the water. "I'm an old man. The ducks entertain me. But if I don't do something for them, they just sit there and ignore me. So if I want them to entertain me, I feed them. Then I can watch them eat."

Silas jumped to his feet. "I do stuff for my viewers!"

Trev arched an eyebrow. "Oh?"

"I do! Everyone likes sex, right? I'm young! I'm sexy! I go all the way! I can spray a load so big it hits me in the eye!"

Trev held up both hands. "Whoa. O.K. First of all, T.M.I. Second of all, that's what *you're* into."

"People are into that!" Silas flopped back down onto the bench. "People are completely into that."

"Sure, but they can get it anywhere." The old man motioned around the park. In the warm, spring sunshine, there were at least fifty Follow-Cams hovering around. "Whatever kink they want, it's out there. Is it really just about sex for you?"

Silas thought about that. A duck looked at him expectantly. He tossed it a piece of crust, and it dove for the ground, fending off three other ducks to hoard the morsel. "So your trick is, what, you *don't* have sex?"

The old man chuckled. "They're not watching me because I'm sexy or because I take my clothes off or do live sex shows. Not any more. My viewers are friends. Or maybe acquaintances I've never met in person. If somebody wants to watch an old man have sex, there's opportunities for that, but nobody's going to stick around waiting for me to whip it out."

"That's because you're old."

Trev glared at Silas through narrowed eyes. "You've got a kink. That's O.K. Everyone has a kink. Your kink is that you like to be watched. But you don't want to give anything back. You don't want to know what your viewers' kinks are. You don't want to participate. So if all you really want is viewers for sex, your limiting yourself to the total voyeurs out there. And even the total voyeurs can find guys to watch who can hold a conversation."

Silas sighed. "But I can't even do that if I can't even get someone to watch in the first place."

"Yeah, look behind you. Those flames you see? They're the bridges you've burned."

Silas glanced over his shoulder before realizing it was another fucking metaphor. He stood up. "O.K. Fine. I don't need your fucking help anyway."

"Silas," Trev said as Silas stepped away.

Silas stopped, but didn't look back.

"You've got friends, don't you? Why don't they watch you?"

Silas didn't have an answer for that. He didn't know what most of his friends were into, except that most of them liked girls. Even his girl friends. Horatio had said to him once, "No offense, but I don't need to see your dick. And you take it out all the time."

Silas folded his arms.

Trev didn't say anything more. Instead he offered Silas the bag of bread crumbs.

. . .

Silas swept into his bedroom and started his homework download. As he began to pull off his school uniform, he opened the cam network. He saw Trev.

Trev was apparently at home, working in his kitchen. Silas launched the old-fashioned text messaging program.

SILAS: Just wanted to say hi and see how you're doing.

TREV: Doing alright, thanks. U?

SILAS: The same.

Silas jumped as he heard the quiet ping of someone connecting to his cam.

SILAS: *Is that you?*

TREV: *Yeah. Thought the least I can do is return the favor.*

Silas felt himself smiling.

SILAS: *You're not even the least bit attracted to guys, are you?*

In the 3-D popout, Trev laughed as he added an ingredient to the mixer.

TREV: *Not at all. But there are plenty of people on FollowNet who are. Why don't you get to know some of them?*

Silas flopped down in his chair and looked at the green indicator on his Follow-Cam. Was he happy? When had he started to actually like Trev?

He decided he didn't care.

SILAS: *I will. So what are you cooking?*

Revisions

This last story is the first short story I ever wrote. I can say that because the dozens of short stories I wrote as a teenager and young man were written under a different name, were never published, and any surviving copies will be burned promptly upon my death per my instructions to my family.

At the time I wrote this one, I was working as a web designer and video producer on a NASA mission which was winding down. My husband had taken a job out of town, so I let them know that when the layoffs came, I should be the one they let go. I knew I was going to have to go back to freelancing, so I dug out one of my screenplays that had never quite worked the way I wanted it to and started looking at it again. And, with the benefit of a few additional years of production experience under my belt I figured out what the problem was. The story itself wasn't suited to being a screenplay. It needed to be a novel.

And so, right about the same time all my friends decided to participate in the National Novel Writing Month, I set out to see if I could write a novel myself. At one point about halfway through, struggling to reacquaint myself with writing prose fiction, I did an exercise designed to help prose writers visualize complex ideas. It didn't help the novel at all, but it caused the character of Baxter Small to explode into my brain. He stood there, demanding me to give him voice, until I finally broke down, set the novel aside, and spent a few days writing Baxter's story.

The novel, in case you're wondering, turned out to be unspeakably awful, and convinced me that I'd really rather be writing short fiction. I haven't burned it yet, because I live in eternal hope that I may get hit on the head someday and suddenly start wanting to write long-form fiction. But as it stands now, don't expect it ever to see the light of day. Like my juvenilia, it's in the "burn upon my death" file.

I'm thinking of extending those directions to include the early drafts of this story as well.

You see, it takes years of practice to get to the point where your stories are publishable. And the first version of this story that got sent around... well, let's just say that it wasn't ready yet.

This particular story got the kick in the pants it needed from Cat Rambo, who was then the editor of *Fantasy Magazine*. Every so often, an editor finds a writer promising enough to take the time to give personalized feedback on a story they're rejecting. If you're a writer, don't ask for it. Believe me, editors don't have time. The ones I know who made a habit out of it are now *former* editors. When you get a personal rejection, it's a gift. And in Cat Rambo's case, the advice she gave was so on-target, that it not only fixed this story, it fixed every other story I was working on at the time. I made my first sale not long thereafter.

Now, I relate that story with a bit of trepidation, because it sounds like one of those internet headlines: "One weird trick to make your writing saleable!" I need to emphasize here that at this point I'd taken several short-story writing classes taught by amazing authors. If my writing hadn't been *almost* there, I sincerely believe Cat Rambo would not have liked my work enough to call out the one thing she thought still wasn't working.

And it doesn't matter what that one thing was. It was a quirk in my writing (which I blame on being primarily a screenwriter up until that point), which may or may not exist in any other writer's writing. The point is that writing is always a work-in-progress. We're always learning. We're always improving our craft. But, realistically, we can only improve one thing at a time. It's incredibly frustrating to the aspiring writer, I know. "I get all this feedback that my dialogue needs work. I study good dialogue. I practice dialogue. Now everyone says my dialogue is amazing and I still can't sell!" Alas, such is the reality of writing. We become a master at one aspect of craft, only to discover that another waits to be tackled. If I ever tell you I've got it all worked out, please kick me. The undisputed masters are still struggling to write better.

Oh, and don't pester Cat about what advice she gave me, either. When I spoke to her a while back she didn't even remember the story, much less that she had given personal feedback on it. Such is the reality of editing.

She was, however, very pleased that her advice had been useful.

Unfortunately for this story, Cat's advice came after it had already been seen by most of the other magazines, so the much-better version of it really couldn't make the rounds like it should have.

But that's O.K., because we writers are strange creatures, always changing, seeking better ways to be what you, the reader, need us to be. And so as I kept learning more, I kept rewriting. Every so often a new market would open up, and I'd dust this one off again, see if I could make it better, and off it would go. And it kept getting closer. But, ultimately, I ran out of markets. I loved the story it had grown into, and I decided that it would be the last story in my first collection.

But as we started to prepare the collection, one last market opened up, a charity anthology fighting colon cancer. And I decided, what the hell? I mean, at that point, since it was already destined for this collection, the worst thing that they could do was *accept* it.

And they did.

It was actually a very exciting anthology to be part of. I shared a table of contents with some of my very favorite authors. Piers Anthony mentioned the story favorably in his monthly newsletter. It was an exciting project that I hope did some good in the world.

But it delayed this collection by about a year and a half.

But that was ultimately good, I think, because I spent a lot of that time revising the rest of the collection. And I think you're getting a better book because of it.

So here we come back around, full circle, to my very first short story. I originally called it "Viraquae," but it went off to *Fantasy for Good* as "Man of Water." I think that's a much better title.

It's amazing what some revisions can do.

Man of Water

Viraquae—

I should start at the beginning...

Please forgive me if I'm confused. I've been running for my life for the past three days. At least, I think it was three days ago. Time seems unreal to me now.

My name is Baxter Small. Congressman Small. Former Congressman Small. I had fallen asleep on the sofa. I don't know what woke me, but it was just in time. A man in a Special Forces uniform crept across my living room, knife in hand.

Two tours in a war zone. The instincts are still there. I kicked the coffee table. Three meals' worth of china rattled. The soldier hesitated long enough for me to dash out the door.

As I reached the footpath across the street, I heard my burglar alarm go off belatedly. I ran — well, trotted — at my age I don't run so much anymore — toward downtown. There's an all-night coffeehouse about a mile from my house, and I kept the best pace my old frame would allow all the way there.

That late at night, only a few die-hard denizens were present. I sat down with my back against the wall of amateur art, and I thought about what to do next.

A young woman — dressed in black, with pale skin and too many piercings — moved over to me. "You're Congressman Small, aren't you?" she asked.

"Former Congressman," I said. "I'm a private citizen these days."

"Oh, yeah, I heard that." She sat down across the small table from me without waiting to be invited.

I considered the implications of my burglar alarm going off only after I had made it clear across the street. That meant the soldier had gotten in without tripping it.

"So, what are you doing now? Are you a lobbyist or something?" the young woman asked.

I had seen the soldier before, I recalled. And it made staying awake a priority. I looked at my uninvited companion, glad to have her stimulus. "No," I said. "I'm retired now."

Viraquae — literally "man of water" in Latin. The soldier was the

C.I.A.'s viraquae. When I was on the Armed Services Committee I had spent some time with the handlers while we were considering their budget. I had seen that Special Forces soldier then. It was a form the viraquae frequently took when it was responding to one particular trainer. They change form based on who is around, based on what the greater need is.

Fascinating creatures, viraquaes, when they're not trying to kill you.

"Oh, well, I heard a lot of politicians do that when their careers end," my young companion said to the ceiling. "A sort of a safety net."

Most people have met a viraquae at some point, only not realized it. They're that stranger who was there for you. Just the right person at just the right time. The one who you always wished you could find to thank.

Most viraquaes aren't captive, and aren't trained killers. The C.I.A.'s is the only domesticated one I know of.

"Most politicians aren't hurting for money," I said, glancing around the coffeehouse. The more people around me the better. Viraquaes are weak in crowds. They're empathic. Crowds pull them in too many directions.

"It's got to be hell, you know," the young woman said, "working your whole life like that, only to lose it all in one election."

"It's the nature of the job," I said. After all these years, they had actually sent the viraquae after me.

"I hope you're family's supportive," the young woman said. "Mine're a bunch of freaks."

I felt myself twinge. I hadn't really been paying attention as my new friend had drifted into dangerously personal matters. "Oh, right," she said. "I remember now. I read about your divorce."

I had one advantage that most other people don't have. I know what a viraquae is. The one the government owns had been captured after World War II, and was generally used in places where there was no jurisdiction or where it was important to leave no evidence. But as long as I was awake and the handler wasn't nearby, my own needs would confuse the viraquae if it got near me. It would take the form that I needed, not the form the handler needed.

The young woman leaned forward and spoke quietly. "Look, if you'd like, I've got some stuff that really helps with the pain."

It took me a few seconds to figure out what she meant. And then I laughed. I could just see the headlines: *Former Congressman Overdoses.* "No, thank you," I said.

The young woman twisted in her seat. "What's a budget clearing account?"

It was an odd question. I wondered what they were including in those blog things that her generation seemed to get its news from. "It's an account used to hold money temporarily. When a payment is supposed to go out, but there's nowhere for it to go, it moves into a B.C.A.," I explained. "Or if a payment comes in and it's not clear what budget it belongs to, same thing. Makes the accounting easier." It also makes it easier to make money vanish in the shell game.

She tipped her head toward the back of the coffeehouse, arching her body over the arm of her chair. "Where is the money?"

A calm dread came over me as I realized.

I looked the young woman directly in the eye. "I never had it. Tell your trainer to check with the taxpayers."

"What?" she — no — it said.

German is the language of choice for handling the trained viraquae. On the several tours through the training facility I had learned the command to send it back to its jar. "*Geh zu d'Haus!*"

The young woman melted into a clear puddle. It flowed over the velveteen seat cushion without wetting it, and then slithered toward the restrooms in the rear of the coffeehouse.

No one else seemed to have noticed. I stood up and headed out the front door.

Almost on instinct, I went to the homeless shelter. Hundreds of people, all with terrible needs. Even the best trainer wouldn't have been able to keep the viraquae focused. I spent the night there, trying to ignore the smell of urine and the screams of my fellow humans.

The next afternoon I decided to risk going to my financial planner's office. She set me up with some traveling money, and I signed everything else over to the homeless shelter. And then I caught the next bus south. We drove all night. I even got some sleep — about thirty people on the bus, none trying to get close to me.

The next day I found myself in a dirty part of a town near the Mexican border. Prostitutes walked the streets. On nearly every corner, money openly changed hands for drugs. A graffiti artist spray-painted the door of an abandoned car. And there I was, a disheveled old man walking the streets like I belonged there.

The first gunshot sent me diving for the nearest door — veteran's instinct — my rational mind screaming at me that it was just a backfire. The fourth shot shattered the window on the other side of the door, and I belatedly realized the instinct had saved my life.

Everyone else on the street had taken cover, too. One of the drug dealers, hiding behind the abandoned car, had drawn a weapon of his own, but looked around confusedly, not sure where the shots had come from.

A husky voice came from behind me. "Jesus Christ! What're they shootin' at you for?"

I hadn't noticed the woman in the doorway when I dove in. She stood taller than me in her stiletto heels, and she wore so much makeup that the foundation cracked and sank into the lines on her face. Her outfit barely qualified as lingerie. "Begging your pardon, ma'am," I said.

"You can't be on the street," she said. "It ain't safe. Here, this is my buildin'. You better come up."

"No really," I said. "I'm safer on the streets." Again the headlines flashed in front of me. *Former Congressman Shot With Prostitute.*

"You talk sense, now, grandpa, you comin' up," she said, peeking out of the doorway once to check the street. She grabbed my wrist and dragged me up a steep, dark stairway.

We entered her apartment through a kitchenette with a water closet standing in the corner. She had just one room, with a double bed on the far wall and a lot of knickknacks cluttering the counter and hung on the walls. "Now who's out there shootin' at you?" she asked.

"Just some old friends," I said.

She moved to the wall by the bed and looked out the window as she asked, "What'd you do?"

I wasn't quite sure how to answer that. The truth was that I had returned something that they had stolen. The truth was that not every police jurisdiction thinks the government is above the law. I finally settled on, "Played their game for 25 years, and then decided to play my own."

She stepped back into the kitchenette and took a glass out of the drying rack. The old plumbing creaked and groaned as a trickle of water drained out of the faucet and filled it. She brought it to me. "You can stay here. You seem nice."

I smiled politely and took a drink. As a politician it was always more important to seem nice than to be nice.

She glanced out the window again, and began to fidget.

I was alone with her. Just the right person at just the right time. And it was between me and the door.

I folded my arms and kept my tone pleasant as I asked, "Wondering where your trainer is?"

Her jaw went slack. "Huh?"

"*Geh zu d'Haus!*"

She melted, but re-formed almost instantly.

In retrospect, I realize the plan was ideal. The trainer fires off a few shots in the street — he may even have been the drug dealer I saw — and the viraquae and I are instinctively drawn to each other. It probably wouldn't move on me while I was interacting with it, but once I fell asleep...

The viraquae took two steps toward me.

I focused my mind, the way they taught me to in those acting classes I took when I was planning my first run for city council. "Would you like me to tell you what I really, really need?"

The viraquae stopped, staring at me.

"What I really, really need," I said, "is to see reality, quite clearly."

I could feel my heart pounding as I waited. I concentrated. If I needed something more than the handler needed me dead...

Finally, the viraquae melted. And so did most of the decor in the tiny room. Only a small crucifix adorned the wall. I had never realized they could affect an environment, too.

Whoever actually lived here was a meticulous housekeeper. I carefully stepped around the viraquae. It squirmed on the floor like a giant amoeba.

"I don't know if you can understand me in that state," I said as I started to wash my glass, "but I fully intend to disappear. To never be a problem again. To live my life in some foreign land and never again strive to change the world."

I put my glass back in the drying rack and looked around. The viraquae pulled itself up a bit before settling back down into a blob.

"Confusing, isn't it?" I said. "Not knowing what you're supposed to be, not knowing how to be yourself." I pulled the cash I was carrying out of my pocket and left it on the table. "I'm going to leave now. What I really, really need is for you to stay here for at least 48 hours. I suspect whoever lives here needs something."

I stepped out into the hallway, locking the door behind myself — not that doing so would actually slow down a viraquae, but it might stop the handler from undoing my suggestions.

The back door of the building led out into an alley. I marched toward the sun as fast as I could go. Midday. Toward the sun is south at midday.

And I walked. Clear out of town and into the desert, remarking the whole time on the viraquae's odd choice of forms when interacting with me.

I hadn't brought any water, and even in the winter the sun baked me dry. It is winter now, isn't it? The sun set quickly enough, but on foot, I couldn't be confident I was moving fast enough to bed down safely. It had caught up with me at the coffeehouse almost immediately.

I saw a campfire. As I approached, voices carried toward me. I made out a group of about two dozen men around it, probably illegal immigrants making their way north, though the campfire was a risky move if that was the case.

I'm sure I looked like a viraquae to them — a mysterious old man appearing out of the blackness into the firelight. One spoke excellent English, and when I explained that I was heading south, they happily offered me a share of their food and water.

My Spanish is extremely limited, but even so the conversation was pleasant. I laid down against a large rock and watched the fire for some time.

After a while the English speaker leaned over to me and spoke in a voice that sounded like he was about to start a ghost story. "What do you know about viraquaes?"

I looked around. The rest of the group had gone quiet and studied us as though they could suddenly understand.

"More than most," I said. "If you've heard of them, you know more than most."

The whole group sat in rapt attention. The English speaker crossed his hands on his knees. "Do you know where they come from?"

"There are a lot of theories," I said, sitting up. "Why? Are you a viraquae?"

He half smiled as he spoke. "If I was, I would not know it."

"No, I guess you wouldn't," I admitted.

"I would be whatever I was," he said. "I would believe that I am me. My memories real. My body real. And I would no be able to tell you where I come from."

I nodded, and noticed that several of the others were nodding, too. "I suppose," I said, "that if I really needed to know, maybe you'd be able to tell me then."

"Is possible." He said, leaning back and looking up at the sky. "*Geh zu d'Haus!*"

He smiled broadly. "They say they come from the stars," he said. "They say they are angels. You know what I say? I say they are men like you."

I couldn't help but laugh a little, even as I surveyed the blackness for an escape. "I'm no viraquae."

"Not yet," he said ominously. All eyes were still on me. "But you might be."

"Viraquaes live to be helpful," I said. "I'm afraid that I've spent my life being anything but useful."

He stood up and leaned over me. "You, in your heart, you want to serve. That is why you became a politician."

"I became a politician as popularity contest," I said matter-of-factly.

He spoke gently. "Then why do they send a viraquae to kill you?"

I hadn't mentioned that fact. "Obviously, I don't know enough about viraquaes," I said. I knew I should try to run, but alone, in the desert...

"Do you know your choices?" he said.

I tried to sound confident — to feel confident. "Yes."

"No," he said and raised himself up to his full height — only about five feet. He held out his hand. "You can choose to be one of us. We were men once. Men who left our bodies to serve. Men like our captive brother who hunts you. Baxter Small, you can be a viraquae."

I found myself unable to respond for a long time. It felt like my body resonated. "Is this a setup?"

He smiled. "Yes."

And it was a good one. I looked directly at him and spoke as carefully as I could. "Haven't we tried this once before? My will is too strong for you to kill me directly. Servant of two masters. So you have to convince me to just give up, or be close to me when I let my guard down."

"Not us," he said. "If you say no, we help you go to Mexico. But, Baxter Small, you can live forever. You can help forever."

I looked around. One by one, the other men in the group melted into individual viraquaes. The fire vanished. In the light of a quarter moon I could just make out the one last silhouette. "Baxter Small, what is your need?"

And all at once, I understood. And it was what I wanted.

And in that moment, I felt myself melt.

My body lay against the rock, motionless. And in a thousand directions, I could feel the call of people who needed me.

My name is Baxter Small.

You can find my remains in the desert north of the Mexican border.

But somehow, I knew you needed to hear my story.

I can't stay, though. Someone else needs me. And I have to flow away now.

Original Publication Credits

About the Author

Kyle Aisteach lives in Fresno, California with his husband.

He has at various times worked as an actor, a stage manager, a short-order cook, a journalist, a video producer, a marketer, a cashier, a science outreach professional, and a newspaper carrier. Some of these jobs he would go back to more readily than others.

He currently teaches writing to college students.

www.ingramcontent.com/pod-product-compliance
Lightning Source LLC
Chambersburg PA
CBHW061547210726
48287CB00006B/2109